good reception

Matt Mills

For:
Bridgette

CONTENTS

0. Rediculousness [sic]

I am an old, deteriorating house.

My rooftop is covered with at least 16 years of moss, and 18 layers of alternating dirt and grime cloud my warped, scratched windows. All told, my dull, crumbling existence creates an abstract storyboard of weathered memories.

No: too vague.

I am a worn and tattered grey rug.

I'm not sure if the greyness came first, last, or somewhere between. I'm a frayed mess of thread and dirt; years of wear and tear leave me thin and worn out. The individual pieces that combine to make me whole beg incessantly to be separated from my very being.

No: too clichéd.

define: clichéd
overused, overdone, stale, commonplace; lacking originality

<!--that sounds about right-->

I am an abandoned, decrepit, yellow-brick, four-story apartment building.

Some might call my bricks gold, some might call them brown, but each description is incorrect. My bricks are yellow.

This much I know for certain.

My crumbling bricks are sun-worn from Augusts past and surrounded by blacktop turned pale from the salt and ice of each year's August counterpart. My walls stand tall but are composed of such a depraved repulsiveness that you have no choice but to look away.

No: too big and confusing.

I am a century-old wall that has been painted over exactly 1618 times.

Unintelligible graffiti covers every centimeter of my degenerating surface. Countless microscopic pieces fall off of my deteriorating surface, floating errantly down to the crack-filled sidewalk below to mix with the dirt, dust and crumbling leaves swirling clockwise with each 16- and 18-mph wind gust. Strangers walk by and unwittingly pick up my microscopic particles and transport them to other places, better places.

I become part of everything by continuously losing a part of myself.

No: untrue.

No one would willingly choose to paint on my wall and my pieces have always been and will always be mine and wholly mine.

I am an antique pickup truck, more junk than collectible.

My windshield is damaged but not completely crushed. I am missing one wheel but prefer it that way, as I do not care much for the other three. My color is forest green, or perhaps a color that resembles forest green. I am not particularly good with colors.

There is, of course, rust peaking through my unknown shade of green in a number of conspicuous places. My rearview mirror hangs upside down, reflecting images in a way that is perhaps 16- or 18-percent skewed. The upholstery of the front bench seat is damaged in multiple spots, exposing innards of unknown origin. The side view mirror on the driver's side lies on the ground directly below where it should be. I'm not entirely sure when this mirror disconnected from the rest of me and succumbed to gravity's call. It could have happened one hour ago or one year ago.

No one noticed.

I surely did not.

<!--warning: objects in mirror are cleaner than they appear-->

No: too promising.

To be antique suggests that you were once worth something or you will be worth something some day. Antiques typically have value, and, even more, are known to gain value over time. Sometimes all an antique needs to reach its full potential - or its full value - is a new owner and that's not going to happen. At least, it's not going to happen here and now.

define: value
a numerical quantity measured, assigned or computed

<!--that might be right-->

I am a horrifying presence.

You see, people don't like me. To be more precise, no living creature particularly cares for me: Insects stay away as if repelled by an invisible field, dogs won't smell me, and birds won't even think of aiming for my head.

I am a wretched individual.

Don't you see? People hate me. In fact, they loathe me. My hideousness often reaches unspeakable proportions. But I'm attempting to speak them for your sake and your sake only. Please understand this: I speak this all for you, for your benefit. I want you to see it all exactly for what it is.

Clarity is 100 percent guaranteed.

You see, when I succeed, they get angry. They get angry like a simmering mob that is just starting to gain momentum.

The angry mob, which has now reached a sufficient size and the appropriate level of madness to become its own entity, realizes that if it loots the used sports store first, the ultimate objective will be easier to obtain. Used ice skates, baseball bats, golf clubs and ski poles will all be at its disposal to be used to further the objective at hand. Perhaps the mob will even luck out and find the outdoors section in the back left corner of the store; now old ice axes, crampons, survival knives and canoe paddles are at their disposal, too.

When I fail, they don't get angry. Instead, they laugh. I'm not talking about a quick smile or a courtesy laugh. No, they laugh with every ounce of their being.

They laugh like when watching the fat comedian tumble down the hill. Every movie, every scene, every skit, every bit, they know it's coming: They know that the overweight funny guy will tumble down that hill that looms just one misstep away. They can hear the noises of slight bodily injury, of future discomfort, of small plants getting crushed and of tree branches snapping. They can see the leaves being tossed aimlessly in the air before it even happens. Still, they laugh. When the fat comedian tumbles, it's still comical.

I am not simply a ridiculous man. Oh no, I am beyond ridiculous. Believe me. In fact, go ahead and reply to my ridiculousness [re:ridiculous] if you wish.

<!--reply all?-->

Be careful not to forward it, but instead reply to it.

To: grey <maxwellgreyson@yahoo.com>;
From: you <hidden>;
Bcc: <undisclosed-recipients>
Subject: re: your ridiculousness

Message:

LOL!

There's no need to tell me how it is. I know it all already up close and personal. I understand it: You detest my very being. If you don't already, you will. Believe me.

There's not a single, minute proton or electron of mine that you would take in and nurture; not a neutron that you would even fake a half-smile at. A warm, home-cooked meal would likely be tossed in my face and then would be followed by an overhead shower of boiling-hot caffeinated cappuccino.

`<!--half-decaf?-->`

I've been here at this one very exact moment hundreds of times before, perhaps even thousands of times before, but it wouldn't matter if this was the very first time. The result would be one and the same.

Trust me, I have seen it all and I still see it now.

What's to say that I will see it all more clearly tomorrow or the day after tomorrow or another day? Is that not like taste-testing tap water each day for the rest of my life?

What am I to do, debate the subtle differences of the tap water week-to-week or day-to-day or even hour-to-hour solely for the sake of discussion?

`<!--and how does your tap water taste today?-->`

To: your entire address book <hidden>;
From: you <hidden>;
Bcc: grey <maxwellgreyson@yahoo.com>;
Subject: FWD: re: his ridiculousness

Message:

LOL! Debate the qualities of tap water? Can you believe this guy? Forward this to 10 friends or you will end up like him!

<!--ridiculers reminding me of my ridiculousness?-->

Really, how ridiculous is that? It's utterly and completely ridiculous is what it is!

But this all is nothing new for me. Perhaps this is all very strange from your nice view in the comfortable loveseat of rationality - and that's understandable on a basic level - but you must know that the same is not the case for me.

I lie comfortably in the hammock of hate.

And, for the record, I do hate hammocks. But, in any case, I lie there comfortably now, letting every muscle, bone, ligament and tendon become part of the threads of the ultimate lounger of loathing.

It was not always this way, believe me. I used to question why, and when and how and then why once more. Acting as the good journalist of perceived hatred, I used to question who, what, when and where? I would even add how and how much for good measure. I used to question it all.

In even my clearest of recollections, I never really did anything to deserve any of this derision. In fact, I have an important point to mention at this juncture, as I'm sure that you're questioning it all: I'm not a criminal and have never been.

I am, I believe, a good and honest fellow who merely has trouble dealing with constant mistreatment from society as a whole. This odd and unexplained loathing all comes despite my valiant attempts to mesh into society like most other souls. There is no standard explanation for the way things are. Believe me. Give me that, for it is absolute truth.

In any case, I have already lived this all many times over. I have seen it, tasted it, heard it, felt it, smelt it.

define: smelt
to extract or separate metals with the use of heat

`<!--that cannot be right-->`

Forgive me my nonsense, as I also forgive those who think that they talk sense.
-Frodrick Gray

I repeat that being loathed used to trouble me - it used to trouble me very much, in fact. I used to question it: Why am I atop the weekly publication of hatred? Why is my mug plastered on the front page of the entertainment section? I'm surely not an entertainer so it must be for the entertainment of the masses.

Simply put, I once hated myself for my uncanny ability to be loathed. Now, though, I'm really in peaceful harmony with it all. I am at peace with all of the pieces that together comprise the puzzle of hatred.

Fact: his hair color is brown.
Fact: her eyes are brown.
Fact: dead leaves are brown.
Fact: people hate me.

But alas I have gone on and on here and, quite frankly, I do not wish to increase your disgust for me at this time - if that is even possible.

Alas, it is time to put an end to this discussion.

define: hateable
meriting loathing due to the [over]use of the word alas

But, if you don't mind, if you can just give me but one more small moment of your time, this will allow me to explain it all the best I can and then we can move along. I know that you're already thinking of fleeing without even a glance over your shoulder. But I assure you that I'll be clear and concise.

People don't like me. You will see. You will understand. Understand that. Perhaps you already see and understand it all? If not, just give me a miniscule fraction of your time and I'll show you. People hate me. You hate me. Don't think so? Ask yourself. Be truthful. Hate is a strong word. I know this. It's OK, I've heard it all before.

In any case, as you will see, I really have no choice in the matter. The bricks are laid out in front of me in a nicely stacked pile and I have the ultimate choice of whether to build or bury. It really boils down to choice, I suppose.

Shall I, in my steadfast denial, claim to see it for the very first time each and every day and concoct a recipe of surprise and breathless amazement to be showered upon the world at large?

Or shall I, in my complete and utter acceptance, wrap my hands around it and exclaim, "hello, old friend!" while wondering who it really is?

Have we met before? Of course we have, I think. I mean, yes we have met before but you seem to have many different faces.

`<!--hello, old friend!-->`

But never mind, I shall go and I shall keep talking, I won't leave off, for anyway I have seen it with my own eyes, though I cannot describe what I saw. But the scoffers do not understand that. It was a dream, they say, delirium, hallucination. Oh! As though that meant so much! And they are so proud! A dream! What is a dream? And is not our life a dream?

Fyodor Dostoevsky

```
function GoToScene(event:imeyeself):void
```

{

I am a 34-year-old trailer with windows of trash bags and duct tape, a frail door with mismatched hinges and a "no soliciting" sign nailed to discolored siding in a way that is so crooked it has to be accidental. The sign hangs in a way that only poor judgment combined with slow, slow time could create. The ability to transport myself - or to be transported by an outside force - is built into the very essence of who I am. I cannot change myself but I can certainly change my location. And I will. I will take my meager belongings and find a more welcoming place to call home.

}

1. My names [sic] Grey

I sit alert
behind the small window
of my mind and watch
the days pass, strangers
who have no reason to look in.

John O'Donohue

"My name's Grey," I say.

I say this because the voice asks what name I go by. The voice says that she prefers to be on a first-name basis and offers up hers in hopes that I will do the same.

"Maxwell Greyson. Maxwell. No, Max. Actually, Grey. My name is Grey. Yeah, you can call me that. Yeah, stick with Grey."

"How do you do, Gray?" the voice asks.

"Good, but it's Grey with an E, not an A."

"Pardon me?"

"My name, Grey, it's spelled with an E, not an A."

"That's interesting, you can tell how I spell a name simply from how I speak it?" the voice asks.

"You don't believe me?"

"No, that's not it. No, no, not at all. I believe you. Are you English, Grey?"

"Yes, I do in fact speak English. How very observant you are."

"No, I mean are you from England? What I mean is, I believe that the English - those who are from England - often spell grey with an

E and that Americans often spell gray with an A."

"I don't know about that but people always get it wrong - always!"

"I see," the voice says. "Is the misspelling of your name an issue that frequently arises when you meet others or when you encounter new people?"

"I'm not really sure. Yeah I suppose so, now that I think about it. Yeah, the vast majority of people do seem to go with the 'A' spelling, now that you mention it."

I sit silently and process the question some more.

"Yeah, you know, they just assume that it's spelled with an A for some odd reason. I've never really understood why."

"And how is it exactly that you can tell whether your name is pronounced with one vowel or the other?"

"It was how you dragged it: Graaaaay."

"OK, how do you do Grey?" the voice repeats. "That was with an E, by the way."

"Yes, I know that was with an E. You were thinking A the first time around, though, weren't you?"

"You know, I'm not sure."

"You can admit it. It's fine, really."

"Truthfully, I'm not sure."

"Yeah, you were definitely thinking A the first time."

"You know, I may very well have been. Honestly, you know, I'm not 100 percent sure what I was thinking at the moment that I spoke your name the first time. But it's entirely possible that I was indeed thinking A the first time around."

"Yeah that's what I figured."

"So how do you do, Grey?"

"How do you mean?"

"How do you do?"

"How do I do what?"

"How are you today?"

"I'm not sure."

We sit and stare for a moment. I'm having trouble processing this whole meeting.

"What do you do?" she pauses. "I mean, what do you do for a living?"

"Well, I guess I drink a lot of coffee. Is that what you mean?"

"Thanks for sharing that but, no, I was referring to employment. Do you have a job?"

"Uh, well I guess I'm kind of a project manager of sorts."

"A project manager? I see. So..." the voice pauses.

"Yes, I manage projects."

"What do you manage, or, rather, what type of projects do you manage?"

"How so?"

"What is the nature of your managing?" the voice pauses and shifts in her chair slightly. "Of projects?"

"Oh, well, the title 'project manager' is, I guess, the best way that I've determined to explain my job to others as clearly and concisely as possible. It's a little hard to explain for some strange reason."

"Why's that?"

"You know, I'm not really sure. I've worked my way through a number of other job titles and descriptions through the years, but I would say that 'project manager' has won out as best title since, I don't know, maybe about two years ago."

"I see," the voice says as she jots something down.

"It's a topic that seems to come up often, so I've had a lot of chances to come up with the best answer," I explain. "And I think I may have finally found it: project manager."

"So you've been - or at least referred to yourself as - a project manager for about two years then?"

"Yeah, I suppose I've always considered myself a project manager but I've probably only been calling myself that for maybe two years. Yeah, that sounds about right."

"OK. What other job titles did you use before that? Or what else have you called yourself in the past?"

"I'll tell you what, I'll give you a detailed list with corresponding witty comments later. My job is ridiculously boring, so let's not focus on that now if that's OK with you. OK?"

"Ridiculously boring?"

"Yes, as you'll find out, I'm quite ridiculous in general."

"Well, we'll see about that."

"Yes we will. Can we move along now?"

"Sure, let's move on for now." the voice says. "What are your hobbies? Or what do you do in your free time?"

"I build stuff, or at least I try to build stuff."

"What do you build?"

```
<!--
I feel half empty inside, and so I build. I'm not the best builder, half
good I suppose, so maybe I fill my entire empty half with half-good,
half-built goods. That would leave me about three-quarters empty, I
think. Does that math work? I'll have to ask Sid.
-->
```

"Or, rather, what types of things do you build?"

"Oh, well my job is really about building things, too. Or at least building is a large part of what I do. I build websites, create them and even maintain them occasionally. I guess I sort of make my mark in the vast online universe by creating and building. But my more exciting builds are of things not related to the Internet."

"That's great, so what other stuff do you build, besides websites?"

"Right now my latest project includes some windows frames. I'm building a set of wooden windows. It's kind of hard to explain, so maybe I can just show you the windows or a picture of them once the project in completed?"

"What made you decide to start this window-building project?" the voice asks. "Is there anything in particular that got you pointed in that direction?"

We sit and look at each other for a time that may have been an instant or may have been a minute or longer. My mind begins to stray.

"What are you building the windows for? What's the purpose of the project?"

"Purpose?"

"Are you replacing windows in your home? Or are you planning to use these new windows for a different building or structure?"

"Oh, I see. No there really isn't a purpose like that for the project."

"So there is a purpose, just not one along the lines of home improvement?"

"Yeah I guess I would agree with that."

"Do you mind sharing the purpose?"

"rx1618."

"I'm sorry?"

"r-x-1-6-1-8," I repeat slowly.

"I'm not familiar with that. What exactly is 'r-x-one-eight...'?"

"r-x-one-six-one-eight."

"I apologize, that is how you said it. I'm sorry, what exactly is r-x-one-six...?"

"One-eight. Let me see, well, rx1618 was here before - or there, actually - but isn't here anymore. I'm building the windows, I suppose then, for rx1618. Yeah, I guess I never really thought about it until now but, yes, the windows are for rx1618."

"Where is rx1618 now?"

"I'm not entirely sure. You know, I don't really want to get into it right now."

"Please, tell me more about rx1618."

"I don't really feel like this is the time or the place for that. Honestly, I don't know if it'll ever be the time or the place. And none of it is really of much importance anyway. Believe me."

Still, we talk more about rx1618. Or, more specifically, the voice tries to get me to talk more about rx1618 but really the voice does most of the talking.

She asks many, many more questions, to be precise, but after a few minutes, the conversation turns.

"I'll recommend the same I recommend to many others in your position," the voice says. "Write rx1618 a letter. You don't have to necessarily give the letter to rx1618, but you should write it. Say what you want to say."

"A letter?"

"Use this exercise as a means to get things off your chest, if you will. Later, you can decide if you wish to give the letter to the recipient or not."

"I don't know. I don't really write letters."

"Perhaps you can give it a try? You can go into whatever level of detail you wish. You can write a very in-depth letter or a short letter with only a thought or two. I have a feeling that you might have a thing or two to say. Am I right?"

"I'm not sure."

"I think this exercise will be beneficial to you right now. What do you think?"

"No, I don't think so. I'm not really interested."

"Please, consider it. Could you attempt to write a short story, a short letter, a short essay?"

"You are certainly persistent."

"Some quick thoughts, even?"

"OK, you know what? I'll give it a try."

"Can you start writing right now? Are you comfortable with that?"

"Yeah, sure, I can do that. Well, I can try, anyway."

"And then we can decide whether or not you wish to share your writings at this time. It's totally up to you whether you want to share it now or ever, for that matter."

17

"OK, yeah, that sounds fine."

I stare at the paper for a while with barely a thought drifting across the emptiness inside, but then the words just flow.

```
//+rx1618

gloe [sic]

I am but one light ray
of one street lamp
in one alley
of one memory
reflecting off
one lid
of one faded
black garbage can;
I wonder if
you might remember
my orange glow?

//-grey
```

I didn't share my writing with the voice today. I generally make it a point not to share things with people who dislike me. And, well, that is most everyone within a 1618-mile radius, at the very least.

Were you not listening, not paying attention, ignoring the truth that is right before your eyes?

She hated me from the very start.

Yes, the voice despised me. Take my word for it this time around.

From the very first moment she laid eyes on me, from the very first second that I entered her office in Fremont, she wanted to turn and leave. In fact, she wanted to turn and run, perhaps even sprint to the Fremont Bridge and leap off the side to end the pain. Or better yet, she would find the quickest route up to the Aurora

Bridge and then take the plunge.

Surely she had visions of sprinting across scorching summer blacktop, barefoot, afraid to turn and look in fear of tripping or losing a step.

It was definitely not one those pleasant visions that are incredibly awesome manifestations of glorious childhood memories. No, it was more like the visions that you get for months after that life-altering, recurring nightmare that told you the truth about the truth.

In her thoughts she tumbled down a random set of cement stairs while fleeing in horror from the mere thought of having to spend more time with my pitiful soul, singing along to the sad chorus only because she is paid to do so.

Spend a few days with me and you will memorize the lyrics and the melancholy tune will be stuck inside the innermost reaches of your ears.

But enough of that already, I'm guessing that you have a pretty good idea of all of that at this point. I'll spare you from having to hear further details.

In any case, she's just a voice. I have no hopes that these visits with the voice, these meetings, if you will, will lead to anything worth anything. But I'll do what I have to do to get by.

I do what I get and get what I do. Do you get it? O if only I could hoist this torch on the highest of tree branches it would light thy path!
-Frodrick Gray

<!--I do not get it-->

I'm sure the voice has a name, but I don't remember it and, after all, she is just a voice - nothing more, nothing less. I have said this already, I realize, but thought it important to offer up a quick reminder. I don't even think the voice really listens to the answers that I offer up in response to her multitude of questions.

She just sits there thinking of the next question and the next question and the next question after that. That much must be painfully obvious to anyone who spends time with her. Is it possible that she is thinking about the next-next-next-next question?

I asked the voice for her email address before I left her office today. It is the digital age, after all. And if I can't get digital access in the digital age, then it's time for me to look elsewhere.

I told her that sometimes things come to me later.

What I didn't tell her was that, in fact, most things come to me later, because I'm not much of an in-the-moment kind of person. For me, it can often take a good bit of processing to find the right answer. My processing speed varies widely but, in the end, is generally on the slow side.

And getting her email address will allow me to follow up with her.

define: follow up
what you say in an email when you don't know what to say

<!--note: follow up on that definition later-->

To be 100 percent honest about my experience with the voice, I liked the writing part but not the talking part so much. That probably doesn't bode well for our future prospects seeing that we're supposed to talk for hours on end about this and that and how this and that combine to make something other.

But the writing - I think I can manage that.

The voice suggested that I write to rx1618 each and every day. I can do that. Well, I think I can do that. In any case, I like the idea. I suppose I have to give the voice credit for that idea, at the very least.

Fact is, I've been thinking about rx1618 a lot these days. And I've got high hopes for my latest project, too, so I've got to keep building and see where it ends up.


```
//+rx1618
```

```
window pain [sic]
```

```
i have a window in the top left corner of the west facing
wall of my bedroom if the night is just right and the time
is just right and the angle is just right the moon will
pour a stream of light directly above me when it all is
just right i glow for a just a moment in time some nights
i lie awake anticipating dozing here and there i wait when
the sun starts rising i close my eyes resting waiting for
another chance to chase the moon
```

```
//-grey
```


The moon is a friend for the lonesome to talk to.

Carl Sandburg

To: grey <maxwellgreyson@yahoo.com>;
From: sid <sidsays0@yahoo.com>;
Subject: zeroes

Message:

grey~

---zeroes 0.1---

I know it now: Life is merely a recurring set of zeroes set in a random sequence so as to avoid nothingness, no? I tried to place the decimal point slightly to the right, followed by non-zeroes, you know? The non-zeroes seemed to represent something in the face of nothing. See what I'm saying? But it didn't really work out. So, in other words, take away the clutter and you have zeroes, like I said, recurring in a random sequence, like I said. Twice two equals four? Absolutely! Two minus two equals? Zero? Well, hello old friend! Where have you been? Right here, you say? Oh how I have missed you!

~sid

---

define: nothingness
that thing that cannot come sooner

<!--that has got to be right-->

maxwellgreyson: BUZZ!!!
sidsays0: hello old friend!
sidsays0: whats the word?
maxwellgreyson: not sure
sidsays0: alright lets go w/ zero then
maxwellgreyson: ?
sidsays0: zero is the word
maxwellgreyson:
sidsays0: :?
maxwellgreyson:
sidsays0: :??
maxwellgreyson: I guess my response should be nothing then
sidsays0: ur starting 2 get it!
maxwellgreyson: starting 2 get what?
sidsays0: ok maybe not
maxwellgreyson: met with her today – finally
sidsays0: who?
maxwellgreyson: the voice
sidsays0: ?
maxwellgreyson: the voice - in fremont
sidsays0: cassini?
maxwellgreyson: yeah the voice
sidsays0: wait, the voice = cassini?
maxwellgreyson: indeed
sidsays0: didnt know 2day was ur 1st mtng
maxwellgreyson: twas
sidsays0: dont flake out on these mtngs man
maxwellgreyson: why not
sidsays0: remember shes a friend of mine
maxwellgreyson: sure thing

sidsays0: seriously, i set this up
maxwellgreyson: i dont even need these mtngs
sidsays0: u do. uv been in the underground 2 long
maxwellgreyson: u mean in my hammock
sidsays0: whatever you call it, i think she can help with ur anxieties & whatnot
maxwellgreyson: thats my word
sidsays0: ?
maxwellgreyson: whatnot is my word - dont use it
sidsays0: sure, but u need 2 talk 2 some1
maxwellgreyson: dont need to
sidsays0: should tho – itll help with ur social anxieties &
maxwellgreyson: whatnot
sidsays0: right
maxwellgreyson: dunno, dont think she has any idea what shes talking about
sidsays0: about what?
maxwellgreyson: anything. everything.
sidsays0: doubtful
maxwellgreyson: no, very probable
sidsays0: thats right uv got it all figured out - forgot
maxwellgreyson: get this, she want me 2 write
sidsays0: write? like an autobiography or what?
sidsays0: Gray Skies?
maxwellgreyson: with an e
sidsays0: The Colorful Gray?
maxwellgreyson: with an E
sidsays0: Gray Matter?
maxwellgreyson: E!
sidsays0: lol – 2 easy!
maxwellgreyson: something like that
sidsays0: u cant even spell man
maxwellgreyson: lol
sidsays0: seriously u cant spell, how r u gonna write?
maxwellgreyson: LOL
sidsays0: got it! The Grey Matter Report
maxwellgreyson: i like that

Welcome to the latest edition of The Grey Matter Report, where Grey fills you in on what matters, what really matters and what's the matter.

This week's term: LOL

LOL (a.k.a. laughing out loud), the acronym that took the virtual world by storm only a few years ago, is now an accepted component of present-day vernacular. But how much do you really know about LOL, really? Consider some of these little-known facts about LOL before you carelessly type those three little, harmless letters next time:

1) No birth certificate for LOL has ever been seen despite claims that the acronym was born in an underground home office more than two decades ago.

2) LOL has accidentally been typed by inattentive conversationalists on numerous occasions, including once when Vici got caught smoking a cigarette and once when Jamie ran away from home [or was it the other way around?].

3) LOL once took a leave of absence for personal reasons only to be seen bar-hopping with a run-on sentence for three consecutive days.

Before you simply type the safe little letters L-O-L without much though, consider how much LOL has changed:

▪ What LOL used to mean: Ha-ha, that is funny. I am actually laughing right now. My laugh may even be truly audible.

▪ What LOL now means: I don't know what else to type right now. Leave me alone. Go away. I hate you.

Things don't change, acronyms do.

Until next time, stay somewhere 'tween black & white.

---

sidsays0: grey the writer now huh? guess i can roll w/ that
maxwellgreyson: yeah, i dunno, doesnt feel right
sidsays0: why not?
maxwellgreyson: will make a fool of myself
sidsays0: not if no1 reads it
maxwellgreyson: tru
sidsays0: well its a safe bet ur a better writer than talker
maxwellgreyson: good point
maxwellgreyson: dunno tho
maxwellgreyson: not sure if im goin back
sidsays0: stick with it man
maxwellgreyson: with what?
sidsays0: cassini - the meetings
maxwellgreyson: the voice will go on?
sidsays0: yes it should
sidsays0: whatever that means
maxwellgreyson: will do my best
sidsays0: dont screw her over, shes a personal friend of mine
maxwellgreyson: whats up w/ the zeroes, anyway?
sidsays0: whats NOT up w/ the zeroes?
maxwellgreyson: seriously
sidsays0: seriously
maxwellgreyson: alright then
sidsays0: its all in the zeroes man
maxwellgreyson: ok if u say so
sidsays0: here, a quick exercise:
maxwellgreyson: wonderful
sidsays0: twice 2 = ?
maxwellgreyson: is this a trick ?
sidsays0: no, twice 2 = ?
maxwellgreyson: 4?
sidsays0: 2 minus 2 = ?
maxwellgreyson: nothing?
sidsays0: incorrect
maxwellgreyson: zero?
sidsays0: maybe
maxwellgreyson: gotta run
sidsays0: l8r

The Mountain hasn't been out for a while now. I can't even remember the last time I saw it. The usual Mount Rainier backdrop of my life has been replaced with an unknown grey horizon. In times like this I'm forced to dig deep into my visual log to remember exactly what's out there behind the curtain upon curtain of greyness. The foghorns are active out on Elliot Bay, though, and I am grateful for that. Audible cues can fill the visual void temporarily.

I'm off to Ballard right now for my weekly woodworking class. This class is giving me some much-needed guidance for my latest windows project. It's held at a cabinet-maker's woodshop that backs up to the old docks filled with rusty fishing boats of various ages, types and sizes.

I endure it the best I can, as the class is full of haters.

Woodworking is my nighttime project of choice these days. I don't sleep much, so the night is generally a good time to take up new projects.

Don't even start thinking about vampires or werewolves anything crazy like that. I just don't sleep very well or very much - nothing more, nothing less. I recently turned the north end of my basement into a workshop to take my newest hobby to the next level.

It was a little tough to get the materials and workers in and out for the basement remodel, but it's safe to say that the location of my house isn't the easiest to get into and out of without a little trouble no matter what you're there for.

Rush hour times in particular are a bit difficult to get in and out, for sure.

It cost about 61805 boosters to buy my place here in Seattle. It was just a simple cash transaction: Not too much trouble, really, but a decent hit to my overall reserves, I suppose. And the woodshop basement remodel set me back another 1051 boosters or so, too.

Oh, right, the boosters. It's all rather simple, really. I'll explain.

//+rx1618

a part [sic]

It is necessary to be far
apart
for when we are near
physicality only creates
a divide
in our togetherness;
if only for now
reach for space
your fingers will feel
the sound of breath
Mine?
If it travels that far

//-grey

To: voice <cassini2358@yahoo.com>;
From: grey <maxwellgreyson@yahoo.com>;
Subject: hello!

Message:

I'm not the best talker but I do like to build. I thought this might help
out with our meetings and whatnot.

www.greywindows.com

-grey

Reception level: Poor (1 out of 4) |

```
function GoToScene(event:imeyeself):void
```

{

I am an outdated cell phone. A technological wonder of sorts, I have one button that does it all. Try to dial 911 and you might see a delivery guy holding a pineapple pizza and a two-liter bottle of mystery beverage at your front door or hear a mobile pet-washing RV honking impatiently at the curb. I'm composed of a host of carcinogenic materials and smell like a mixture of burnt rubber and body odor on top of body odor. I own but two ringtones and both are prone to cause dogs to bark and rodents to scurry. My owner claims that I will be recycled but I'm not buying it; a garbage dump is the only logical destination. Indeed, I'm destined to experience a slow and painful death next to a crumbling clay pot, a cracked glass shelf and a decomposing apple partially covered with plastic wrap.

}

2. I'll take too [sic]

To conform inwardly is to deviate; to deviate inwardly is to conform. Conform to what? To the deviation, of course, or lack thereof.

Frodrick Gray

Ever since I can remember, I always wanted to live on one of those patches of grass in the middle of on-ramps to the highway. Let me explain: I'm not talking about the median but rather the circular patches of land that exist within on- and off-ramps.

That is, I'm not referring to the traditionally rectangular land masses that separate north-going traffic from south-going traffic or east-going traffic from west-going traffic. Many people often think that I'm talking about the median, but, really, living on a median never did interest me at all.

No, I was always interested in the circular patches of land that add a little nature to the otherwise concreteness of on- and off-ramps to highways or roads. I suppose that some of these circular land masses are probably too large to be considered "patches" but that's neither here nor there.

This is what I wanted. I was sure of it. I can even say that it was an honest dream of mine.

I always figured that a nice patch of grass in the middle of an on-ramp would be an exceptionally pleasant and peaceful place to see things come and go without any kind of consistent or predictable pattern. It would be like watching the world's irregular heartbeat from a front-row seat in the most serene of outdoor arenas.

One doesn't have to dig too deep to uncover the countless invaluable benefits that living at such a residence would offer to its fortunate inhabitants.

Patch Court highlights:

- Not too quiet
- Not too dark
- Not too much action
- Not too little action
- Wide variety
- Constantly changing parts

If I was forced to give one of those "what do you want to do when you grow up" presentations in elementary school, I surely would have stood up in front of the class and proclaimed truthfully and emphatically that I hoped to live on the patch of grass in the middle of an on-ramp some day in the very near future. I would have thrown it down poetry slam style with the class alternating cheers and nods of approval.

I should note here, though, that this is all just a theory. The reality of it all is: *if* I ever spoke, *then* I would have put it as eloquently as possible.

It is very possible that I was, in fact, supposed to give that very presentation in elementary school, and if so, I have no memory of it at all. I certainly don't remember giving that exact speech, but I can't rule out that I was supposed to give it or even that I attempted to give it.

They called it selective mutism and they probably still call it selective mutism. I don't know exactly what it was but I do know that I just didn't feel much like talking for a few years.

This much I know for certain.

<!-- :| -->

In any case, my dream, vision, goal, whatever you may call it, came true not long ago. I bought the patch of grass in the middle of the ramp on the southeast corner of the Ballard Bridge. Traffic heads north from there, and, oh, what a glorious piece of land it is! I even got a view: You have the Cascade Mountains to the east and the Olympic Mountains to the west.

1618 Patch Court: It's my own personal circular valley of on-ramp splendor. I built a three-story house there and, indeed, that's where I lay my head to rest at night.

And so I lay my head on the pillow of indifference, concocting wild dreams of differing deference.
-Frodrick Gray

I understand the next logical question here, so let me summarize to the best of my abilities. Reminder: my abilities are pretty feeble and some [most?] would even call them pathetic. It wasn't all that difficult, really, to buy the patch of land and build a house on it. Really. I just hired the right attorneys for the right amount of boosters. Boosters can go a long way, believe me.

Oh right, the boosters. I'll get to that shortly.

In any case, it went up for some kind of vote, as many things in the Seattle area tend to do, and it somehow passed. "It" being that a resident of Seattle would be permitted to purchase the land of that very on-ramp and build a residence on that very plot of land.

define: pros & cons
A list created and rigged solely to further a specific agenda

Pros of building a residence at 1618 Patch Court:

- Will bring in additional tax revenue
- Will ease workload of city landscaping crew
- Is really just a creative adopt-a-highway initiative
- Great for community morale
- Is aesthetically pleasing
- Will decrease the chance of a tent community popping up at that location
- Will deter wild packs of dogs from attempting to take over that part of town

Cons of a residential structure existing at 1618 Patch Court:

- None that I can think of

I didn't vote but I did build. Well I didn't really build much myself but I managed the building. And now Patch Court is where I call home.

I suppose it's time to tell you about my career, my work, my job; explain to you how I earn money, exactly what I do, precisely how I spend my days.

The quick answer: I build websites.

You have already thought of the worst, haven't you? You can freely admit these things at this point. Remember, the whole hatred thing is all out in the open now and I am surely at peace with it all.

But, I must know, have you sunk to the depths and thought the worst of the worst? Not yet, right? Already you have? Oh no, you've thought of the worst of the absolute worst, haven't you: thief, criminal, illegal-this, immoral-that? Spammer? Yes, spammer! You think that I'm a spammer, don't you?

To: you <hidden>;
From: grey <maxwellgreyson@yahoo.com>;
Cc: your entire address book <hidden>;
Subject: re: that link yu always wanted!

Message:

Don't click the link for non-illegal stuff below, or else. Or else! OK, OK click here just this one time. Only this one time!! This is a once-in-a-lifetime e-mail and you'll never hear from me again. Unless you want more non-illegal stuff. In that case, let me know. Cheers friend!

No, that's not the spam that I sent? You did indeed receive that spam but that's not the one that I authored?

OK, yeah that last spam is really a bit tame in the grand scheme of things. I'll admit that I've seen much more creative spam - as an innocent bystander, of course.

Yes, this must be the spam that I sent to your inbox last night at 2:12 am, right? Or to clarify: this is but one of the many spams that I've sent. Oh, and I'll still send many more spams to your defenseless email account regardless of your personal preference and sad attempts at opting out and filtering, right?

To: you <hidden>; 16-other-people-with-frighteningly-similar-email-addresses <hidden>;
From: grey <maxwellgreyson@yahoo.com>;
Subject: new shopping,new life, friend!

Message:

Dear life long friend!

I would like to introduce to you a good company who trades mainly in electornics. They provide the best in service to customer s and,what is more,the price is a suprising happyness to you! Click here Now nor never :o) !!

No, that's not the spam that I sent, either? You are still concocting tales of my deceitfulness? Oh I see, you're thinking that I may even be scripting a brand new spam email at this very moment to be delivered at a later time to infiltrate your innocent inbox when all rational, law-abiding, honorable, and useful beings are fast asleep dreaming of waking to good things in their inboxes.

I see, yes, you must be confident that it must be one of those elaborately ridiculous banking-fraud scams, right? I mean, how many of those bank-account-stealing swindles does one really need to hit a home run on to obtain the big payday - one, maybe two, or maybe three at the very most? It's a ridiculous scheme that is just the right fit for a ridiculous individual such as myself.

And, of course, you think that I'm just the right kind of untrustworthy, scheming filth of a person to send out a identity-theft banking scheme to every mother in town. To every grandmother in town, you say? Or even to every grandmother in the entire country?

To: you <hidden>;
From: grey <maxwellgreyson@yahoo.com>;
Subject: Urgent and Confidential; !! Reply Soon !!

Message:

Good day mate,

Firstly, I most apologize for sending such an urgent notice containing such sensitive private information via e-mail instead of Certified through the official Post-mail offices of America. Dear old friend, we have never met, and I humbly ask your acquaintance and assistance with a very important opportunity of economical importance.

I am a pirate who hails from Australia. You need not fret, sir, as I am a pirate of the good kind and pleasurably request of you to discover the abandoned sum of $16.18 Million U.S. funds into your bank account for the time period of 27 days. The afore mentioned $16.18 million was buried in my chest for many years after a tragic boat crash took the lives of all crew members, including that of my paternal grandfather Oskar.

After 27 days, banking law in Australia intently stipulates that the lump-sum can be dispersed at the account holders preferability. For your aide and co operation, you we agree to compensate in the sum of 40 percent, with the remaining 60 percent going fourth to an official bank account of high standing. It is my understanding that you are an individual of high stature who is greatly respected by peers and, I, having found your email address on a forum discussing the merits of canine training, am reaching out to you slowly and surely with palms facing down for assistance.

It is of the utmost importance that you kindly reply to this email in a timely manner and supply us with the minimalist information request'd below, after which you will be contacted by the Senior Director of the Bank of Seas with farther instruction.

1.] You're full legal name
2.] You're residence of legal squatting
3.] You're personal fax line numeral
4.] You're age and occupation
5.[a] You're bank name and location
5.[b] You're bank account numerals
6.] You're mother's maiden name
7.] The names of all pets that you have owned

Aye matey and top regard,
Sir Frodrick Gray

Believe me, you are not the first to throw me haphazardly into the spammer heap, and you surely will not be the last to do so. And all of this comes with no evidence at all. Why? I have no idea, really. Like I said, I no longer question this type of occurrence. No longer do I expend valuable energy attempting to play detective and unravel absurd mysteries such as these.

What is the point of questioning that which has no sensible answer in this world before our eyes? I'll say it and keep saying it: I am really at peace with it all.

Remember the hammock?

"HOW DO YOU DEW?"
Screenplay by Maxwell Greyson

ACT 1, SCENE 1

EXT. GRASSY PATCH OF LAND- SEATTLE, WA - DAWN
(PRESENT)

GREY and GUY stand barefoot in the damp grass in the early morning hours as the sun rises slowly over the foothills of the Cascade Mountains to the east as the clouds part and a new day is about to begin.

GUY
What do you do?

GREY
Hey, are your feet getting wet at all? (He's looking down at his bare feet with a confused look, shaking his head slowly from side to side.)

GUY
A little I guess, but, anyway, I need some answers, man.

GREY
Mine are - it feels kind of nice, doesn't it? It must be dew or something. Do you think it's dew?

GUY
Yes, my feet are a little wet.

GREY
I think it might be dew.

GUY
Yeah, yeah, dew, fine - but anyway - what do you do? Seriously, I really have no idea. Like no idea at all.

GREY
I'm an online entrepreneur, I suppose.

GUY
Yeah, yeah, right, me too! On-Trey-Prey-Nure. Right here (pounds chest). What the hell does that mean, anyway? Like what *exactly* do you do? (picking up his left foot off the ground, he tries to shake off the dew)

GREY

Online marketing?

GUY
What's that, online marketing? You market online? So, you're like some sort of Internet advertiser or what? Dude, that makes no sense.

GREY
Uh, yeah? Go with that. Yeah, go with Internet advertiser.

GUY
Ah, so you're a spammer? OK, yeah, you're a freaking spammer!

CUT TO BLACK

No, you're not choosing to journey down the well-traveled spammer route? You may want to reconsider and just go ahead and join the crowd. It's simple: all you need to do is follow the signs (clearly marked, at that).

`<!--reach fork in the road, continue on-->`

No? OK, you must be sure, then, that my websites are filled with what you might call "questionable" content, or perhaps content that is not "suitable" for all audiences. Yes, I know you're thinking it. Let us just get it all out in the wide-open, vast valley of truth, shall we?

Click HERE if you are at least 18 years of age (because clicking definitely proves your age!)
Or click here if you are under the age of 18.

Adult entertainment? Seriously? That's all that you can come up with? That's quite an unimaginative imagination you have there. Perhaps your brain has taken a personal day or an extended vacation of some kind. Please do try a little harder next time.

"HOW DO YOU DEW?"
Screenplay by Maxwell Greyson

ACT 1, SCENE 2

EXT. GRASSY PATCH OF LAND- SEATTLE, WA - DAWN
(PRESENT)

GREY and GUY are still standing barefoot in the damp grass as the
sun rises behind the Cascades. They're still discussing what GREY
does and also the morning dew.

GREY
No, I'm not a "freaking spammer," as you call it. I don't spam,
never have spammed and never will spam.

GUY
Yeah right, man, I've heard it all before!

GREY
What are you from Hawaii or something?

GUY
What're you talking about, man? Dude, you never make sense.

GREY
You love spam so much, I was just thinking that maybe you were
from Hawaii or something.

GUY
Listen dude, I don't have erectile dysfunction, so lay off! I don't
care what kind of magic your pills will bring - take me off your
list!! I opt out!!!

GREY
Funny, yeah I'm not a spammer. To tell you the truth, I wouldn't
even have a clue how to send out that many emails. I did once

accidentally forward an underwear sale to my entire address book, but that's about as close as it gets.

GUY
Hey, what kind of underwear was it? Was it for boxer briefs? I got that!

GREY
In that case, you're welcome.

GUY
Yeah, right. Well, then what do you DO? Come on man, time's a running out. You're killing me here. Dude, this dew is all over the place.

GREY
This dew will not come off! (shakes foot)

GUY
Last chance, dude, or else I'll just come to my own conclusions.

GREY
Web development?

GUY
Porn? Seriously?!

GREY
Listen...

GUY
Where do you have tryouts, casting calls or whatever?

GREY
I think I may try to bottle this (he squats, feeling the dew between his fingers). So clean, so fresh, so pure.

GUY
Seriously, can I get in on the next casting call?

GREY

Have you tried the hammock yet? (points to hammock)

FADE TO BLACK

THE END

It's fine, really, that you think these ridiculous things. But why exactly do you think these things of me, anyway? Nevermore, I am peace with it all. You can now clear your head of these unscrupulous thoughts.

I won't even go into the absurd depths of your terrible, unspeakable thoughts. Scratching the surface has been quite enough, and, honestly, I do not wish to visit those depths and, in turn, paint myself in even more of an off-putting light.

Run a virus scan if you must.

I realize that I haven't given you an answer yet as to what I do for a living. Believe me, I don't wish to string you along but it can always be helpful to give a little background, and, to be completely honest, I have a lot of time on my hands these days.

So, to be completely truthful, perhaps I did want to string you along after all. But, really, can you blame me with all of those unreasonable thoughts and outlandish theories floating around in your head?

In any case, the answer is much simpler: Cell phone antenna boosters. I sell antenna boosters for cell phones.

That's right, I sell cell phone antenna boosters, or "boosters" for short, online. Well, I don't really sell them but I'm involved in the selling of them. Well, I'm only superficially involved in the selling of them. That is, I really only refer people to the actual sellers. Well, in reality I usually refer people who are looking for antenna boosters to another company, and then that company, in turn, refers those people to an actual company that sells actual antenna boosters.

Conclusion: I sell boosters.

In case you're not familiar with cell phone antenna boosters, I'll give you a quick overview. A cell phone antenna booster is small grey/black decal with a funky pattern and a mysterious molecular structure that you place either carefully on the battery inside of the cell phone, on the outside of the phone itself, or perhaps even in both places if you are so inclined.

Once this peculiar and mystifying pseudo-sticker is attached to your phone, you'll be immediately rewarded with a stronger cell phone signal, less interference, fewer dropped calls, and a more enjoyable cell phone experience overall.

Do they work? Are my cell phone antenna boosters as good as advertised? Do they boost your signal? Will these fine antenna boosters truly take your reception level from bad to good or good to great?

They certainly look the part. Their appearance is almost like a tiny plastic version of a complex circuit board and using them certainly hasn't hurt my signal. Those reasons are good enough for me.

So, yes, they work. They work very well.

Currently, I have 16 boosters stuck to various parts of my cell phone, and they combine to form a sort of scaly, futuristic skin of sorts. Hence, my phone is known affectionately as the snake.

Some used to call what I do affiliate marketing and some still do call it just that. I used to call it affiliate marketing - and I tried to call it many other things at many other times - but now I simply call it project management.

Plain and simple: I'm a project manager.

Here, for your reference, is a handy list of job titles that I've used to explain my profession, and, along with them, the most common public translations for those job titles.

- **Online marketer:** Lowlife spammer; e.g. one who steals a toy from a small child.

- **Online advertiser**: Lying, lowlife spammer; e.g. one who steals candy and a toy from a small child.

- **Web developer:** Dishonest, lowlife computer freak; e.g. one who steals money out of the piggy bank of a small child.

- **Affiliate marketer:** Scumbag, lowlife computer freak; e.g. one who steals the money from the piggy bank of a small child and then shatters the piggy bank in front of child.

- **Online entrepreneur:** Lazy, lying lowlife, and possibly a scumbag spammer; e.g. one who lies about everything, all the time, to everyone.

- **Project manager:** Undetermined.

How do I know these definitions so well? Stand here in these shoes for 24 hours and you will cease asking such questions. I can see it in their eyes, read their minds, and feel the seething words that are waiting to be tossed in my direction.

In any case, I now go with "project manager." It's equal parts vague and detailed. It says "don't ask any more questions" without raising any flags. It says "leave me alone" with the asker actually wanting to leave me alone.

That's the key, you see. I don't want my chosen job title to say "leave me alone" with the asker actually wanting to know more. That can be a problem. "Project manager" can be processed very easily without actually being processed beyond surface level. Managing a project can be a tough task or an easy one, depending on the details of the project itself. But no one ever wants to dig below the surface very far, so a project manager I am.

It is, in many ways, perfect, much like my patch of grass surrounded by continuous traffic traveling in circles was supposed to be.

define: project manager
one who is responsible for the progress and performance of the project

Repeat after me: project manager.

<!--nod head slowly but surely-->

My profit is $16.18 per booster sold. I sell approximately 423 per day. These numbers have been proven over time and there really isn't much variance. I don't need to consult with Sid or anyone else to confirm that $16.18 x 423 x 365.25 equals a lot of dollars. Or, at least, that simple mathematical equation right there produces a result that equals a lot of dollars for a simple project manager.

define: law of averages
Regulation that stipulates that one must make use of both the mean and median in order to remain compliant in all numerological practices

I must admit that referring virtual people to virtual places where they can virtually purchase antenna boosters for their cell phones is about as exciting as it sounds. For more mind-blowing, finger-tingling insight into the glorious, enthralling world of cell phone antenna boosters, simply nanozero it.

Head over to nanozero.com and nanozero for:

- boosters
- antenna boosters
- cell phone antenna boosters
- cellphone boosters
- mobile phone antenna boosters
- cellphone antenna boosters
- boost me now

To the 16 of you in the world who are unfamiliar with nanozero, let me fill you in quickly. It's the one and only search engine worth its weight in virtual silver. It's the search engine that I use, you use, your neighbor uses, we all use it. Why? Relevancy is the key to nanozero's success. You see, nanozero.com sorts through all of the mess and confusion on the Internet. It filters the World Wide Web, strains it, if you will, and presents you with one single result.

That's right, billions of web pages exist out there, but nanozero will present you with the *one*, the only, the *only one* that matters.

nanozero.com:

- Our search button doesn't even say search
- We only put the search box here because we *had to
- Two results is one too many
- Where you are always the one
- Three results is two too many
- Absolute nanozero: www = zzz
- Miss out on the world's misinformation
- The world wide "what's that?"
- The first ever search go kart
- Don't be live
- Live, live, live (say it in the mirror)

As far as boosters are concerned, I'm that one and only result. Well, my website is that one result, to be exact. Regarding cell phone antenna boosters, I'm really all that matters. Well, not me, but my website selling antenna boosters. Or my website that refers people to a place that sells boosters, whether directly or indirectly.

How did I get the coveted number one spot in nanozero's results? You're still thinking those crooked thoughts?

Simple: I managed that project perfectly.

Quick, close your eyes. Think of the stock photo of the slightly overweight, happy looking fellow sitting at his recently dusted computer desk with a nice crisp-looking monitor and delicious-looking cup of coffee. You can see it, right? He is sitting there in his pajamas - you hope they are his pajamas - without a care in the world.

<!--what if those are not his pajamas?-->

For some reason, he's very pleased to be clicking on something on the screen.

<!--what if he wears those clothes all day?-->

But you can't make out exactly what is so pleasing on the screen. The angle of the photo is such to create an air of mystery. But he's obviously pleased to be sitting there in his comfortable clothes with his coffee mug. His teeth are really white, too. OK, have that picture in your head?

That is me. He is I. We're the same guy, really. That stock photo has a comfortable home in reality: My computer desk on third floor of my home on my very own patch of grass encompassed by traffic traveling in a circular motion.

Although I must admit that the stock photo and my life are not exactly carbon copies of one another. That is, I'm not really overweight and I don't recall feeling overly joyous for more than a handful of clicks in my life.

But I do like coffee. My teeth are not really white anymore (the coffee), but I do have a computer desk that I sit at occasionally. The desk is not very clean, my monitor is old, and, well, you get the picture.

Right now, I work one hour per day. I sell boosters. I work on projects.

I take my sweet time with it all.

\\+rx1618:

labore [sic]

I will rest my feet
On the sturdiness of labor
Daydreaming today's visions

In someone else's
tomorrow breeze
Comparing to those
of what should have been

\\-grey

define: labor
hard work; an endeavor that takes great effort

<!--have you seen my hammock?-->

To: voice <cassini2358@yahoo.com>;
From: grey <maxwellgreyson@yahoo.com>;
Subject: 2day

Message:

v- cant make our apptmnt 2day. sorry-crzy busy at wrk. slammed! will
write ltr -g

I've got plenty of ways to pass the time, and, more importantly,
pass the time in a more enjoyable and productive way than sitting
in the same room with the voice for an hour. I suppose my favorite
place to pass the time these days is Cafe Entropy, an old cannery
converted into a coffee shop in Ballard.

As if you could kill time without injuring eternity.

Henry David Thoreau

Everyone is very friendly with each other at warm and cozy Cafe
Entropy, but I, unfortunately, seem to be excluded from that air of
kindness. The regular barista over at Cafe Entropy, Ruby, knows
everyone who frequents the joint by his or her first name, knows

his or her favorite drink, favorite color and the temperature at which he or she typically breaks a sweat.

I, on the other hand, have been visiting Cafe Entropy every day for two years and have yet to be acknowledged beyond the most basic of levels.

One large drip coffee, please.

I generally stay for an hour or two, often pacing back and forth along the counter where many people sit and pretend to work. At least I don't even try to pretend. If Cafe Entropy had a hammock, I would gladly lie in it all day long.

<!--do they really all have the same laptop? how is that possible?-->

Those don't look like comfortable clothes that they're wearing, either. I don't think these counter dwellers fall into the same category as the guy in the stock photo with his pajamas and stainless-steel desk.

In any case, I haven't been the recipient of acknowledgement at Cafe Entropy just yet but surely it'll happen someday soon. I'm confident of it! It's time for a refill before I head home.

Headline: Local man frequents coffee shop despite barista's silent ridicule of his drip

Finding ways to pass time has become a hobby of mine. Cafe Entropy helps out a lot with this but I have other avenues of time-passing, as well. It's not all sunshine and cloudless skies, though. Having too much time, though, can also bring in a lot of unwanted action to your life, so you need to be able to shut down when necessary.

Believe me, when others get the idea that you have a lot of time on your hands, it can get complicated quickly. I've become rather adept at sounding busy these past few years.

Here's a quick primer on how to sound busy, free of charge:

Quick and easy guide to sounding busy, by Grey

1. Careful selection of descriptors for your current state is essential.

OK	busy	very busy
Good	overloaded	crazy busy
Better	buried	swamped
Best	insane	slammed

2. Grammar plays a major role.
i. complete lack of punctuation can be okay in that itll work out well in some instances but its not really necessary if you know what I mean what do you think
ii. another tactic ... is using - completely, random "punctuation" which, can create: a sense of rampant; agitation...

3. Length must be scrutinized.
i. one proven method is to go with run-on sentences (see #2, part i) but it's important to note that this method can completely backfire in that your intelligence can be questioned but perhaps not, it's almost like why doesn't anyone know the difference between loose and lose?
ii. a better tactic is to go with shorter sentences and include abbreviation wherever possible.

#1 (average)	I am so very busy at work that I cannot even find the time to spell out all of the words right now. Talk to you later. Goodbye best friend forever.
#2 (better)	I'm so swamped at work that I can't even spell out the words right now. ttyl bff.
#3 (best)	slammed @ wrk: cant even spl out wrds - l8r!

It is my ambition to say in ten sentences what others say in a whole book.

Friedrich Nietzsche

maxwellgreyson: BUZZ!!!
sidsays0: hello, old friend!
maxwellgreyson: canceled on the voice today
sidsays0: come on man
maxwellgreyson: :?
sidsays0: its only the 2nd one
maxwellgreyson: yeah well
sidsays0: well what?
maxwellgreyson: im pretty slammed over here
sidsays0: right, right, of course
maxwellgreyson: insanely swamped
sidsays0: yeah well its only the 2nd meeting man
maxwellgreyson: nice u can count
sidsays0: indeed
maxwellgreyson: thought u only counted to 0
sidsays0: tru
maxwellgreyson: dont u need to take your pet 0 out for a walk or something? feed it?
sidsays0: give it a chance
maxwellgreyson: itll surely bite me
sidsays0: no cassini - give her a chance
maxwellgreyson: the mistake was showing up once
sidsays0: y?
maxwellgreyson: 0 is the number of choice, right?
sidsays0: no man, u arent paying attention
maxwellgreyson: sorry what were u saying?
sidsays0: funny.
maxwellgreyson: agreed
sidsays0: so what r u gonna do?
maxwellgreyson: dunno
sidsays0: lemme guess, head over to cafe entropy?
maxwellgreyson: already did
sidsays0: give it up, man, you have 0 chance of being rubys friend
maxwellgreyson: dont want 2 be a friend
sidsays0: is that right?
maxwellgreyson: just a 1/2 friend
sidsays0: 0% chance
maxwellgreyson: disagree
sidsays0: :0
maxwellgreyson: why?
sidsays0: not hip enough, grey, time 2 move along
maxwellgreyson: :1

sidsays0: not hip enough
maxwellgreyson: 0% chance of that
sidsays0: people dont like u man, its tru
maxwellgreyson: its gonna happen! believe!
sidsays0: ur not getting a convert here
maxwellgreyson: tx
maxwellgreyson: brb
sidsays0: l8r

To: grey <maxwellgreyson@yahoo.com>;
From: sid <sidsays0@yahoo.com>;
Subject: re: zeroes

Message:

grey~

---zeroes 0.2---

I know what you're thinking: And what exactly is zero, anyway? You
were thinking that, no? I will answer that first question with a question
of my own: What does it matter what the definition is if you already
know it as an old friend? You know it as the oldest of friends, in fact. I
could most certainly put some words on some paper to define zero, as
it were, but why not simply point my finger instead? Or perhaps I
could take zero in my hand and feed it nothing ever so gently. Would
you like to hold my pet zero? Careful now, there's no telling how
fragile my pet zero might be. But what about the other zeroes, you
ask? How are they to defend against nothingness without so much as a
single helping hand? See, this is where the definition gets tricky. When
your definition turns into an explanation, you've definitely gathered
too many extra words that will do nothing but muddy the pristine
glacial runoff. I'll just point instead: Look!

~sid

The gaze of emptiness exists only in a summer twilight haze.
-Frodrick Gray

It's definitely time to take a leisurely break in my hammock in my backyard. I guess I don't have much of a traditional "back" yard on this here circular patch of land, but it is a yard.

While lying in the hammock I often daydream of what it would be like to be included in Ruby's inner circle of friends. I can't help but hope that maybe one day my daydream will transition seamlessly into a real dream. Oh what a glorious dream that would be!

And then perhaps that real dream could transition to reality, you know? I wouldn't expect a seamless transition on that switch, but it could happen, right? What emotions would pass through when she said my name right after I strolled into Cafe Entropy? How would my temples tingle when she asked me how I was doing?

And so I rest on this tangled web of cloth, dozing here and there, creating visions and prophecies in succession, debating each one's qualities and hoping that they effortlessly merge into the most extraordinary of dreams!
-Frodrick Gray

Sleep comes easy in the hammock. I close my eyes and drift off to a parallel space. After an hour or so, I wake up suddenly with eyes wide open.

I just woke up remembering that I remembered Ruby's face in a dream.

Ruby!? Why!? What does it mean?

I just wanted to be a half-friend or even a quarter-friend and nothing more. But now that I remember her face I'm stuck with a mix of emotions so foreign that I have no words to describe what I feel.

This all is absolutely ridiculous and I can't even process it correctly right now. Falling out of my hammock, I run inside to attempt a sketch with paper and pencil. It's no use; I can't draw.

But I remember. I remember!

\\+rx1618:

shure [sic]

your beauty often sits
quietly perched
on the shore of solitude;
perhaps that
is what makes your beauty
stay a while longer

\\-grey

To: voice <cassini2358@yahoo.com>;
From: grey <maxwellgreyson@yahoo.com>;
Subject: hello again!

Message:

I'm sorry that I missed our meeting today.

In any case, this is basically my job here, or what I do for a living.
Have you thought of boosting your reception?

www.antennaboostersrus.com

-grey

Reception level: Average (2 out of 4) ||

```
function GoToScene(event:imeyeself):void
```

{

I am a forgotten face. Go ahead, close your eyes and attempt to draw me. Your brain pen will run out of ink before you have a chance to reconstruct even a fraction of my profile. Please do not hit your pen repeatedly on the table for better results, as this will not produce the desired effect. My features simultaneously blur and lump together in a heap of indescribable dark matter. Sure, I still exist, but not in visual memory of any kind. That is, as nothing but pure information, I exist in some other space, waiting patiently to discover the most direct path to the next reasonable destination. Floating aimlessly in this other space, I plan to enter the nearest black hole and impress my likeness on its container for eternity.

}

3. A see [sic] of nothing

But I stress that the universe is mainly made of nothing, that something is the exception. Nothing is the rule. That darkness is a commonplace; it is light that is the rarity.

Carl Sagan

I saw Ruby's face! I remember Ruby's face! I remember what she looks like!

Do you understand what this means? Do you comprehend the significance of this one simple event that seemingly mixes into the stew of apathy simmering quietly on the stove of everyday life? I saw her face in a dream and I can see it now if I simply close my eyes!

It doesn't matter if within a dream, a daydream or somewhere in between - there it was, her face: I saw it, I see it, and I remember it. I remember it!

This has never happened before. Not ever. Fact is, I don't even fully comprehend the implications of this single remembrance right here and now. But I do know that this is definitely a significant event.

This much I know for certain.

define: prosopagnosia
face blindness; an inability to recognize faces

Prosopagnosia is a condition that I've had since I can first remember. In all honesty, it's strange but I didn't even realize that I suffered from this peculiar deficiency for quite some time. A good number of confusion-filled years passed before I filled in the missing blank pieces with partial bits of information obtained from here and there, and gathered them together into a finished theory of incompleteness. Or perhaps I assembled a generic rough draft that evolved through time, if not a detailed theory.

`<!--hello for the first time yet again, old friend-->`

In any case, Prosopagnosia has always been a part of me, like feet or toes or toenails or corns.

```
define: prosopagnosia
corns
```

I got so used to not remembering what people look like that it just became part of me. I often forgot that my prosopagnosia existed until I stepped on it at just the right angle with just the right amount of pressure. At that point of temporary agony, I remembered full and well as I hopped around in pain and tried to recover as quickly as possible.

Think back to when you were a child. Now think of your backyard. That backyard was what all backyards were like, right? In your mind, the Earth was nothing more than a large patch of land. So, everyone saw the same backyard, played games in the same backyard, right? Your tree was the same as all of the other trees that existed across the globe. Why wouldn't it be? Your grass was the same color as your neighbor's grass and the other guy's grass and the grass outside of the gas station. Your life was merged with every other life out there. You didn't think it, you just knew it. Everyone saw things just as you did and lived the same experiences that you lived each day.

I thought that when everyone closed their eyes they saw everything except faces, just like me. I didn't even think about it, really. I just knew it. Why would it be different for anyone else?

Think of someone you know very well. Now close your eyes and think of his or her face. Think of the fine details that you store to recognize this person; the subtleties that define your memory of who that person is. Think of the small variations that differentiate that one person from all of the other people you have ever known, or even all of the people that you have ever met. Got it?

Now think of a reality police TV show. You know, one of those where tiny hidden cameras capture footage of arrests and altercations where the faces are greyed out and blurred. The driver is being given a field sobriety test but all you see is a pair of jeans and the spider-web tattoo on his back. Or is it his chest? You can't tell. His face is indecipherable from a cloud rolling in to block the sun. Indeed, my memories are filled with inappropriately dressed, typically shirtless drivers getting slapped with felonies and misdemeanors of varying levels of severity.

Not even in a daydream can I remember a face.

Forgive me my daydreams, as I also forgive those who think that they dream, whether 'tis day, night or somewhere 'tween.
-Frodrick Gray

Not until this very moment have I ever been able to recall a face. In the past, this inability to recall faces caused or at least contributed to quite a few mishaps; new haircuts, new wardrobes, significant weight loss or weight gain, even different locations all posed problems.

I would walk right past people I had known for years and look old acquaintances in the eye having no idea who they were. I must admit that this deficiency increased the difficulty of my life an immeasurable degree.

Ruby? Ruby!

I close my eyes now and see her face. I saw it then and I see it now. What a spectacle! I've somehow found spectacles for a ridiculous mind. But how? And why?

Headline: Local man's fleeting moment turns into breakthrough of some sort

Now for the real question: how should I break the news to Ruby?

I mean, Ruby and I have never really spoken aside from the counting of change and the ordering of large drip coffees (and large drip-coffee refills), but this is my chance to break through. Is it perhaps my one and only chance? With this breakthrough, we can finally become the best of friends like I've always known we could be.

```
define: BFF
bit-map-based first fit
```

```
<!--that has got to be wrong-->
```

```
\\+rx1618:
```

```
the won [sic]
```

```
You know you're the one
Don't you know?
I've seen you before, you know
You don't understand;
I don't see much
But I've seen you before
Don't you see?
```

```
\\-grey
```

Listen, I'm not talking about Ruby and I running hand-in-hand through a field of wildflowers and galloping in slow-motion to a structure of white lattice and perfectly manicured green vines. I'm simply talking about a nice, pleasant harmony here. I mean, I'll even settle for "best acquaintances" or something along those lines.

She can call up at midnight and ask life advice from Grey, her loyal friend and trusted confidant. Well, I suppose that the midnight call might take it a step above best acquaintances, but I'm OK with that, too. I'm prepared to grab hold of it, no matter what form our budding friendship ultimately takes.

Why am I so unjustly and unfairly banished from such simple pleasures that come included in the fine print of the life contract for everyone else? No longer!

Nevermore, I'm really at peace with it all. I only mention the whole unfair banishment for the sake of explanation, conversation even. Surely you're not going to strip that from me as well? Have I reached the level of ridiculousness where I'm not even permitted to converse, to engage in small talk for the sole purpose of providing a basic explanation?

In any case, I've come up with some ideas of how to approach the topic with Ruby. I've created a short list of statements that'll send me on the fast track to becoming a member of Ruby's trusted inner circle.

re: breaking the [fabulous] news to Ruby:

- I dreamt about you last night!
- You were in my dreams last night!
- I saw you in my dreams last night!
- Where were you last night? I already know - in my dreams!
- When I close my eyes, I see your face!
- I saw your face last night while sleeping, can you believe it?
- Hey, I woke up and remembered your face!
- I remembered what you looked like while in bed!
- I was in bed and thought of your face!

None of those lines really seems to have that perfect ring now, so maybe I'll just wing it on the fly. Sometimes it works out better that way, you know?

Problem is, I'm not really great with quick one-liners unless I have slightly more than 16 hours to contemplate all possible choices and eliminate those of poor quality, consolidate the list to a more manageable amount, and then test out the lines one-by-one.

I understand that this lack of improvisational skills doesn't exactly bode well for me to perform admirably in an uncomfortable setting, but I don't really have much of a choice.

Ah, enough of this! When am I ever going to get a better chance than this? The time is now to begin the first few steps up the seemingly endless staircase that leads to the summit of Ruby's ultimate confidence and admiration. Breaking through the red tape will be the hardest part; after that it'll be smooth sailing ahead.

<!--this much I know for certain-->

maxwellgreyson: BUZZ!!!
sidsays0: hello, old friend!
maxwellgreyson: great news!
sidsays0: west seattle is breaking free & forming its own country?
maxwellgreyson: uh
sidsays0: that IS great news!
maxwellgreyson: no, great news on the grey front
sidsays0: love it when u talk about urself in 3rd person
maxwellgreyson: good, b/c there is great news on the grey front!
sidsays0: plz do tell
maxwellgreyson: i remembered a face last night - in a dream
maxwellgreyson: can you believe it??
sidsays0: not sure
sidsays0: wait, is this your prosopagnosia stuff? the face blindness?
maxwellgreyson: indeed!
sidsays0: well that is good news. how did it happen? or what happened? or whatever
maxwellgreyson: not sure, but ul never guess who
sidsays0: who?
maxwellgreyson: any guesses?
sidsays0: dude who threw the mango smoothie @ ur head?
maxwellgreyson: no
sidsays0: ur old neighbor friend who always screams LAZY! when he sees u?
maxwellgreyson: incorrect
sidsays0: dude from the concert who head-butted u 4 no reason?
maxwellgreyson: wrong
sidsays0: fast food guy who refused to sell u a hotdog?
sidsays0: again 4 no reason
maxwellgreyson: nope, thx for gr8 memories tho
maxwellgreyson: forgot about the hotdog incident
sidsays0: got it - guy with the tiny bike who threw it on the ground in the middle of the street & kept yelling U WANT A PIECE?!
maxwellgreyson: no
sidsays0: a few faces from the angry mob that started throwing empty beer bottles at u?
sidsays0: yet again 4 no reason

maxwellgreyson: when was that?
sidsays0: the 1 time u tried 2 ride ur bike?
maxwellgreyson: oh right
sidsays0: so ... ?
maxwellgreyson: ruby!
sidsays0: oh no
maxwellgreyson: oh no? no - great news!
sidsays0: not great news
sidsays0: dont tell her man - ive already seen u struggle enough w/ my own eyes
sidsays0: & thats not even counting the stuff u dont tell me
maxwellgreyson: awesome thx, ur a great friend
sidsays0: seriously man dont tell her, she already cant stand u
maxwellgreyson: yeah yeah yeah
sidsays0: its gr8 news tho
sidsays0: remember any other faces now?
maxwellgreyson: no
sidsays0: like maybe people who dont hate u?
maxwellgreyson: & who would that be?
sidsays0: good point
maxwellgreyson: alright gotta run
maxwellgreyson: time for a caffeine boost
sidsays0: no its not!
maxwellgreyson: smooth sailing ahead
sidsays0: thats my least favorite greyism
maxwellgreyson: good
maxwellgreyson: SMOOTH
maxwellgreyson: SAILING
maxwellgreyson: AHEAD
sidsays0: thx 4 yelling it
maxwellgreyson: NP!
sidsays0: u need 2 go 2 cafe entropy like u need me 2 write 'Hate Me' on ur forehead
sidsays0: again
maxwellgreyson: LOL
sidsays0: dont go to freakin entropy man
maxwellgreyson: brb
sidsays0: dude
maxwellgreyson: l8r
sidsays0: grey!
sidsays0: BUZZ!!!
sidsays0: BUZZ!!!
sidsays0: BUZZ!!!
sidsays0: :|

Sid lives in West Seattle, so he won't be able to get out to Ballard fast enough to stop me from swinging by Cafe Entropy to spread the good news. He knows this, he knows that I know this, and I know that he knows that I know this.

Sid says that West Seattle is more Seattle than Seattle and he might be right. Indeed, he may very well be on to something there because I have no idea what that means. I generally take his word for it no matter what he's talking about.

The entire west wall of his loft in West Seattle is a chalkboard. And he actually writes things on the chalkboard, things like equations and whatnot. I mean, that alone puts him an indeterminate number of notches ahead of me in regards to pretty much every possible character trait. Believe me, I have never had even the smallest clue, the slightest inkling even, of what a semi-intelligent person might do with a chalkboard if given a blank slate and a fresh piece of chalk.

"THE CHALK BORED"
Screenplay by Maxwell Greyson

ACT 1, SCENE 1

EXT. ELEMENTARY SCHOOL CLASSROOM - MORNING (PAST - 1985)

GREY sits quietly at his desk while TEACHER and another student return from the hallway. The room is quiet and all eyes are on TEACHER. She slowly turns and looks at the chalkboard as she re-enters the room with the sullen-looking student at her side. TEACHER's face quickly morphs into one of anger and disapproval as she turns to address the classroom.

TEACHER
OK, class, very funny (shaking head). Who drew the clowns on the chalk board? I was out of the room for grand total of two minutes!

Quiet laughter is heard but no student answers the question directly.

TEACHER
Maxwell (she looks directly at GREY), did you draw clowns on the
chalk board again?

GREY
[...]

TEACHER
Maxwell, did you draw clowns on the board?

GREY
[...]

TEACHER
Maxwell?

STUDENT 1
Maxwell did it (pointing)!

STUDENT 2
Yeah it was Maxwell (pointing)!

The classroom erupts into a confusion of confessions and
accusations, with multiple students pointing out the silent GREY
as the culprit.

TEACHER
Let's go Maxwell (taking GREY by the arm), out we go!

GREY turns to look at laughing classmates as he is escorted out of
the classroom.

FADE TO BLACK

THE END

For the record, I didn't draw any clowns on the chalkboard in the
classroom that day. Nor did I draw clowns on the chalkboard any
other day, for that matter. Sure, I got blamed for the clown

drawings, but, in reality, it was Sid who put the chalk on the board and created the masterpiece.

It was always Sid. Always.

I'll admit, I often took the blame for Sid's antics back then but, really, it was a small price to pay to have a loyal friend like him at my side.

If only I could shrink Sid to pocket size and carry him around with me! I'd have to get my hands on a tiny tin container, though, so that I could shut him up in there when necessary. No need to worry, I would certainly poke a few pin holes in the lid of the tiny tin can for air flow. I wouldn't want to be cruel or anything, but, really, where are the rules for how to treat a tiny pocket friend?

Generally speaking, I take Sid's word for most things and trust his opinion completely. But this remembrance that I experienced last night is more than a little unique. I think the right path to take going forward is also probably a bit unique if, for no other reason, because of the sheer uniqueness of the situation.

Sure, my vision may be a bit narrow, perhaps like looking down a small underground tunnel even, but I feel as though I see more clearly now since the dream.

Since remembering a face - Ruby's face to be exact - I see everything with a level of clarity that I never thought I'd be able to reach. I won't go so far as to say my vision is now crystal clear but overall clarity is definitely improved.

I'll head over to Cafe Entropy now and begin my journey to the center of Ruby's stage, a voyage that will include a healthy dose of undying admiration and unbridled joy from the likes of Ruby and her closest friends.

Headline: Local man attributes newfound 20/20 vision to half-caf/half-decaf

She has not yet been born:
she is music and word,
and therefore the untorn,
fabric of what is stirred.

Silent the ocean breathes.
Madly day's glitter roams.
Spray of pale lilac foams,
in a bowl of grey-blue leaves.

Osip Mandelstam

Hold up, what's this other barista doing standing behind the counter? I mean, I don't think this person is Ruby (see also: prosopagnosia) but it could be. No, I'm pretty sure that this person right here in front of me now is *not* Ruby.

Has my vision been clouded more than I ever imagined?

No, that's definitely not Ruby.

Where is she? She's always here.

"Hey, what can I get for you?" the imposter barista asks.

"Hello, Uh, I'm a … Uh … I think … is Ruby working today?" I mutter.

"No she's not here, is there something I can get for you?" she asks.

"Uh yeah, sure, I'll have a … will she be in later?"

I can't think straight.

"I'm not really sure, I'm new here."

<!--insert awkward pause-->

"Would you like to order something?"

"Oh yeah, sorry, I'll have a large drip coffee."

"A large drip coffee? That's it? Anything else?"

"No, yeah, no that's it. Thanks."

<!--my time is bent-->

"Do you want to leave a message for Ruby or …"

"No, that's OK, yeah … uh … just tell her Grey said hello."

"Hello?" she asks. "That's it?"

"Oh, and that I have something important to tell her."

"And your name is what again?"

"Grey."

"OK, sure thing Gray, that'll be $1.68."

"It's with an E."

"What is?"

"Grey - my name - it's with an E not an A like you said it."

"Got it. Grey with an E. That'll be $1.68," she holds out her hand and stares blankly.

I drink the coffee so fast that my throat burns, but I don't really feel pain, only discomfort that will turn into pain later.

define: lyfe[sic]
this; discomfort that will turn into pain later

I feel that every eye within a stone's throw is staring at my every move, studying my every step, listening intently to my every syllable.

I started saying and thinking things like "a stone's throw" recently. It makes me feel more sophisticated.

I need to get out of here. It's time to abort this failed mission and head over to Green Lake for a nice peaceful jog. Yes, it's definitely time for that. But first I better head home and check up on the boosters. I've been slacking with the boosters.

To: grey <maxwellgreyson@yahoo.com>;
From: sid <sidsays0@yahoo.com>;
Subject: re: zeroes

Message:

grey~

---zeroes 0.3---

What's that? I'm sorry old friend, I can't hear you. The silence is too much for you these days? Or should I say too little? Go ahead, move the decimal point away from the zero a little bit farther. Move it farther, not further, mind you. If you go moving it further then we've got a whole new set of complications on our hands. But go ahead and move it. Move it only enough to produce the highest decibel level, though. Correction: move it far enough to produce the highest comfortable decibel level. Comfort is always key, old friend. Surprisingly, a zero followed by a decimal point, followed by zeroes eradicates silence. Correction: it *can eradicate silence. In the end it can produce true harmony or pure noise - which do you prefer?

~sid

---

sidsays0: BUZZ!!!
sidsays0: hello, old friend!
maxwellgreyson: ?
sidsays0: meet us at entropy in an hour
maxwellgreyson: was just there
sidsays0: oh no
maxwellgreyson: dont worry
sidsays0: u didnt!
maxwellgreyson: didnt say anything
sidsays0: oh good
maxwellgreyson: ruby wasnt there

sidsays0: close 1
maxwellgreyson: still gonna tell her tho
sidsays0: still advise against that
maxwellgreyson: still dont care
sidsays0: ok well meet us there in 1 hour
maxwellgreyson: us?
sidsays0: u, me, cassini
maxwellgreyson: the voice?
sidsays0: yes we r all meeting up
maxwellgreyson: cant
sidsays0: 3 of us
maxwellgreyson: swamped over here
sidsays0: dont want to hear it - not gonna let u screw this up
maxwellgreyson: how would i do that?
sidsays0: by not showing up for mtngs
maxwellgreyson: only missed 1
sidsays0: yeah 1 of 2
maxwellgreyson: tru
sidsays0: meet us there in 1 hour
maxwellgreyson: fine
sidsays0: good
maxwellgreyson: gives me another chance 2 tell ruby the good news anyway
sidsays0: no it doesnt
maxwellgreyson: :??
sidsays0: :|
sidsays0: see u there
maxwellgreyson: fine
sidsays0: cya
maxwellgreyson: fine
sidsays0: l8r
maxwellgreyson: l8r

I'm actually relieved to see the imposter barista still there in place of Ruby when I return to Cafe Entropy. Sid and the voice are already seated at a table talking and have a large drip coffee sitting on the table waiting for me.

"Hey, sorry about missing our last meeting," I say.

"No problem, Grey," the voice says. "I understand that things come up. I deal with scheduling conflicts every day. It's part of life for me."

"Yeah, that's definitely what it was - a scheduling conflict," I say.

Sid stares.

"How long have you two been here?" I ask.

"We just got here a few minutes ago," Sid says. "So, anyway, I thought it might help for all three of us to meet because I've known both of you for a long time and I'm obviously the one who connected you two."

"Thanks, yes, I think this is a good idea," the voice says.

"Yes, definitely a good idea," I echo.

"I want this to just be an informal meeting, Grey," the voice says. "Not like one of our sessions. I guess our goal here would be for me to get a better understanding of your background and also for you to start feeling more comfortable with our meetings and everything."

"I'm already comfortable with everything."

"No you're not," Sid says.

"Yeah I guess not," I admit.

"So, I've known Grey a long time - like a really long time," Sid says. "He's admittedly always been a bit odd, but I'll also admit that we've always been friends."

"Yeah, well you're a bit odd, too," I say.

"True. But anyway, I've seen you slipping more and more into the 'underground' as you like to call it."

"You mean lying in my hammock?"

"Sure, your hammock. I forgot. So, anyway, I've seen you kind of

71

recede back from society due to your anxieties and, as a friend, I wanted to help. So I connected you two together."

<!--a tear would trickle down my cheek if it could-->

"Thanks for the background, Sid," the voice says. "So Grey, I deal with helping people with social anxieties on a daily basis. This is what I do for a living and I'm confident that I can help you."

"How can you help me when you already hate me?"

"I don't hate you, Grey."

"Surely your opinion of me is not a favorable one."

"Actually, I must admit, you were far more normal than I expected based on the way that Sid described you."

Headline: Local man looks normal, but isn't - really isn't

"Great, thanks Sid."

Sid laughs.

"I didn't lie about anything," Sid says. "I just told the honest truth."

"That people hate me?" I ask.

"Yes, that people hate you," Sid says.

"People don't hate you, Grey" the voice says.

"Yes they do," I say.

"They really do," Sid says, nodding his head.

"Sid, you're agreeing with Grey here?" the voice asks.

"Yeah, you see, people really do hate Grey. It's always been a total mystery to me - well, maybe not a total mystery but a mystery nonetheless."

"Yeah a mystery," I echo.

"Some people have that invisible likeability, right?" Sid says. "Well Grey has the opposite of that."

"I find that hard to believe," the voice counters.

"Believe it," Sid says. "It's the truth."

I nod my head and raise my eyebrows.

"People don't like me at all."

We talk some more about hatred, dislike and whatnot as I sip my drip coffee. At least now the voice will have a better understanding of my ridiculousness.

Now I'm really ready to go for run.

I looked up today and the sky was green – it's not supposed to be green. I then looked down and the grass was brown - it's supposed to be green. How long shall this ghoulish invader sit in thy home of Mother Nature? It is decided: I shall be color blind from this moment forward.
-Frodrick Gray

Running has become a favorite hobby of mine in recent months. I use the term hobby loosely here, but then again, one could argue that using terms loosely is but another hobby of mine. I generally switch it up between running the hills of Queen Anne and Magnolia to help train for some high mountain adventures and running the flat 3-mile flat circle of Green Lake for a more leisurely experience.

I haven't exactly had any high mountain adventures just yet, but I will some day, I think. The hills are nice to run when I really feel like suffering.

Headline: Local man shows that he can suffer with the best of them

Running Green Lake has its perks, too. It's a good place to put in a few miles while just melting into the crowd people and disappearing into a cloud of your own thoughts. It can be chaotic but peaceful at the same time.

Each Sunday I stretch out my run and make it more of the long-distance variety. From Patch Court, I run to Green Lake. Once at Green Lake I run the lake once and then head west to Ballard. Once in Ballard, I end my run at the farmer's market there.

Here, at the Ballard farmer's market is where I buy my organic produce for the week ahead. I had a personal nutritionist get me on the organic-produce-buying craze a few months ago. He sold me on the mind/body/environmental benefits of buying organic produce. He made a very compelling case during our private consultation.

"Is your green supporting green or are you simply being green by avoiding going green?" he asked repeatedly.

Or maybe I heard the green speech on one of those late-night infomercials. I honestly can't remember. It may have been an infomercial for a hammock that doubles as a reusable grocery bag. Yeah, actually I'm not sure that I ever had a consultation with a human. Not in person, anyway. If I had to vote, I would put my mark next to the hammock/grocery bag choice. Yeah, there was no consultation and I kind of made up the line with four greens in it. But I do buy a lot of organic produce.

I have yet to eat any of it, but, oh, do I support local!

This much I know for certain.

Welcome to the latest edition of The Grey Matter Report, where Grey fills you in on what matters, what really matters and what's the matter.

This week's term: Going green

Attempting to go green is the new black. Along with presenting a strange color pattern, this can also cause various problems for you if you are not presently going green in every single aspect of your life.

Here are some quick tips to get you started and help you fit in:

- Do not drive your SUV to get coffee at the corner the next time you need a caffeine boost. Your neighbors will see you and hate you for it! Instead, drive your SUV to a coffee shop a minimum of two miles away to avert disaster.

- The next time you're taking your bag of paper scraps, plastic bottles and aluminum cans to throw in the trash can (because the recycling bin is way too far away), stop and think for a moment: Can this wait until nighttime so that it'll be tougher to ID you?

- The next time you are asked "paper or plastic?" at the grocery store, ask for doubled plastic bags. This way you'll have twice the bags to bring all at once to the bag recycle bin at the grocery store. You'll look like an absolute hero.

- If you forget to bring your plastic bags to the bag recycling bin at the store, simply throw them in the trash after dark (see above).

- Use green face paint whenever possible, not just on St. Patty's Day. Everyone loves face paint.

Until next time, stay somewhere 'tween black & white.

"What's this in your pocket?" the officer asks as he pats me down in a not-so-gentle manner.

I refrain from spouting out any ill-timed jokes and remember that I brought a fairly large wad of cash with me to buy my weekly supply of organic produce at the Ballard farmer's market. I'm aware that this batch of organic produce was a sure bet to start its decomposition process shortly after purchase in my basement refrigerator but that's not important right now.

<!--purchase/transport/store/rot/rinse/repeat-->

"Oh, yeah, I forgot about that. That's just cash," I say, pulling the money out of my right pocket perhaps a bit too quickly.

"Whoa, whoa, whoa," the officer says while involuntarily placing his hand on his gun. "Hand that to me very carefully."

"Sure," I say and place the roll of money slowly but surely into his outstretched hand.

"Just cash? Interesting, you say you're just going for a run at Green Lake but you have hundreds of dollars of cash in your pocket?" he asks.

"I don't recall saying that I was 'just going for a run' at all," I say defiantly. "And, in any case, it's just 20 boosters or so?"

"Boosters?"

"Nevermind," I say. "If you must know I was going to buy my weekly supply of organic produce after my run," I say.

"Organic produce?" the officer asks, half-amused. "Yeah, me too. Maybe I'll go buy some organic produce myself after I throw you behind bars. I might need some all-natural fuel to replenish the energy lost dealing with a clown like you. What do you recommend? The carrots? The tomatoes?"

<!--I never even drew the clowns-->

"Where can you even buy organic produce around here?"

"Oh, well I always run up to the Ballard farmer's market on Sundays and buy my weekly supply of organic fruits and vegetables."

"The farmer's market in Ballard, you say? That's pretty far from here. I think your story has more than a few holes in it."

<!--here we go-->

I had jogged maybe a half mile before I felt a large presence closing in behind me on the crowded path. At first I thought it might be a group of moms with jogging strollers or perhaps an angry mob of cyclists on their way to a Capitol Hill donut shop/tavern/tattoo parlor/book store but it was actually a police car coming after one person: me.

The officer had driven his squad car up directly adjacent to the paved path on the grass and was slowly approaching me. I finally glanced over and he motioned to me specifically to talk to him off the path, so I confusedly obliged.

When the officer stepped out the car I made note of his name immediately: Officer Higgs. Making note of officers' names is a practice that I have made a first order of business throughout my years. Remember, people tend to strongly dislike me, and that doesn't make for many high-quality meetings with police officers or other law enforcement officials.

This much I know for certain.

"Please step into the back of the vehicle, sir," Officer Higgs insists.

"Wait, what is this all about?" I protest half-heartedly.

It's obvious that, for whatever reason, Higgs is not going to let me walk away from whatever is happening right here, right now.

"A older gentleman was mugged of his briefcase here a few minutes ago," the officer says. "He said it was a white male with a gray shirt on who stole his briefcase and then took off. His description sounds an awful lot like you."

I look down and see my grey shirt and then look down at my hands, palms up.

"His briefcase you say?" I ask, looking down at my empty hands.

He raises his eyebrows and motions to the back seat of the squad car with a subtle forward movement of his head.

I reluctantly take a seat in the back of the squad car. I have no choice, really. Officer Higgs would love nothing more than to be forced to toss me violently into the back of the car. Listen, I've been down this road before. And if I'm going to lie in the hammock of hate, I'd rather not be bruised and battered. The usually comfortable strings of the hammock can end up feeling as though they are piercing delicate tissue.

"Listen officer, I appreciate what you're doing, but you've got the wrong guy," I say from the back of the squad car.

"Yeah, OK, keep quiet back there for a minute," the officer says while picking up the handset for his radio.

I keep talking: "Listen officer, I have a lot of respect for police, and I know you're just doing your job, but you've got the wrong guy."

The officer places the handset back down and begins another series of questions.

"What's your name?"

"Maxwell Greyson."

"Maxwell? Grayson?" he repeats as he writes it down.

<!--don't mention the A, don't mention the A, don't mention the A-->

"Yes," I confirm. "Maxwell Greyson. You can call me Grey."

"OK, Maxwell," the officer says. "Where do you live?"

"Hard to say, it's kind of Ballard, kind of Queen Anne, kind of Interbay, kind of ..."

"Your address, please?" Officer Higgs says forcefully.

"1618 Patch Court."

"Is that right?" he laughs.

"You know the place?"

"Everyone knows the place," Higgs says. "It's the hideous looking tall, skinny thing sitting there in middle of the on-ramp to the Ballard Bridge. Yes, I'm familiar with it."

"That's the one," I say cheerfully.

"I'll tell you what," he says. "I don't know a lot but I do know that that is *not* your house. I know that you do *not* live at 1618 Patch Court."

<!--this much I know for certain?-->

I start to say something but he talks over me abruptly and loudly into the handset.

"I think I've got the guy - 99 percent here - going to bring him over to the victim for direct ID."

The old guy looks pitiful. He is wearing a plaid, wool suit and thinks that he was on his way to work at Green Lake at 4 pm and got mugged of his briefcase by some young guy with a grey shirt on. I can only hear little bits and pieces of Higgs' conversation with him from within the car.

I wouldn't be all that surprised if this old guy has no idea what his name is right now. Sometimes you can see how lost someone is by one simple glance in the eyes. I was able to get a few solid glances in, so I got a good, long preview of the empty valley within.

Old Man looks into the squad car and looks right at me. I see him shake his head from left to right. Left to right, left to right. Higgs hurriedly comes over and opens the door so O.M. can have a better look at his supposed attacker. The old man looks me over carefully once more and then again once more for good measure.

"I don't think that's him, he looked different" O.M. says. "I don't know, I'm not sure anymore," He actually scratches his head. "I have no idea."

I'm truly thankful that not everyone suffers from prosopagnosia. At least O.M. came through in the arena of facial recognition. I'll give him credit for that much, at least, although I suppose that I should be a little upset that he contributed directly to getting me into this predicament. Regardless, I cannot help grinning.

Higgs, on the other hand, is not thankful or pleased, nor is he grinning. He's not amused one bit.

Headline: Local man mugs briefcase from senior in plaid suit, buys $323 of organic produce

Here you go again with those bad habits. I can hear the distant murmur from your head questioning me and wondering about the depths of my ridiculousness. How is it that you already have issues with these bad habits? Please do clear your mind of those devious thoughts, right now at this instant.

I didn't steal anything from any senior citizen with memory-loss issues and an outdated wardrobe. I know nothing of a briefcase, a mugging, an attack, a robbery, or anything of the likes. It's ridiculous that I even have to travel down this road of qualified truth at all, but, alas, it is how it is. People loathe me, you see, and as tiresome as it is to you hearing about it over and over and over, think of me.

For once, please think of me!

Officer Higgs decides to take me in to the police station despite the negative ID from Old Man. I didn't protest. What would've been the point of that, really? I did ask if we could stop at Cafe Entropy on the way to the station but that didn't help much, either.

I end up spending a few hours in a cold holding cell, I believe, simply because Higgs made a choice to loathe me.

The holding cell, strangely enough, has nothing but an old radio in the corner. I try and try but it's tough to get a good signal without interference. Perhaps he's hoping for inadvertent strangulation by electrical cord?

When they release me they give me back my wad of cash and cell phone and send me on my way back to Patch Court - by foot, of course, without so much as even an attempt to explain why they brought me in.

The snake is claiming that I missed 16 calls while I spent quality time with Higgs. The words are right there on the tiny screen yelling at me: 16 missed calls.

It must be some kind of mistake or error or a malfunction of some sort. The stinging sensation behind my eyes is relentless and my head aches to the point of nausea. Right now, I need to get home as quickly as possible so that I may also recover as quickly as possible.

For now, at least, the snake takes a back seat to the hammock.

Sixteen calls? Sixteen?

Ten voicemails? Ten? Seriously?


```
\\+rx1618:

ryght [sic]

Your right angles
are no longer right
but in a perfect way
Imperfect particles fall
and become earth
unnoticed
Listen
I would not change you
You are now a billion
shades of red
Absorbing and reflecting
```

light rays
and consuming the clouds
Look
Go ahead, float above me
I see you now

\\-grey

To: voice <cassini2358@yahoo.com>;
From: grey <maxwellgreyson@yahoo.com>;
Subject: eye myself

Message:

Sorry that I missed our meeting again. This time it was truly out of my control. I'll have to explain later – it's too much to write. BTW, did you know that I have no idea what you look like? When I close my eyes it's all gone, erased. This, too, is true.

www.prosopangnology.com

-grey

Reception level: Poor (1 out of 4) | ⅲ

```
function GoToScene(event:imeyeself):void
```

{

I am a brain in a vat. I'm not certain what liquid my vat
contains or what exactly my vat is constructed of but I'm
certain that I am a brain and I'm also certain that I am
in a vat. I can guarantee nothing more, nothing less. I
have no way of confirming that my left is indeed my left,
that my left is really my right or that it is, in fact,
neither my left nor my right. Colors are really just
shades of grey, with each color a twisted illusion of time
and space that is but one component of the current
construction of now. None of this is real, or, better
yet, it's all very real but with differing levels of
truth. An uninvited guest, I overstay my welcome yet
again. I'll sleep on the couch, really, I won't mind. Or
even a thick rug on the floor will do just fine. I may
leave a stain, though, like a slug or whatnot.

}

4. Nowhere [sic] I'm going

Thinking is another attribute of the soul; and here I discover what properly belongs to myself. This alone is inseparable from me. I am - I exist: this is certain, but how often?

Rene Descartes

I'll never forget the first call. Or, more precisely, I'll never forget the first voicemail. Remember, I wasn't able to answer the first phone call because I was in temporary custody at the local police precinct for an apparent mugging of a 90-year-old, reality-starved business man wearing a plaid, wool suit in summer weather.

To be quite honest, I don't remember my exact initial reaction to listening to the first voicemail, although I can predict with a high degree of certainty that the reaction combined a non-unique form of extreme confusion with some sort of blank hope that the message was an unfortunate, strange, one-time occurrence.

Half-sleeping on cold concrete in the basement of a tired old police station for hours with nothing but an ancient AM/FM radio made it difficult to have any kind of well-defined sensory reaction to the first voicemail.

The voice in that first voicemail is forever burned in my brain. The voice is that of an older man who is confused and perhaps more than a little frightened. His voice is muffled and the message itself is difficult to understand. The message itself is a sort of half-statement, half-question mixed with a sort of severe disorientation but yet also filled with an alarming sense of finality.

Voicemail: "I, I want to know, uh, where I'm going to?"

I already listened to the message many times over, and, in fact, just listened to it again. I cannot stop listening to it.

I hold the snake with trembling hands, trying to focus, trying to make sense of it. I recently added one more antenna booster to the snake, so it now makes use of a total of 16 boosters in all. The 16 boosters pretty much cover every single centimeter of the phone.

I've always wanted to know exactly where I was headed. Nowhere, you say? Nevermore, I prefer to simply travel to and fro in an elaborate looping pattern, projecting a sweet-tasting, lukewarm delusion for all to bask in.
-Frodrick Gray

The caller showed up on my phone as "unknown caller" so the location/origin of the call is uncertain. I'm listening to the voicemail over and over in hopes that I might actually recognize the voice of the person who left the message.

You see, on the flip side of my facial recognition deficiencies sit my voice recognition abilities. That is, if my facial recognition ability sits on the cold, damp concrete of a holding cell, then my voice recognition ability sits comfortably in the nearest recliner with three remote controls within arm's reach.

If I look at a face a thousand times, the last time I see it would be the first time yet again. For the vast majority of physical life I have loathed my face blindness; I have detested my lack of ability to remember faces, to remember what people look like. But prosopagnosia is something that I learned to live with. I adapted and found ways to deal with this unfortunate problem.

But if I hear a voice a thousand times, the last time I hear it would, in fact, be the thousandth time. I can remember a voice like the call of a crow; I'll notice a slight change in pitch, a slight difference in tone. If it is there, I hear it and I feel it. And once it is gone, once it leaves, I will always remember it. The instant it returns, I'm aware of it.

Now what? At this moment my mind is filled with one familiar face and one unknown voice. I currently float in uncharted territory.

Thing is, this is not the only time, not the only call, not the only message. It was the first time, but not the last time and definitely not the only time. The calls are now coming in with regularity.

VM: "I, I want to know, uh, where I'm going to?"

There doesn't seem to be any kind of pattern to the incoming calls, though - at least not any kind of pattern that I recognize. The calls and messages are all very unpredictable and irregular. Why me? Why now?

I can't do a thing to help. At least I haven't figured out how - yet.

maxwellgreyson: BUZZ!!!
sidsays0: hello, old friend!
maxwellgreyson: got the strangest call last night
sidsays0: ruby called?
maxwellgreyson: lol
sidsays0: she wants 2 b ur bff?
maxwellgreyson: LOL
maxwellgreyson: no, seriously – got this messed up voicemail
sidsays0: messed up voicemail? from?
maxwellgreyson: kinda hard 2 explain
sidsays0: higgs wants to meet you at the bike racks @ 3pm?
maxwellgreyson: no idea, some guy
sidsays0: some guy? explains a lot, thx
sidsays0: gr8 story
maxwellgreyson: I think some dead guy
sidsays0: whoa hold up a sec here man
sidsays0: :!
sidsays0: dead guy?
maxwellgreyson: yep
sidsays0: :0
maxwellgreyson: :1
sidsays0: what did the caller id say?
maxwellgreyson: unknown caller
sidsays0: well thats good
maxwellgreyson: ?
sidsays0: at least it didnt say dead caller
maxwellgreyson: unknown caller
sidsays0: maybe its the snake playin magician on u?

maxwellgreyson: dont think so

sidsays0: u sure?

maxwellgreyson: dunno

sidsays0: what did the dead guy say?

maxwellgreyson: "i want to know where im going to"

sidsays0: ok, so what exactly makes him a dead guy?

maxwellgreyson: i dunno man its messed up

maxwellgreyson: u just have 2 hear it

sidsays0: dead people cant really talk

sidsays0: usually

maxwellgreyson: is that right?

sidsays0: yes it is

maxwellgreyson: r u sure about that?

sidsays0: yes i am

maxwellgreyson: well this dead guy talked

sidsays0: wait, how do u know hes dead?

maxwellgreyson: dead or dying or – u just need to c for urself

maxwellgreyson: or hear for urself

sidsays0: ok, sure, ill check it out

sidsays0: always wanted 2 hear a voicemail from a dead guy

maxwellgreyson: its ur lucky day then

sidsays0: indeed

maxwellgreyson: my phone is ringing off the hook all of sudden

sidsays0: snakes been busy has he?

maxwellgreyson: indeed!

sidsays0: oh yeah? all dead people?

maxwellgreyson: dunno man

sidsays0: what do u know?

maxwellgreyson: dunno - that theyre all unknown callers

sidsays0: sounds about right

sidsays0: hey! its what uv always wanted

maxwellgreyson: yeah right, a bunch of unknown calls

maxwellgreyson: from dead people

sidsays0: no man, some good reception

maxwellgreyson: yeah i dunno about that

sidsays0: stop by & ill listen to the message

maxwellgreyson: ok

sidsays0: will let u know what i think

maxwellgreyson: ok, cya

sidsays0: head on over 2 the real seattle

maxwellgreyson: already here

sidsays0: no ur not

maxwellgreyson: yeah yeah yeah
maxwellgreyson: l8r
sidsays0: l8r

To: grey <maxwellgreyson@yahoo.com>;
From: sid <sidsays0@yahoo.com>;
Subject: re: zeroes

Message:

grey~

---zeroes 0.4---

Battle of the zeroes - who wins? Is the winner simply the zero that is most absolute in its quest? Or the most absolute and the most focused? Perhaps that is so, perhaps not. But I do know with a low degree of uncertainty that the roundest zero often claims to be victorious. Aim for perfection of circularity: at least this is what I have gathered with some rather roundabout methods. When two zeroes collide, what occurs? The short version: chaos followed by an overlapped existence. The zero composed of the most perfection takes front stage in the hall of perception. Is there any other front stage? That is, if perfection comprises the perception of the zero, to an absolute degree, is there really any room for doubt? In the end, it is an overlapping victory that varies depending on the direction of wind. There's no breeze today, you say? There's nothing I love to hear more!

~sid

VM: "I'd love to hear from you. Be sure to give me a call now. Have a good day now, goodbye."

Why? Who are you? And why would you love to hear from me? And what exactly do you want to hear from me? And what am I supposed to talk with you about?

I don't want to give you a call.

Let me explain something first and foremost here: I'm not used to receiving this many phone calls. If one was to engage in the study of individuals who have racked up the most unused minutes on their cell phone plans over a two-year span, I'm confident that I would end up in the top one percent of the top one percent.

Headline: Local man boosts reception in order choose to avoid even more calls

I'm simply not used to problem solving at a high level. Antenna Boosters 'R' Us is pretty low on the list of businesses that utilize top-level problem solving techniques.

List of most stressful occupations (descending order):

- Doorman at vacant building
- Chicken roaster at vegan restaurant
- Tailor at nude commune
- Nightshift barber at retirement community
- Project manager at Antenna Boosters 'R' Us

It's as though I'm feeling with my eyes and seeing with my ears for the very first time.

```
\\+rx1618:

sole [sic]

I see behind eyes
But feel with eyes closed
When the vision appears
I linger a while
But not for long
Afraid of souls meeting
at the wrong time;
Can you see it?

\\-grey
```

My head is absolutely pounding. Every centimeter of the skin covering my skull is stretched to the absolute maximum. I can usually narrow down the possible causes of a headache to a short list of two or maybe three candidates, but today's different. Today, the possible causes are seemingly infinite.

That last email from Sid alone is enough to force me to consider purchasing an extra-large bottle of some type of extra-strength pain reliever. Sid often finds a way of interjecting an extra, unneeded dose of something into nothing.

It's time for a coffee break.

I am an idealist. I don't know where I'm going but I'm on my way.

Carl Sandburg

"Hey, Grey, I hear you left an important message for me," Ruby says.

<!--she knows my name!-->

"Yes! I mean, I do. I mean, I did," I say, taken aback and failing miserably to conceal my joyous surprise.

<!--or maybe I was just described as the peculiar fellow who paces to and fro with drip coffee every day-->

"I've been eagerly awaiting your arrival - please tell me more," she doesn't even attempt to disguise her sarcasm.

<!--did I just mention something about a peculiar fellow?-->

I can't get any words to come out.

"What'll it be?"

<!--I feel laughter somewhere behind me like a swarm of gnats-->

"Can I get a large drip coffee?" I say as I swat at the invisible gnats. "I need my morning coffee to function properly, you know?"

<!--how does she not know my order by now?-->

"That's right, a large drip coffee. How could I forget?"

<!--/how does she not know my order by now?-->

"It's 4 pm but, OK, I'll get your *morning* coffee," she says staring right through me.

"It is? Oh, I must've lost track of time."

<!--am I standing near a swamp?-->

She comes back in what seems a nanosecond and places the coffee in front of me with a small thud on the counter.

"This one's on the house."

<!--inner circle forthcoming?-->

"Oh. Wow. Great. Thanks."

We stand there looking at each other for a short while and then she brings up the topic once again. She seems a bit impatient.

"So what's up? You had some important news to tell me, I hear, or something important to tell me?"

"Well, I sort of had this dream."

<!--an amazing, incredible, indescribably spectacular dream!-->

"A dream? Good, I love dreams. What happened?"

"Uh...well..."

"Hey maybe we could grab one of those books of dream meanings and figure it all out for you. I love doing that," she says.

"Well...it's kind of hard to explain. Let me try the coffee first." I taste the coffee. "It's good. Yes, very good, as usual."

"The dream?" she asks impatiently.

"No, the coffee. Good coffee. This right here is a good cup of coffee."

"So what was it about?" Ruby asks.

"Uh...yeah, it was about me. And..."

She stands there actually tapping her fingers on the counter. I never knew people actually did that. A feeling of dread overtakes me and travels to every part of my body. I feel it in my toenails.

<!--destined for existence solely in the outermost of circles-->

"I was a robot."

<!--tap-tap-tap-->

"You were a robot?" she asks. "In the dream?"

It seems, strangely enough, as though the mention of the robot dream has actually piqued her interest. Well, momentarily, at least.

"Yeah, so I was like this robot in my dream - which is a dream that I always wanted to have going way, way back. And so I realized - in the dream - that I was a robot."

Her stare is scorching my eyebrows.

"You see, I've been waiting a long, long time, an eternity it seems, to have this very robot dream because I've always wanted to be a robot. Well, maybe not in real life but in a dream, you know?"

"Sure, you always wanted to be a robot - got it."

"OK, yeah, so I've always wanted to dream about being a robot, you know? Or so I thought. I was never really interested in being a robot in reality, but I thought that being a robot in a dream would be pretty amazing, you know?"

"OK, so you were a robot in a dream. That's it?" she interjects impatiently.

"No, that's not it. No, no not at all. That's definitely not it." I take a long drink. "So, you see, in the dream I was a robot but it really didn't matter at all that I was a robot. Do you know what I mean?"

"No, I don't."

"I was a robot in the dream but it was almost as if I wasn't really a robot … in the dream."

"And you needed to tell me this urgently? Why?"

"Let me explain a little more: You see, I guess I had always dreamed of dreaming that I was a robot because I thought it would be an amazing dream filled with amazing robot feats and amazing robot events and amazing robot-like happenings. It had to be amazing, right? I mean, imagine what kind of amazing things a robot in a dream could accomplish, right? I mean, a robot in real life can accomplish a lot, but a robot in a dream? Now we're talking about a whole new level of amazing."

I take another long drink of coffee and feel the air deflating out of the invisible, inflatable boat that I sit uncomfortably in at this moment. I'm actually now standing and swaying, waiting for the next decent-size wave to come along and send me tumbling to a wet grave.

"But in the dream all I did was walk around telling people that I was a robot. That was it: nothing more, nothing less. It was terribly boring, ordinary, commonplace. I would just walk up to people in my dream and say 'I am a robot' but then nothing would happen. I didn't process any information at super-fast speeds or show any incredible feats of strength. I was not super fast. I was not super strong. I was basically a robot with no robot-like qualities to speak of."

Ruby stares.

"I just walked around saying 'I am a robot' to strangers."

"That sounds awful."

"Yeah, I mean, I was pretty much the most unrobotic robot that you could ever imagine. Actually, I think I may have been the most unrobotic robot perhaps even in the vast history of the entire dreamscape. Well, maybe that's a bit much, but you get the point. It was akin to walking around and approaching people with an empty clipboard asking them to sign their names on a nonexistent petition asking for a guaranteed lifelong mundane existence of tasting tap water each and every day and then debating the qualities of that tap water by means of a daily roundtable discussion."

<!--tap water? seriously?-->

"Tasting tap water?" she says. "You know, tap water does taste different depending on where you live."

"Yes! It does, doesn't it?"

"Why is that?"

"I don't know, but I do know that my dream was unfortunate."

<!--tap-tap-tap-->

"An unfortunate dream," I say. "That's all."

"I'm sorry, I missed the urgent part of that dream somewhere in between robot and tap water," Ruby says.

"I forget," I say.

"Well, that's definitely a strange dream. But what may even be stranger is the fact that you had to tell me about it."

"Believe me, I did have a reason for telling you, but, sorry, I can't remember it now."

She stares.

"I did, believe me."

"OK then Grey, I'm really glad you let me know about this urgent situation, or dream, or whatever."

<!--she does know my name!-->

"Hey, you know, you're the first person in a long time to say my name the right way."

"Grey?"

"Yeah, you said it correctly - with an E instead of an A. Not many people get it right."

"Well..." she starts to say something, squints her eyes a little, shakes her head slowly and turns to walk to the back of the shop. "Good luck with the next robot dream then. Maybe you will be super-strong or whatever you said next time."

<!--secret trap door to inner circle cracked open again!-->

"Hey! I just remembered why I wanted to tell you about the dream!" I say it loudly so that now all eyes are on me, if they weren't already.

<!--It was you! In the dream I kept telling you that I was a robot!-->

"Ruby!"

<!--
And I know it was you! I remembered what you look like! For one moment in time I wasn't blind!
-->

She is gone.

<!--I am a robot-->

My phone is ringing: unknown caller.

I don't have time for this right now. I need to head over to my appointment with the voice. Ruby disappeared to the back of Cafe Entropy, so I leave in hopes of actually making it to the appointment on time today. I admittedly have not been the best client lately.

<!--this much I know for certain-->

Read my time between the lines.
-Frodrick Gray

"Thanks for letting me know about your condition, your face blindness," the voice says as I sit down in one of her comfortable chairs. "Thanks for sending the website over."

"Sure."

"That must be a challenging thing to deal with and I'm eager to learn more about it and also about how you've learned to deal with it. And thanks for emailing over all of the other websites, too. I've enjoyed them and they really do help to provide more insight into you and your life."

"Sure, yeah, I thought it might help us out here, you know?" I say. "Sometimes things come to me later. I'm not so much an in-the-moment kind of guy."

Her chair right here, right now feels pretty good and comfortable. Who needs hammocks?

"You certainly create those pretty quickly. How long does it take you to create one of those?"

"Create what?"

<!--I buy my hammocks for about 16 boosters each-->

"The websites, Grey, how long does it take you to create one of the websites?"

"Oh, right. Sorry. It depends, I guess. I don't really sleep all that much, so that helps with the whole time thing. I can only watch so many late-night infomercials. It's better to just create sometimes. Have you ever seen the green guy who's always yelling incessantly about going green or being green or whatever?"

"No, I can't say that I have. I'll let you know if I do. But they're a great help here - the websites are - so please do keep sending me your work."

"Sure thing."

"So you've never been able to remember faces at all?" she asks.

"No, not until very recently."

"You experienced a change recently?"

"Sort of, yeah, I mean, I made some progress with the whole prosopagnosia thing, I guess."

"Is that right? Wow, that must've been a great moment! What happened?"

"I remembered a face, just one face."

"Whose face did you remember?"

"It was a friend, I mean, an acquaintance. Her name is Ruby."

"I don't think you've ever mentioned Ruby before, have you?"

"No I don't think so."

"Tell me about Ruby."

"There's not much to say, really," I say. "She's just works at that coffee shop that I go to all the time. It's the one you, me and Sid met at a while back."

"You said you're acquaintances, not friends, right?"

"Yes, definitely."

"What do you think about the fact that the first face you have recognized, or at least the first that you may have recognized in a long while, is that of an acquaintance and not someone you have known all of your life?"

"I don't really think all that much of it, to be honest."

<!--100 percent honesty guaranteed?-->

"OK, well, what else can you tell me about Ruby?"

"Not much. It's really all very unimportant and uninteresting, to tell you the truth. We should probably just move on. OK?"

"Well, I'll have to disagree with you about that all being uninteresting and unimportant but we can move along for now. However, I would also like to take this time to point out something to you that you may or may not be aware of but is necessary at this juncture. I feel it's necessary so that we can move forward and progress in our sessions here."

"I'm a little nervous here. Don't tell me: You bought an antenna booster from Antenna Boosters 'R' Us and it didn't work out too well?"

<!--each of these sessions is costing me 6-plus boosters?-->

"No, it's nothing like that. I did buy an antenna booster from your site, but I don't think I'm prepared to review its performance just yet. I need to give it a little more time to see if my reception improves."

"OK, well I'm glad to hear that. I'm all about the customer, you know."

"What I wanted to bring up is your refusal to go into detail about specific topics. In our discussions here we have come across three people in your life: rx1618, Sid and Ruby. Obviously some of these people may be closer to you than others, but each time I attempt to get any information about any of these people, no matter what the specific subject matter of the conversation is, you quickly turn the conversation to another subject. You quickly end the conversation and move to a completely unrelated topic. It's important that we dig a little deeper into your life here - and even your interpersonal relationships - in order to have any chance at achieving real results at all."

<!--like using green to go green-->

"It's not like I refuse to talk about anything. I just don't think that stuff is all that important. That's all. There's really nothing more to it than that, I swear."

"OK, well, I'm bringing it up now because I do think that these topics are very important. So, if you'll agree, perhaps we can go a little deeper on some of these topics in the future - starting today. Starting right now, even?"

"Yeah, OK, sure thing."

"OK, then, let's rewind a little bit here. What else can you tell me about Ruby? How long have you two known each other?"

"Well, Ruby is the barista at Cafe Entropy, which is a coffee shop that I have been regularly visiting for more than two years now. She's not exactly the nicest person in the world. Or, to be more specific, she's not the nicest person in the world to me. Yeah, she actually hates me, you know, loathes me, despises my presence. She is extremely, almost freakishly kind to every single person who comes through the doors, except me."

"What makes you think that? Why do you think she doesn't like you?"

"I don't think it, I know it. It's the same with her as nearly every person I meet or otherwise encounter out there. People just don't like me. People like to hate me and people also hate the idea of possibly having to even pretend to like me. It's been that way ever since I can remember lacing my own shoes, which I can't even remember, by the way."

"How are you so sure?"

"Don't act like this is a surprise to you, like you aren't fully aware of it already."

"Well, I don't hate you, Grey, and that should count for something."

`<!--and what does your tap water taste like?-->`

"Thanks, I appreciate that, but if we're going to go the honesty route here, I'm not sure that I entirely believe you," I say. "But, again, thanks for the kind words. I do appreciate the kind words. Really, I do."

"Grey, this is not a debatable topic. I don't hate you."

"OK, well Sid has known me for a long time. He's known me for a long, long time, in fact, especially by my standards. And you know what? He told you himself: people do not like me. When we were kids, Sid used to say that I must have 'hate me' tattooed across my forehead. I've actually heard him say that very sentence so many times that it makes my stomach churn just saying the words. In fact, he wrote 'hate me' on my forehead with permanent marker more than a few times. Once it took me three days to get it off. My forehead was raw from the scrubbing."

"That's not a very nice thing to do. Has Sid always treated you like that?"

"Like what?"

"Like writing 'hate me' on your forehead with permanent marker?"

"Yeah, pretty much."

`<!--only, if only, little Sid were in my pocket right now!-->`

"And yet you consider Sid a good friend of yours?"

"The best."

<!--can you hear the soft knocking on the tiny tin can?-->

"I'd love to hear more details about your friendship with Sid. But right now I'd like to go back to the face blindness. So, going back to Ruby, you said that you now remember or recognize her face. Did you see her outside of the coffee shop or how did it all happen? Where did it happen? I'd love to hear the details - this is a big moment for you, I suspect."

"Oh, well, I first saw her - recognized her - in a dream and I can still see her now if I want. If I close my eyes, I can picture her. I can actually remember what she looks like."

I close my eyes and there she is: Ruby!

"This is really all new to me and I'm not really sure what to do with it or make of it."

"That's definitely exciting news, Grey! Hopefully I can help you figure what may have brought this change on, and perhaps we can replicate your success with recognizing Ruby and it can help you with others. How nice would it be if you could recognize more people? I suspect that this would be a good thing."

"I wouldn't exactly call my remembrance of Ruby a success."

"No?"

"Well, she still hates me and, you know, I tried to tell her about the dream but it didn't go too well. I thought it might help with the whole loathing thing, but, no, not really."

"What happened?"

"Well, in my dream I was a robot. And ever since I can remember, that's the one and only dream that I always dreamed of having. I always wanted to be a robot in a dream and see what it would be like, see how it would feel. In the dream, I was a robot telling Ruby that I was a robot. And that's when I saw her. She wasn't faceless like the rest of the people in the dream."

"OK, and you told Ruby about this robot dream?"

"So, yeah, I told her how I finally had this robot dream but it ended up being really disappointing because I didn't end up doing any amazing robot-like stuff in the dream. All I did was walk around and tell people that I was a robot. But no one seemed to care and I was really rather unrobotic."

"That's an interesting dream, Grey. You'll have to tell me more about it. How did Ruby respond?"

"She didn't think it was interesting, that's for sure. I think she was rather bored with it all, to tell you the truth."

"Well that's too bad. I wonder, is it possible that she was more interested in it than you thought? Maybe you misread her response a little?"

"I doubt it. Listen, I know we talked about 'opening up' or whatever but I think we've gone far enough at this point. There's no need for me to relive a painful conversation at this point. Can we move on?"

"Yes, OK. I thank you, Grey, for opening up. Even if it's difficult for you, I assure you that it's for the best. It's for the best both here in our conversations and out there, in conversations with others," she points to the window.

"How's work going? Is there anything else that you would like to discuss since we last spoke? It has been a while - about three weeks now - so I'll just open it up to you at this point."

"OK, well, not much has been going on, really, I don't think. Oh, well, I mean, I sort of got arrested for mugging a 90-year-old man of his briefcase on the way to work at Green Lake and then I also keep getting voicemails from dead people, or dying people, or something like that. But that's about it, really."

The voice sits up straight in her chair and turns her head slightly to one side. Twice she starts to say something but it never materializes into audible speech.

"Yeah I guess those probably need a bit more explanation, huh?" I say.

`<!--this much I know for certain-->`

"Yes, I think so."

"OK, well, I went for a jog at Green Lake a few days ago, as I often do. It's a nice place to go for a jog, you know?"

"Sure."

"Anyway, this cop pretty much pegged me for the mugging of a 90-year-old man who was wearing a wool, plaid suit and who was also heading to work at Green Lake at 4 p.m. on a Sunday afternoon."

"Green Lake has offices?"

"No."

"Somebody mugged him, though?"

"Probably not. I don't know. Maybe?"

"What happened to his briefcase? Did they ever find it?"

"He probably never had one."

"What made the officer think that it was you who mugged the poor old guy? Did he say why he singled you out?"

"Indeed, what did make the cop think it was me? Indeed! People hate me. People don't like me. You see what I'm saying? Would that ever happen to you? I think not. Did it happen to anyone else at Green Lake that day? Not that I am aware of. You see, I have this uncanny ability to be loathed, and, while it does provide entertainment at times, it really is a huge pain most of the time."

"Wow, what an ordeal that must have been. How did it all end?"

"Yeah, well, in the end the old guy said point-blank that he didn't think I was the guy who mugged him but the cop took me in to the station anyway and threw me in a holding cell for like six hours or something."

"Can he even do that?"

"Probably not."

"What happens now?"

"Nothing, I guess. I mean, I didn't mug anyone and the old guy said that it wasn't me, anyway, so there's not much there. But who knows, really. Believe me, in my experience anything can happen."

Headline: Local man in need of home remedies for removal of permanent marker from skin

"Well let me know if you continue to have any trouble, OK?"

"Yeah, sure. I mean, why?"

"Perhaps I can be a character reference for you or help out in some other way."

"OK, thanks."

"So what's this with the phone calls now? Did I hear you correctly when you said something about dying people calling you on your phone?"

"Oh, right. Yeah, well, when I was in the holding cell, you know, for stealing some old guy's briefcase and then making it vanish into thin air while I contemplated what organic produce I was planning to buy, I started getting all of these unknown calls to my cell phone. I didn't know it at the time because I didn't actually have my phone with me in the holding cell. Anyway - long story short - all of these strange people are now leaving me voicemails on the snake with cryptic messages and riddles and whatnot."

"The snake?"

"My phone."

"Oh. What type of cryptic messages and riddles?"

"And whatnot."

"Excuse me?"

"And whatnot. You forgot to add 'and whatnot' to the end of your sentence."

"I'm sorry, what type of cryptic messages and riddles and whatnot?"

"Yeah, you know, like 'figure out who I am' and 'decipher my mysterious message' and 'here's a vague clue for you, detective' type of stuff."

"Are you saying that someone is playing a prank on you? Sid or someone else you know?"

"No, definitely not. These are real people. I know it. I can feel it. They're reaching out to me for some odd reason, and I can't figure out what that reason might be."

"And the dying part?"

"Well, it just seems that these people are either dead or dying or something like that. It's really freaking me out, to be completely honest."

"Well, from what I've heard thus far, that's a normal response to have, I assure you of that," the voice says.

"What, freaking out?"

"Yes, freaking out. Freaking out is a normal response to what you are describing. I think a lot of people, if they were in your position right now, would be freaking out right now. Or they would at least be confused and unsure of what to do."

"OK, well I'm confused and unsure and freaking out so where does that leave me?"

"What do these people say in the messages that they leave for you?"

I take the snake out of my pocket and play six messages for the voice on speaker phone:

VM: "I, I want to know, uh, where I'm going to?"

VM: "I'd love to hear from you. Be sure to give me a call now. Have a good day now, goodbye."

VM: "I like it here, I want to stay."

VM: "Do me one favor: Tell him that I knew it was his worst day."

VM: "I don't know where I am right now, can you come and pick me up, please?"

VM: "From where am I supposed to gather what is to be gathered? It's empty."

After the final message ends, we sit in complete silence for a moment. Although I do think I hear the Fremont Troll babbling in the distance.

"What do you think? Am I crazy or what?" I ask.

"It appears as though you are, in a way, stuck in the middle right now," the voice says.

"Stuck in the middle?" I ask. "Of what?"

"I think that's probably the very question that we need to work to find the answer to," she says.

"How do we do that?"

"I'm not exactly sure but I'm confident that we can find the right path," she says. "We'll give it our best shot to get to the bottom of this all and get you some answers. I'm just being honest here like you, Grey. We'll work hard to get you some answers, OK?"

"I like the sound of that. I think."

As I walk home from Fremont to Patch Ct, I listen to the voicemails over and over:

VM: "I, I want to know, uh, where I'm going to?"

VM: "I'd love to hear from you. Be sure to give me a call now. Have a good day now, goodbye."

VM: "I like it here, I want to stay."

VM: "Do me one favor: Tell him that I knew it was his worst day."

VM: "I don't know where I am right now, can you come and pick me up, please?"

VM: "From where am I supposed to gather what is to be gathered? It's empty."

The snake is rattling again: unknown caller, again.

I let it go to voicemail, again.

They won't stop calling me.

\\+rx1618:

meddle [sic]

I stand in the middle
of now and then
time, not standing still
slows considerably
a slow gaze
reveals stars bright and dim
in the middle
now

and
then
it was here that I realized
never before this moment
had I been
here and there
at the same time

\\-grey

To: voice <cassini2358@yahoo.com>;
From: grey <maxwellgreyson@yahoo.com>;
Subject: my destined;ation

Message:

I have no idea where I'm going and I'm even starting to wonder where I've been.

www.nowhereimgoing.com

-grey

Reception level: Above average (3 out of 4) |||

```
function GoToScene(event:imeyeself):void
```

{

I am a dysfunctional pocket watch. My problems cannot be narrowed down to a single cause or to a single event, nor can they even be described in a single sentence. My battery died long ago and leaks ever so slowly, my face displays an intricate pattern of fine cracks, my chain is rusty, and somehow sand has infiltrated my innards. The time that I keep always crawls when least convenient and skips full minutes to shorten any rare periods of contentment. Sure, I'll tell you the time, but I cannot guarantee that I'll give you the answer you've been looking for. I prefer to spend the majority of my time in a pocket or a bag or even a drawer, safe from the wicked gaze of the sun.

}

5. Stuck in the meddle [sic]

Life overcomes life.
The sound fades out.
Something is always missing.
There's no time to remember it.

You know, it was better before.
But there's no comparing
how the blood used to whisper
and how it whispers.

Osip Mandelstam

I can say with a high degree of certainty that this is, in fact, the first time that I've been here and there at the same time. Or, at the very least, this is the first time that I've realized that I am, in fact, here and there at the same time.

`<!--this much I know for certain-->`

Problem is, I can't seem to recall ever being in the middle before. I'm sure I've been in the middle at some point, but my mind has no official record of existing in the middle of anything or of inhabiting any sort of middle space.

I've spent most of my time at the bottom, near the bottom or even beneath the bottom. It's certain, in any case, that the word "bottom" is most definitely a main component of my main description.

`<!--I do solemnly swear that I am a bottom feeder-->`

Existing in this middle ground, or this middle space, if you will, is a new experience that I've yet to fully grasp. But I can say that I'm beginning to accept this middle space, if, for no other reason, because I feel as though I don't really have much of a choice in the matter.

I walk down the sidewalk crushing dead leaves into tiny remnants of what they used to be, floating along in my newfound middle space. The breeze seems different, as if it's hitting new outer nerves that used to be covered with room-temperature plastic wrap. Various colors now pop from trees and I can see the smallest parts of visible life circling in on my narrow, cold, dull vision of everyday life.

But must I embrace this newfound world wholeheartedly without any answers at all? Is this all something that I must partake in without questioning it at all? Must I really gather all of the materials and create a brand new, perhaps even less comfortable, hammock to lie in at this very instant? My current hammock just reached a new level of comfortableness and it took quite a bit of effort to get to that point.

<!--rx1618: weave me a peaceful world-->

"What can I get for you, Grey?" Ruby asks. "You know, I should probably know your order by now, shouldn't I?"

"Yes, you should."

"Let's see here, I think it's probably a ..."

"Yeah I've only been coming in here about every day for...forever," I say.

"That's right, you have been a regular for a while now - what like a couple of months?"

"Years."

"Year? What, you've been a regular since the start of the year? That sounds right, I guess. I was off by a few months, though."

"A few years. I've been coming here for a few years."

"A few years?"

"Yes - years. Plural. You see, I've been frequenting your fine establishment of caffeinated beverages here for at least two years."

<!—yes, finally got to use the fine-establishment-of-caffeinated-beverages line!-->

"Are you sure it's been that long? Two years?"

"Yeah, I'm pretty sure it's been that long. Yeah, in fact, I'm certain of it: two whole years."

"Oh, OK then. What is it, a red eye?" she asks.

"I do?"

"You do?"

"I don't use eye drops, although I don't sleep much, so maybe I should start. Those infomercials that I watch are probably not helping, either. Like the green guy says: 'don't be green about having to spend green to go green' or whatnot."

"Red eye?"

"No, the green guy - from the infomercials," I say.

"What green guy? I'm talking about your drink: Is it a red eye?"

"What drink?"

"I give up, what's your drink?"

"Oh, just a large drip coffee. That's all, thanks," I say. "What's this about red eyes? Do you have a mirror handy?"

"A red eye is drip coffee and espresso mixed in the same drink," she explains. "I thought that was your drink for some reason."

"You know what, make it a red eye! That sounds good for today. I'm all about being in the middle today."

"OK, I'll have it for you in a minute."

"Don't forget the red glove," the old woman says as she walks by on her way out of Cafe Entropy.

She walks so close behind me that I feel the direction of the air change as she passes by. The door closes behind her softly and she's out of sight in an instant.

Just like that, she's gone.

"Don't forget the red glove?" I ask to no one in particular.

"It's called a red eye, Grey, not a red glove," Ruby says.

<!--she said it with an E again!-->

"Yeah, I know, I was just repeating what that woman just said to me," I explain. "She said not to forget the red glove or whatnot."

"Who said what? What woman?"

I turn and take a look around. The place is empty. Not only is the woman long gone but all is silent and still. The usual laptop clones aren't even pushing up their glasses in a synchronized cyber dance per usual. Cafe Entropy is eerily quiet.

"Who is she? Do you know?" I ask.

"Who?"

"Nevermind. It was just a joke," I try to change the subject. "A bad joke, I guess."

"Why are you talking about red gloves? Do you always go around telling bad jokes and mumbling about robots and gloves?"

"I didn't mumble about robots."

"Well, about red gloves then?"

"No, not really. I save them all for your fine establishment of caffeinated beverages here."

<!--twice!-->

"At least you know what we serve here, I guess. We do have decaf, too, you know."

"Ah yes, of course, decaf."

<!--can't think of a decaf joke-->

"So, anyway, do you live around here or something?" she asks.

<!--she wants to know where I live!-->

"Uh, yeah, I mean, as the crow flies it ain't too far from here," I say.

I decided to start using words like "ain't" a lot more because it makes me sound more unsophisticated. I thought it might help.

"As the crow flies?" she repeats with confused amusement.

I decided to start saying things like "as the crow flies" a lot more because it makes me sound more sophisticated. I thought it might help.

"Yeah, I mean, it's not too far. I don't fly like a crow - I'm not a crow - but I wish I could fly like a crow, you know? Maybe just for one day, at least. Caw!"

<!--caw?!?-->

She slowly backs away from the counter. I don't think she even realizes that she's backpedaling in slow motion - no, in super-slow motion. Not even in my robot dream did I do anything in super-slow motion!

"Yeah, so as the crow flies it's probably about eight tenths of a mile or so from here. I ain't exactly sure. Or maybe it's more like nine tenths of a mile, depending."

"Depending on what?" she asks.

"How straight your crow flies?"

<!--is that a laugh?-->

"Well, I don't have a crow and I don't think I've ever heard anyone caw like a crow before," she says. "But, anyway, where did you say you live again?"

<!--definitely not a laugh-->

"I live right around the corner, really, just over the bridge there - at 1618 Patch Court, to be exact."

<!--now that is definitely laughter-->

"You need some original material, Grey."

"Organic material? Like cotton or what? I do go to the Ballard farmer's market, you know."

"No, *original* material, I said. As in, your jokes are not original. Like, I think you need new material for your stand-up routine or whatever it is that you do here."

Headline: Peculiar fellow paces to and fro at local coffee shop, practices lame stand-up routine

"You know, I've heard people refer to me as 'the funny guy' a few times."

"I'm not surprised. But, anyway, you're like the tenth person to use the 'I live on Patch Court' joke this week. It's really not funny."

"Good because I prefer a cotton/polyester mix for my t-shirts."

"What?"

"62/38 on the cotton side is the perfect ratio."

"I'm not talking about t-shirts, I'm talking about your bad joke about living on Patch Court."

"It's not a joke. Well, I guess I was joking about the whole crow thing but I really do live at 1618 Patch Court.

"Seriously, do you know who does live there?' she asks. "So many people claim to live there that I have no idea who really does."

"Me. I do."

She stares.

"Really, I do. I swear."

"Right, so you and the ten other people that made the joke all live there together? What is it like a commune over there? A commune right there on Patch Court? Wow, who knew?"

define: commune
to feel at one with; to be in touch with

<!--feeling in touch with my lack of community-->

"No, it's just me. It's definitely not a commune. I live there alone. But I do have a hammock."

This much I know for certain.

She stops listening and moves along to other customers who had arrived during the commune portion of our frayed and disconnected discussion. They all seem a little confused but also quite uninterested in it all. Our conversation is over.

"It's comfortable. I like it," I say as I walk out the door. "It's a good hammock - and it's mine."

The voice is right - it appears as though I am stuck in the middle here, too. I'm stuck somewhere in the middle of Ruby's inner circle and her outer circle, I suppose. Ruby, if you were Saturn, I would be sitting patiently in the gap between the first and second rings.

Ruby, Ruby, Ruby, I know that you want to let me in; deep down inside you want me to be part of your inner circle! You do, I know this. I can sense it. Perhaps you want me to be included simply for the sake of entertainment. Dare I even say you may allow my admittance solely for the sake of ridicule?

That's OK, I can live with that.

I'm surely at peace with my ridiculousness, and nothing you can say or do will make me any less ridiculous, any less foolish, any less ghoulish, nor can it transport my soul to the land of sensibility.

To: grey <maxwellgreyson@yahoo.com>;
From: sid <sidsays0@yahoo.com>;
Subject: re: zeroes

Message:

grey~

---zeroes 0.5---

The zero in the middle is almost always the most overlooked. Listen, I'm not talking about some clichéd middle-child analogy here. This is important stuff, not some bad TV show fodder to fill the role of mundane small talk at tomorrow's proverbial water cooler. The zero in the middle is often the most overlooked. This is often the case with a lot of things, no? Well, I say that zero is no different. Why is it that zero is always looked at differently? Twice-two minus twice-two plus two: The answer is two but there's a zero in the middle there, no? Go with the crowd and forget it, right? Don't mention it - don't even look in that direction. Move along. The middle zero rests comfortably in the unknown space. That's the zero that ends up in my pocket, carried to a better existence and placed gently in the bowl on my shelf. It will sit there with all of the other forgotten, misplaced zeroes. What are you doing? Stop looking in that direction! Move along, I said! Forget it, I said! After all, it is merely a zero, no? Have you never seen a middle zero before? What does it matter if it's here or there?

~sid

VM: "Mailbox Peak is the destination. There's something waiting for you at the summit."

Mailbox? Peak? Destination? Waiting? Summit?

The voice on the message sounds almost like a recording, but I can't tell for sure. My head aches yet again. Maybe it was the red eye? Or is it these relentless voicemails that are the main cause of this endless suffering?

maxwellgreyson: BUZZ!!!
sidsays0: hello, old friend!
maxwellgreyson: calls r still coming in
sidsays0: really? how many more?
maxwellgreyson: lost count
sidsays0: man that phone really has some good reception
maxwellgreyson: thats 1 way 2 put it
sidsays0: whats another?
maxwellgreyson: dunno but im starting 2 get really freaked out
sidsays0: freakin?
maxwellgreyson: yeah something like that
sidsays0: how do they call u from underground?
maxwellgreyson: :??
sidsays0: the dead guys, how do they call u from down under?
maxwellgreyson: australia?
sidsays0: no 6 feet under
maxwellgreyson: lol
sidsays0: never understood that part
maxwellgreyson: LOL
sidsays0: i know your definition for lol, btw
maxwellgreyson: Good
maxwellgreyson: LOL lol LOL lol LOL
sidsays0: what did the ghoul say on the latest message?
maxwellgreyson: dunno, but i really dont know what 2 do
sidsays0: why dont u go clear ur head with 1 of those torturous runs that u do?
maxwellgreyson: i wish
sidsays0: dravus st is calling ur name
maxwellgreyson: im afraid 2 go running now
sidsays0: rightfully so
sidsays0: cops are waiting @ every corner
maxwellgreyson: dont want 2 c higgs right now
sidsays0: dont blame u
sidsays0: what r u running 4 anyway?

maxwellgreyson: training

sidsays0: what r u training 4, a marathon or something?

maxwellgreyson: no, for the mountain

sidsays0: THE mountain?

maxwellgreyson: yes that 1

sidsays0: hold up - rainier?

maxwellgreyson: indeed

sidsays0: it would seem to me that training for mountain climbing

sidsays0: especially attempting to climb THE mountain

sidsays0: would involve more actual mountain climbing

sidsays0: or training ON the mountains at least

maxwellgreyson: good pt

sidsays0: never heard of mt greenlake

maxwellgreyson: good pt x 2

sidsays0: maybe u should start hitting up some smaller peaks

maxwellgreyson: good pt x 3

sidsays0: actually training on a real mountain, u know?

maxwellgreyson: might do just that

sidsays0: cops might find u there 2 tho

maxwellgreyson: also a good pt – ur full of good pts 2day

sidsays0: yeah well at least stay away from greenlake 4 a while

maxwellgreyson: u dont have 2 remind me that

sidsays0: good

maxwellgreyson: been thinking of trying out mailbox peak 1 of these days anyway

sidsays0: whoa!

maxwellgreyson: :?

sidsays0: who is this?

maxwellgreyson: :??

sidsays0: mailbox peak?

maxwellgreyson: yeah mailbox peak

sidsays0: :0

maxwellgreyson: :1

sidsays0: how does 1 maxwell grayson know about such a hidden gem of a trail?

maxwellgreyson: its with an E, not an A

sidsays0: 2 easy!

maxwellgreyson: LOL

sidsays0: plz do tell, old friend

maxwellgreyson: hey man i know things - give me a little credit here

sidsays0: no credit given

maxwellgreyson: im all over mailbox peak

sidsays0: who told u about it?
maxwellgreyson: no1 – i just know some things is all
maxwellgreyson: i do know some things sometimes u know
sidsays0: yeah well, its a good hike - tough tho
maxwellgreyson: np for me
sidsays0: its right up past north bend off 90
maxwellgreyson: yeah already knew that
sidsays0: no u didnt
maxwellgreyson: did
sidsays0: didnt
sidsays0: & u know theres actually a mailbox up there right?
maxwellgreyson: yeah real funny
sidsays0: :0
maxwellgreyson: :1
sidsays0: no there is, seriously
maxwellgreyson: will b sure 2 check the mail 4 u
sidsays0: please do
maxwellgreyson: outta here
sidsays0: good luck
maxwellgreyson: l8r
sidsays0: lemme know how it goes
sidsays0: & bring some 1st aid supplies
maxwellgreyson: :|

I nanozeroed Mailbox Peak and got some basics about what to expect but there really wasn't all that much information about the hike or the trail or the mountain or even the general area around the mountain.

It can, at times, be tough to find good information on nanozero. That is, of course, unless you're talking about antenna boosters. In the case of cell phone antenna boosters, all is well on the nanozero front. Nanozero definitely knows its stuff when it comes to antenna boosters. As far as boosters are concerned, nanozero has it covered like a glove.

<!--red?-->

In any case, Mailbox Peak does sound like a pretty intense hike for someone with limited trail experience. But it should be manageable, I think. After all, I do manage projects. Tomorrow morning I'll go and see what it's all about firsthand. I need to break in some of this new climbing gear that I bought for The Mountain anyway. The gear has been sitting in my basement with tags on for a few months now. Or has it been a few years already? It's been a while.

<!--this much I know for certain-->

Tomorrow, Mailbox Peak will indeed be my destination, but today I'll stick with the hills near Patch Court. The hills were tough when I first came to Seattle and I used to avoid them at all costs but I now take them on willingly.

I still vividly remember the first time I took the long walk home. I planned to stop here and there but simply kept walking. Today I plan to turn back the clock a bit and take the long way home. It'll be a nice long, leisurely route home. I'll just pick a general direction and go.

And so I stroll.

You call it a hill. I call it a hill. So we're really not that different after all, aye mate?
-Frodrick Gray

After a few hours, I approach the top of the hill and see the house. It looks a bit rundown but that's not what catches my attention. The house is dark, very dark, except the front porch. It's a covered summer porch or something along those lines. The light in the porch is dim but just bright enough to sit and read under.

I have to look hard to see her: the red glove woman from Cafe Entropy earlier! She's reading from the dim light of her porch while the sun sets behind Puget Sound, behind the jagged Olympics. I stand at a distance and watch her glow in front of a magnificent backdrop.

I see her now: the old woman who reads at night.

I can't say why I chose to be on this hill right now. But I'm here.

I watch her read for a short while and then turn and head back down the hill. All of my senses are in a hypersensitive state. I feel it all with every ounce of my being: every breeze, every chirp, every slight change in humidity.

At the bottom of the hill, I sit on a bench to catch my breath. For some reason, I'm more tired from going down the hill than I was from going up. It starts to rain a bit, as it often does here, but it's not particularly noticeable. Rain in Seattle is often more like a fine mist than a downpour, and we all end up forgetting to notice at some point.

I sit on the bench for a few minutes, feeling half paralyzed. It's as if the reserves of my reserves have been entirely depleted. How am I going to manage Mailbox Peak tomorrow if I can't even handle these modest hills?

Suddenly I hear small and slow footsteps. It's almost a shuffling sound of sorts. Too tired to look up, I wait for the person to pass by with eyes focused on the sidewalk stained green. Two feet stop directly in front of me and I slowly raise my eyes to meet hers. It's her: the woman who reads at night.

But I just saw her reading in her porch.

"I might need a hand here, young man, if you wouldn't mind," she says to me.

She looks up the hill and motions uphill with a nod of her head.

"Oh dear, I've walked this hill many times but it's getting dark and it's a little slick with the rain. So, if you don't mind..."

"Of course," I say as I stand up. My legs wobble slightly but I can feel my body slowly recovering.

She takes my arm and we start walking methodically up the hill. The grade is such on this hill that the sidewalk has raised grooves to help prevent slipping. I trip on the raised sidewalk grooves a few times but she has no trouble with the uneven terrain. It's as if she could walk this route flawlessly with eyes closed many times over.

"You're not from around here, are you?" she asks.

"Uh, well sort of. Yes and no, I guess."

"Where are you from, young man?" she asks.

"I live not too far from here - right over the hill," I point to the northeast. "But I'm not really from around here."

"I've never seen you around before."

"I'm around."

"Such a kind young man you are. Thank you for helping out an old lady like myself."

"Sure, of course," I say.

The mist feels soothing on skin hot from the uphill struggle. Lying down in a hammock of clouds would be perfect right about now. I close my eyes and take a deep breath, feeling great about my good deed and momentarily forgetting every single bother in my world.

"Would you be my son?" she asks.

Startled, I stop walking and open my eyes wide, turning to look at her. She nearly falls.

"I'm sorry, what did you say?

"Will you be my son?" she asks again.

"Uh, yeah, well, I suppose that I could..."

"Such a nice young man walking me up the hill so that I don't slip."

"But how would that work exactly? I mean, what..."

"Not everyone would do that you know. Not everyone would take the time and effort and have the common decency to walk me up this hill. Not my darned son, that's for sure."

"You have a son?"

"Yes, but he's only really waiting for me to die so that he can have the house. He's of no use!"

"Oh, well, I don't think I can take over for your real son. I'm not very good in a replacement role, you see. I mean, I have a hard enough time getting a passing grade as myself."

"Sure you could, it's real easy. Just be yourself. That's all you really need to do."

We arrive at her house on the top of the hill. I already know which house is hers but she doesn't seem to notice.

"What did you say your name was again?" she asks as she lets go of my arm.

"I didn't say. But my name's Grey."

"Grey? I like that," she says as she turns and walks to the house.

<!--with an E!-->

She walks into the front porch, turns out the light and walks in the front door. I never hear the door close. Just like that, she's gone.

I stand motionless looking up into the night sky. A wide variety of grey clouds float high and low and foghorns can be heard in the distance. After a few minutes gazing up, I feel a large presence behind me inching closer and closer.

I turn and see the police car right behind me. It appeared suddenly, as if an apparition. The squad car stops and the driver's door opens: it's Officer Higgs. Of course it is. I can tell by the way he walks.

"Sir, is this your residence?"

I'm standing in the middle of the front lawn, still staring up into the night sky.

"Sir, can I ask what you are doing here at this residence?"

He doesn't know it's me yet. Maybe he won't remember? Maybe he has prosopagnosia, too? He walks closer and his eyes light up.

"You? Again? What are you doing here at this residence, Maxwell? I thought you lived on Patch Court?"

"My name's Grey."

"We received a few complaints about an unknown male walking up and down the same hill mumbling incoherently and staring up into the sky. Were these callers describing you, Maxwell?"

"I've walked up and down this hill a few times but I'm not incoherent. At least I don't think I am. Can you understand me?"

"Yes, I can understand you," Higgs says.

"I think you've got the wrong guy - again."

"That's doubtful. I'm pretty sure that I have the right guy and I'm pretty sure I had the right guy last time, too," Higgs says.

"No, I think you've got the wrong guy - again."

"What are you doing here at this residence, then? Is this your residence here?"

"No, I don't live here. I just walked the nice old lady home up the hill. She asked for help when I was sitting on the bench down there. She lives here, you can ask her. Go ahead," I motion to the front door.

"You walked the old lady home? Is that right? Maxwell, this residence has been uninhabited for more than a decade. Come with me."

"What are you talking about, I just…"

"Please step into the back of the vehicle."

"But…"

I take a good look at the house and notice that the yard is completely overgrown with weeds and invasive vines. The house itself is in complete disrepair: the roof is covered with moss, the siding is in horrible shape and the shutters have fallen crooked on some of the windows. It really does look as if no one has lived in the house for a decade.

But I know the truth. I know she's in there, and I know that she sits on the porch and reads at night.

There's no need to tell Higgs this; it'll make no difference to him. He sees what he wants to see.

I step into the back seat of the squad car and Higgs takes me to the station for further questioning. He ends up keeping me at the station for a few hours and then lets me go with some sort of warning for trespassing.

As soon as I'm out the door of the police station, I set out on a direct path. I know the exact direction that I'll be heading: back to the top of that hill, back to the house, and back to see the old woman who reads at night.

My legs ache. I've walked a tour of there and back and there again. But the destination is all that really matters at this point in time. I walk more slowly than usual but eventually end up at the house on top of the hill. I'm not sure of the exact time. All I know is that it's not morning yet. It's dark and she's not there. She's not reading; she's nowhere to be found.

I walk closer to the front door, and notice a name on the mailbox attached to the house: Kaluza-Klein. The mailbox, of course, I need to look inside! Why didn't I think of this before? The red glove is inside. Of, course the red glove! It's a smaller, one-size-fits-all, red glove made of some kind of stretchy, synthetic, wooly-looking material.

In the mailbox, along with the red glove is a dirty, old postcard of Mount Rainier. It's addressed to:

Ms. Kaluza-Klein
1921 General Way
Seattle, WA

The postmark is from 1993 and the postcard is unsigned, although it does have a single sentence written with broad strokes in red ink: Mailbox Peak is the destination.

I stagger back a few steps wondering if I'll have enough left in me to make it up Mailbox Peak tomorrow. It's time for the long, slow trek back to Patch Court.

And so I stand there at the top of the hill, out of breath, the thick Seattle air cool with mist as only Seattle air can be. The air conforms to my body in a way that's neither soothing nor burdensome. It's there, part of me here and now at the same time. It's dusk and the clouds seem to be rolling in heavier and faster than usual.

I float at the top of right here and now.

<!--this much I know for certain-->

I can't seem to catch my breath and a weak northerly breeze enters the neckline of my shirt, penetrating my skin and sending shivers down my back and arms.

I think I want to leave but I can't.

My feet are frozen in glacial ice. My feet throb, but it's nothing compared to the bent tune playing in my head right now; it's a combination of stretched time and compacted noise.

\\+rx1618:

dzire [sic]

tonight it was midnight but it felt like noon and i cannot
really explain it but with the full moon and warm blanket
of clouds a black cat walked in front of my path or maybe
it was a skunk but i saw no white stripe up a ways a man
walked his white dog but in the absence of rays an orange
glow came from the house where the old woman reads but she
did not read tonight she has not read for a while all in
all a searching something searched and a lost one lived
the sign blurred and with the wind nonexistent desire
appeared missing since i can first remember

\\-grey

*And, in the first place, I will recall to my mind the things I have
hitherto held as true, because perceived by the senses, and the
foundations upon which my belief in their truth rested; I will, in
the second place, examine the reasons that afterward constrained
me to doubt of them; and, finally, I will consider what of them I
ought now to believe.*

Rene Descartes

Everything is wrong, all of it. Nothing is right. Everything I've
imagined and seen and thought and known and sensed and felt
and heard and said and wanted and had.

It's all wrong.

Time seems to have changed its meaning or, at least, time doesn't
have the same meaning that it used to have.

Everything up until this point is false, misconstrued, inaccurate,
misunderstood, incorrect, misread, misinterpreted.

I turn on the TV and see programming from last week. The green guy is nowhere to be found. All I see is dust and the visual components of white noise flashing before me in slow motion. I think there must be some sort of multileveled misunderstanding here.

Have no fear, friends, for what we have here in front of us is a simple case of missed understanding. 'Tis not the first nor the last time.
-Frodrick Gray

I did. I missed understanding.

I could die 1618 deaths and the emptiness would keep surfacing like cracks on 50-year-old pavement. The blackness would fade and the brightness would dim. I know one thing for certain: these depths of loneliness are the lowest of lows.

If my pen wrote, "you are going to live this life over and over into infinity," I would erase those words, delete them from consciousness. I would obscure each word many times over with dark clouds and bury them in the sky, floating above me.

But if my pen wrote, "this is the end, there is no more, this is it," I would crush the paper up and throw it away, run it over, stomp it, smash it, burn it to nothingness. I would throw unlit matches into the mix to reignite the flame every other instant. The smoke would clear and nothing would have changed.

I want this to end.

I don't want *the* end.

I just want *this* to end, now.

Nothing before this moment is real and I need some help sorting it all out. I don't know how this journey will end but I know there's only one place to start it.

Everything begins with every second that follows this very instant in time.

\\+rx1618:

Tyme [sic]

I have always had a hard time
figuring out when today ends
and tomorrow begins
Draw a line in the sand
where today ends
and another
where tomorrow begins
Read between the lines
The tide will wash it away
If not today,
then tomorrow

\\-grey

To: voice <cassini2358@yahoo.com>;
From: grey <maxwellgreyson@yahoo.com>;
Subject: do you happen to have the time?

Message:

I am having a really hard time being on time lately. I need a better
way to tell time. Can you help me that or am I way off base here?

www.tymeloss.com

-grey

Reception level: Excellent (4 out of 4) ||||

```
function GoToScene(event:imeyeself):void
```

{

I am a fallen tree decaying in an old-growth rain forest
in the Pacific Northwest. My rings are too many to count,
and, besides, I'm too rotten to even estimate how many
lines - thin or thick - might exist. I'm home to a handful
of vile creatures that thrive on the dark and moldy forest
floor; I maintain a basic existence solely to provide the
occasional roof or meal to these dreadful creatures. In
fact, the only organisms that dare come in close contact
with me are those that exist in 3 a.m. nightmares and
forgettable 2 a.m. half-memories. Shake your head and hit
it ever so lightly to rid of it - each hit decreases the
percentage remaining. I'm slowly decaying into
nothingness.

}

6. Mailbox peek [sic]

I used to measure the heavens, now I shall measure the shadows of the Earth. Although my soul was from heaven, the shadow of my body lies here.

Johannes Kepler

Fact: I was able to gather some basic information about Mailbox Peak by nanozeroing it.

Mailbox Peak:

- Approximately 2.5 miles from the trailhead to the summit
- About 4,000 feet of elevation gain from start to finish
- Parts of the trail contain grades of 40 to 60 percent
- Main hiking trail is often riddled with deep, muddy patches
- Trail can be tough to navigate in some sections

Opinion: My rudimentary math skills plus the sum total of my outdoors experience combine to tell me that I'm looking at about 6 miles roundtrip to the summit and back (taking into account getting lost three or four times) with steep inclines and, for me at least, extremely difficult terrain. Mailbox Peak looks as if it will definitely test the limits of my mountaineering skills despite that fact that it's little more than a steep hike.

At least it looks that way on paper. And, for me, it usually looks better on paper than it appears in reality.

Fact: One can surmise that police squad cars cannot fit onto the main hiking trail at Mailbox Peak, so Higgs is rendered invisible for the duration of this climb.

Fact: It will undoubtedly be a major struggle to reach the summit of Mailbox Peak.

Opinion: This much I know for certain.

My thighs burn with each step up the trail and it's only the first half mile of the ascent up Mailbox Peak. The air temperature is cool - maybe 44 degrees or so - but my skin is hot to the touch and my clothes are already soaked through with sweat.

I'm not sure if it's raining or misting or if there's any precipitation at all. It doesn't matter much at this point. I'm wet, the trail is wet, and every single part of every single thing associated with my excursion appears to be wet through and through.

The presence of a steady rain will make absolutely no difference to what exists right now. Dampness already governs and there's little hope for immediate change. A thin layer of fog shrouds the trail, making it seem as if I'm swimming through the forest step by step.

I walk along miming the breaststroke for a moment, hoping that no one appears out of the trees to point and laugh. The trail is a little muddy but I haven't encountered any terrain that I would term difficult in this first half mile.

I hit a second wind, so to speak, at approximately the one-mile mark. It's a bit too early to be getting a second wind, but I'll take what I can. After a quarter mile or so of this unusually flat section I stop and look up at a steep array of switchbacks ahead.

define: switchback
A trail leading up a steep incline with a series of alternating, ascending paths that may include turns of up to 180-degrees

In my world of novice mountaineering, switchbacks are essential for hiking steep terrain and I often welcome the site of them. But this set of switchbacks in front of me right now does not look of the friendliest kind. In fact, it looks of the kind in which your friendship ceases immediately following your last step. You helped get me here, sure, but I don't have to be fond of you.

Sid talked about completing the dreaded 97 switchbacks at Mount Whitney out near Lone Pine, CA last summer, and if Sid can complete Whitney's switchbacks without a problem, surely I can conquer this modest set of switchbacks on modest Mailbox Peak.

Headline: Local man refers to torturous ramps of earth and stone as 'switchbacks'

After two switchbacks, it's time for yet another short break. I've already lost count of how many stops I've made so far. The sun is peeking through here and there, and the air temperature is slowly rising.

It's hard to tell how many more switchbacks are left, but, more than anything else, I can't wait until I can stop trying to predict how many are left. Failed predictions can be so much more painful than the here and now.

<!--left in front of right; right in front of left-->

I pause for another break and lean haphazardly against a damp tree trunk. Tipped over into the tree trunk, I have absolutely no say in how I'm positioned. The edge of my shoulder digs awkwardly into the bark protruding from the trunk, causing my fingers to tingle.

I don't want to sit down because I'll get too cold and my legs will cramp in multiple spots.

I don't want to take off my backpack because when I put it back on it'll press cold, wet, heavy clothes squarely against my back and make my body shiver down to the bone marrow.

I don't want to eat because my stomach is churning air and bile and I need to save what little food I have for the summit.

I don't want to drink water because I need to ration it better. I've drank too much already.

Oh, how I would love to debate the subtle differences between the taste and quality of tap water from the same location on different days right about now. And all while lounging on a comfortable recliner with four or five pillows adding to the sheer coziness of the chair, too!

I'll just lean against this tree instead.

Struggle is mandatory, progress optional.
-Frodrick Gray

A group of three hikers all looking a little grey around the edges, two men and a woman, emerge out of the thin layer of fog and pass by with a few subtle nods of the head. Each climber is carrying a backpack about two-thirds his or her size and the three of them seem to take steps in unison as they travel effortlessly up the trail.

<!--synchronized mountaineering-->

Their packs tower over their heads as they ascend. You could fit at least a 1618 or so tiny Sids in just one of those backpacks - even if each tiny Sid came with his own tiny tin can. I doubt that these climbers carry tiny tin cans in those packs, though.

To be quite honest, I don't even know what's supposed to be in a backpack when hiking a trail of, say, five miles and 4,000 feet of elevation gain. Stale English muffins and two liters of tap water probably won't cut it.

This much I know for certain.

I wait a bit to avoid crossing paths with the three sneering hikers again. It's unlikely that I'd catch up with them on the trail, but, in any case, I decided that it would be better to wait a while so that I don't have to encounter them again. I know that they're laughing at me inside right now anyway. So why would I willingly offer up more material solely for their entertainment? It's painfully obvious that they're having trouble containing their amusement.

Why does it always come to this? Really, what is the point of such mockery?

Yes, I'm aware of my utter ridiculousness, but there's really no need to secretly and quietly mock the absurdity of me being on this trail right here, right now. Need I be reminded of my ridiculousness at the turn of every corner, at the top of each switchback while I gasp for air with hands on knees?

hiker1: could u believe that guy?
hiker0: LOL! I KNOW!
hiker1: it looked like he fell against that tree back there and decided to just stay there daydreaming about comfortable, cozy recliners or something
hiker0: COZY RECLINERS! ROTFL!!!!
hiker2: Maybe he was just thirsty, wishing there was a tap water supply nearby
hiker1: no, definitely not! he was dreaming about hammocks or recliners
hiker0: LOL! LOOSER! HAMMOCKS!
hiker1: yes, he was definitely dreaming of recliners!
hiker0: LOL! LOOSER! RECLINERS!
hiker2: I feel bad, we should have offered him some water.
hiker0: AND PILLOWS TO! LOL!
hiker1: why would we offer him water?
hiker2: Well, we have more than enough for us, that's for sure.
hiker1: forget water, you should've given him some fashion tips
hiker1: seriously, did you see his clothes?
hiker0: I know! LOL! Is this dude 4 REEL or what?!
hiker2: What was wrong with his clothes?
hiker1: uh, yeah, he pretty much looked like he was about to go play the pauper
hiker2: the pauper?
hiker1: yeah, at the nearest renaissance fair
hiker0: LOL!!!!
hiker1: & he ended up at mailbox peak by accident!
hiker0: PAWPER and the REN FARE!
hiker2: A pauper?
hiker0: ROTFL!
hiker1: dude, he even had like a sack for a backpack!
hiker1: a sack!
hiker0: A SACK! LOL!
hiker2: He didn't have a sack, I think your memory is failing.
hiker1: No that dude is a FAIL!

hiker2: He had a regular old pack. I mean, maybe it was a little old, but it wasn't a sack.

hiker1: and he had like a bandana on or something, what is he a pirate or something?!

hiker0: AYE MATEY! LOL!

hiker1: *a pauper pirate

hiker0: AYE!! WALK THY SWITCHBACKS AND THEN GO LAY UNDER THAR TREE!!!

hiker2: OK, I guess his clothes were pretty bad.

hiker2: But we should've asked him if he needed anything.

hiker1: like what, rope?

hiker2: Not funny.

hiker0: YES FUNNY(!)

hiker2: No, like food, water, something?

hiker1: the only thing we could've done was tell him to leave

hiker1: and go do Mt Si or something

hiker0: YAH LOOSER – GO TO MT SI ALREADY!

hiker1: someone did Mt Si in high heels on lunch break the other day

hiker0: YAH while on a conference call! LOL!

hiker2: You guys are crazy. Mt Si isn't even easy at all.

hiker1: oh yeah?

hiker2: It's actually kind of hard. It's like 3500 feet up or something isn't it?

hiker0: 3500 in HI HEALS! LOL!

hiker1: well he had no business trying to deliver the mail

hiker2: Good one, how long did it take you to come up with that?

hiker0: dont get it

hiker2: You know – Mailbox Peak, delivering the mail

hiker1: neither rain, nor sleet, not snow, nor paupers

hiker0: NOR TREASURE HUNTS!! ARRGGHH!!!

hiker2: That pirate stuff is really stupid.

hiker0: LOL! LMAO!!!

Those three greying overachievers just flew up the steep trail as if it were a stroll on First Beach. It'll take me at least five times as long to go the same distance.

I start up the painful switchbacks again and, after what seems to be many hours, I pause for another uncomfortable standing break atop the trail of zigzagging inclines below. I'm done with the switchbacks but surely not finished with the ascent.

<!--left in front of right; right in front of left-->

The trail is a little hard to find at times, but I can see the tracks from my three ridiculers pretty easily at some of the critical spots. I'm not much of a tracker but it's pretty easy to spot these six footprints.

<!--arrive at fork in trail, proceed-->

Two-dozen rolled ankles, five-dozen stumbles and a half-dozen flat-out falls later, I arrive at the top of Mailbox Peak. The snake tells me that it took about 5 hours to reach the summit.

I have arrived at the destination, so to speak.

I sit down on the nearest, flattest rock and dig into my backpack for a meal of stale English muffins and a small ration of somewhat cool tap water.

Only a moment of peacefulness passes until I can hear their voices getting closer. It's the three hikers, the three haters, the three ridiculers. They must be heading back down the trail. Perhaps they are coming from the real summit and I'm pathetically sitting here right now on a false summit. That, of course, would only increase the height of my ridiculousness in their eyes.

Surely my level of ridiculousness is already off the charts but, believe me, it can be raised another notch or two. Not only are they still mocking me with shallow, unoriginal pirate and fashion jokes, but now they'll be able to add a few one-liners about the bum sitting at a false summit looking all pleased and whatnot.

Nevermore, I am really at peace with it all. They will say what they will say.

The first two hikers walk by quickly without a word and a barely a glance at my pitiful, temporary camp built on a foundation of stale English muffin crumbs. I bet their jaws are aching after hours of ridicule. The third hiker comes along with a gallon of water in an old milk carton and sets it down on the ground about a foot away from my foot.

"We thought you might need some extra water for the return trip."

"I, uh, thanks. Don't you need it?" I ask.

"No, we each hiked up with six of them in our packs and we just dumped them all out for the hike down, but we thought you maybe looked a little thirsty so we saved one for you. If you don't need it that's fine, I just wanted to see if you might be able to use it."

"Thanks, that may be one of the nicest things anyone's done for me," I say.

"I doubt that, but it's no problem."

"No, seriously, that is probably the nicest thing any one person has ever done for me," I say. "Maybe ever."

"Well, no problem. Well, be safe on the return trip. Take care."

"What are you doing hiking up Mailbox Peak with all of those gallons of tap water in your backpack, anyway?"

"Oh, we're just training for The Mountain."

"Rainier?"

"Yep."

"That must be pretty heavy, a lot heavier than tiny tin cans I bet."

<!--do not mention the tiny tin cans again-->

"Yeah, I think each gallon weighs around eight pounds, so it gets pretty heavy."

"Do you want a muffin?" I ask as I hold one out. "They're English. The muffins - they're English muffins."

The English muffin falls to the ground. It bounces a few times and then settles down next to my foot, atop the foundation of crumbs.

"Thanks, I think I'll pass," the hiker says and then turns to head down the trail. "We already ate a few things up here while resting."

"Hey, is there really a mailbox up here?" I ask.

The hiker stops, turns around and comes back.

"Yeah I know, my friend told me that there was one but I bet he was probably just messing with me. Sorry."

The hiker points right over my head: "It's right behind you."

I turn and take a quick glance. The mailbox sits maybe 16 or 18 feet directly behind me.

"My name's Grey," I say holding out my right hand, fingers spread and pointing to the sky.

<!--with an E-->

"Murray."

"Do you guys live around here or something?" I ask. "It seems like this probably isn't your first time on the trail."

"No, we live up in Everett but try to make it out here to Mailbox once or twice every year."

I turn and look behind me. The mailbox is still there.

"All right, I better catch up to my group. Be safe."

Fact: Sid actually told the truth for once.

Opinion: He probably still threw in a few half-truths to even things out a bit.

I slowly rise to my feet and walk over to the mailbox. I don't really want to know what's in there but, then again, what else am I up here for? I'm not about to struggle my way up here eating only stale English muffins and absorbing the scorn of overachieving mountaineers to *not* look in that ridiculous mailbox.

<!--this much I know for certain-->

My breath is visible as I open it and look inside: two red gloves and another postcard!

One of the red gloves matches the glove that I found in Ms. Kaluza-Klein's mailbox. The other glove is also red and made of a similar material but isn't identical to the other two.

The postcard is another old one with a picture of Mount Rainier on the front. It has no addressee and has one simple line handwritten in red ink of the back: "The Mountain: Everything not forbidden is compulsory."

\\+rx1618:

stranger things have happened

\\-grey

define: strangeness
a property of elementary particles characterized by a quantum number that depends, strangely enough, on the relative number of strange quarks and anti-strange quarks

\\+rx1618:

you are no stranger to me

\\-grey

My brain shuts down, as I'm too exhausted to try and decipher this latest riddle. Thoughts completely cease.

Compulsory? I have no idea what that word means. It sounds like something Higgs would yell at me or threaten me with. I'll have to nanozero it when I get home.

And not only is this all some sort of agonizing riddle but I found the latest clue in a mailbox on some random peak in the Cascades all while being mocked by a pirate-loving trio of backpackers with poor spelling skills.

I'm too exhausted to even attempt to figure anything out at this point.

I lie down next to the mailbox, placing my cheek directly on the cool dirt below. It feels more comfortable than any recliner I've ever sat in, with or without additional pillows.

I wake up shivering fiercely from the tip of my toes to the top of my head, ready for the trek down to civilization. The snake tells me that my quick nap took up about an hour, which means that I need to get moving quickly in order to reach the trailhead before dusk.

I stop by Sid's place in West Seattle after returning from Mailbox Peak and fall asleep on his couch. I've been known to crash here on this very couch from time to time, although it's been a while since I awoke here with the sunrise.

I just hope that I don't awake with something written on my forehead in permanent ink.

The only caveat to Sid's hospitality is that I must, once morning comes, hear his latest theory on this or that, his latest theories on both this and that or, even more likely, some combination thereof.

He's always working on some type of thesis or theory and I'm often the recipient of his rough drafts and subsequent smoother drafts.

That reminds me, I haven't put much time into my woodworking project lately. I've been neglecting it, for sure, but it'll have to wait for now.

But I'll find time for the windows soon enough.

\\+rx1618:

deter mine [sic]

Divvied now or embraced later?

Press once or press it an infinite sum or perhaps until
infinity, it is really just one of an endless array of
intricate choices to be made that allude to having an
endpoint of some kind, but, really, what kind of
conclusion - what type of finality - can it own when its
existence lies solely on choice itself?

```
<!--
Fibonacci:1,2,3,5,8,13  \n
1,2,3,5,8,13,21,34,55,89,144,233
-->
```

\\-grey

To: voice <cassini2358@yahoo.com>;
From: grey <maxwellgreyson@yahoo.com>;
Subject: 2 is 1 too many

Message:

I heard that you still use that other search engine? Seriously? It's time
to join the herd!

www.nanozero.com

-grey

Reception level: Excellent (4 out of 4) ||||

```
function GoToScene(event:imeyeself):void
```

{

I am sideways man. I'm an old friend of the most
questionable kind. When describing me to others, the word
friend is used simply out of obligation and, although the
opposite may be true, this fact may never be spoken of. On
the surface I'm a curious but perhaps acceptable fellow,
but come a little closer and you can smell the stew
boiling. I wear a shower curtain as an overcoat and stand
at the bus stop, periodically taking one large step into
the street to curse a late bus to no one in particular. My
closet is filled with items typically found on the free
table after a weekend-long garage sale. I hang jeans from
my shower curtain rod to block stray water drops and use
oil and vinegar as shampoo. I sprinkle soap chips on my
iceberg salad and wallpaper my bedroom with used coffee
filters. I'll remove a lamppost from the ground and use it
to dig a shallow trench 162 inches long in the back of
this here community garden. It's decided: I shall lie here
on this cool cushion of earth forever.

}

7. Twin berth [sic]

No, I was no one's contemporary-ever.
That would have been above my station.
How I loathe that other with my name.
He certainly was never me.

Osip Mandelstam

I awake to the sound of foghorns and the smell of freshly-brewed coffee. Sid has already filled the chalkboard with lines of material and I know that he's only getting started. And once he gets started, it can be a little tough to get him to stop. Sid lives near Fauntleroy, so at least I can peek out the window and watch the ferries travel to Vashon Island and back. But that'll get old after a while.

"Check this out: History repeats itself, right?" Sid says. "It always does if you wait long enough. Sometimes you have to wait just one hour or 20 minutes or 20 seconds, but sometimes you have to wait 20 million years. But history will repeat itself."

"Right. History repeats itself. Got it. Like me ending up on your couch or the Trojan Horse or whatever."

"The Trojan Horse incident was not repeated, Grey."

"Oh, now I finally understand why that instructor failed me."

"Here's a better example: Tic-Tac-Toe. It's just a bunch of X's and O's, right? Wrong. It's so, so much more. I believe that there are about 26,000 different possibilities of how a single game of Tic-Tac-Toe can play out."

"That's a lot X's and O's," I say.

"Yeah, well let's assume that the 26,000 number is correct, or that there is, at least, one correct number of total variations to the way in which a game of Tic-Tac-Toe can be played out. OK?"

"Uh, yeah, sure."

I often agree just to keep things flowing and, more importantly, to avoid unpleasant scorn. I've experienced enough ridicule in the past 24 hours.

"So, the number of possible start-to-finish Tic-Tac-Toe games is finite. That's established. That is, there's a specific number of total possibilities of how one individual game of Tic-Tac-Toe can occur."

"Yes, I know what finite means."

"OK, well, that, in turn, means that as long as enough time passes, each and every one of those 26,000 variations will not only occur once but more than once. Each variation will be repeated. It isn't as if each variation occurs just once and then disappears forever. No, each variation is very real and will occur again - and again and again and again. In fact, each variation will not only repeat once or a handful of times, but each one will actually be repeated an infinite amount - if given enough time."

I nod my head in total agreement. Yes, indeed, I know exactly what Tic-Tac-Toe is. I think I may have even been good at that game at one point. So simple, yet so complex at the same time!

"So that all leads to the next logical question: Is the universe finite or infinite? The simple question 'finite or infinite?' brings multiple variations to what can occur and is, in fact, the perfect stepping stone to finding the path to the truth.

"Stepping stone, yes," I say and nod in agreement.

<!--:?-->

"Well, I'll get right to it: I posit that the universe is indeed infinite, but also that there's a finite number of ways in which matter can interact, much like the Tic-Tac-Toe example that I just used. And if the universe is indeed infinite, but there is a finite number of ways that matter can interact and ultimately arrange itself, then what we have here right in front of us must be repeated somewhere out there in the universe, right?"

Sid draws an O with an X on top of it on the chalk board.

"That is, there are only a set number of possible ways to arrange particles in space, and if the container that holds those particles - the universe - is infinite, then the patterns in which those particles are arranged must be repeated. They must be repeated."

Sid writes "they can be repeated" on the chalkboard, crosses out "can" and replaces it with "must." He then circles the "must" that he just wrote.

<!--is it better to start with the x or the o?-->

"You're thinking about Tic-Tac-Toe still, aren't you?" Sid asks.

"No, not at all. I'm just taking it all in: finality vs. infinity and whatnot."

"Finite and infinite, Grey," Sid says. "Finite versus infinite."

<!--is it better to start in the middle square or one of the corners?-->

"Grey? You there? Hello?"

"Yeah I'm listening, carry on with the container stuff. Hey, do they have plastic in outer space? You know, plastic containers and whatnot?"

<!--start with an x in the top right corner - yes!-->

"Grey, stop thinking about Tic-Tac-Toe. I can't even imagine if I used Othello as the example instead," Sid says, shaking his head in disgust. "Then you'd really be lost in your head, that's for sure."

"Oh yeah, I like Othello. That's a good game. Wait, what's the tagline again?"

"For what?"

"For Othello - it's great. I can't remember it exactly."

"The tagline for Othello, also known as Reversi in some countries, by the way, is something about being easy to try but tough to master."

"Yes! That's it! Love it!"

"Kind of reminds me of this friendship," Sid says.

<!--I forgot how much I love Othlello!-->

"So let's recap here: I posit that the universe is indeed infinite, or perhaps that the universe is actually finite but it is so large that for our purposes we will just consider it infinite. In either case, space is infinite as far as we are concerned here, right?"

<!--is it better to start an Othello game as black or white?-->

"Oh man, what did I do now? Grey! Stop thinking about whether it's more advantageous to be black or white in Othello and pay attention here. This is important stuff!"

"What are you talking about? I'm not debating white vs. black in Reversi. I don't even know what you're talking about. I hardly remember that game."

"Since when do you call it Reversi? You just heard that for the first time 20 seconds ago."

"Not true."

"OK, if you were indeed listening, then go ahead and explain to me what I was just talking about. A brief summary will suffice. Go ahead."

Sid stares with that disappointed-teacher kind of look. Now I've seen two people actually tap their fingers on a counter while waiting impatiently.

"Well, I mean, I don't really get it," I say. "I mean, you can't just say 'it is either one or the other but we'll just say it's one and not the other" without knowing. Don't you need to know?"

<!--:??-->

"Are you talking about how I said that the universe could actually be finite but we're just going to consider that it is infinite regardless?"

"Yes. Yes I am."

"That is actually a good question. You really were listening, I think. Or you may just be lucky. But, anyway, whether space is infinite or not is really of no consequence. Even if space does have limits it may act as if it doesn't because there are parts that we will never see – they're too far away. I'm talking about a scenario where the expansion of space pushes the limit beyond our scope. You do know about the Big Bang, right?"

<!--definitely choose black, you get to go first!-->

"You're still thinking about Othlello, I can tell. Remember, Grey, I beat you 162 straight times," Sid says.

<!--I forgot how much I hate Othello!-->

"I was just making a point that really isn't even of much relevance here, but, anyway, let me summarize for you. Some astronomers and physicists still debate whether space is infinite or finite. On one side, they argue that space literally goes on forever. If that's the case, then what I'll get to next will hold up. The other side of the argument is that the universe does not expand indefinitely. If space has a fixed size then some of what I'll say may not hold up. But, then again, space could be finite but so incredibly large that some of what I am going to say would, in fact, hold up. That's all I was saying."

"OK, I give up! Space is infinite! It is definitely infinite!"

"If it makes you feel any better, that really smart guy who came up with the theory of general relativity and all that thought that space was infinite."

"I kind of lost track of what you were saying. That's too much math for me to process."

"Let me guess: I lost you somewhere between Tic-Tac-Toe and Othello?"

"Yeah, maybe. But, like I said, it's too much math for me."

"First of all, it was not too much math. It was hardly any math. Second of all, math is not just numbers on paper, or numbers on a chalk board, Grey. Mathematics will bring clarity; it will bring answers to this right here, right now. You must allow yourself to see it. And if you work hard enough, if you push to the limits and then some, you will see that it can explain this right here and also that way out there."

"Right here and way out there - got it."

"So, what we have here must be repeated out there. It must be. Grey, do you think that this universe that we're in right now, or this one that we believe that we are in, anyway, is the only one?"

"No, I guess not. No, I guess I don't think that this right here is everything, I guess."

"That's a lot of guesses, but that's OK. So, let's bring it up one minor level here. Is there, perhaps, another universe or are there maybe even a bunch of universes?" Sid asks. "What would this mean for us or for the possibility that other life exists out there? What if there isn't just one universe or even a handful of universes but rather a multitude of universes, you know?"

"No idea."

"Grey, I think the simple evidence that I just laid points clearly to the fact that our universe could really be just one single part of a much broader entity. That is, our universe may be but one of a multitude of universes that populate what really is more of a broad multiverse.

"Multiverse?"

"As I mentioned many times already, the simple evidence points to the conclusion that what we have in front of us here, what we are immersed in, is probably not unique. That is, this very situation right here right now could be happening elsewhere in unison. We could very well be just one peg in an enormous, insanely large multiverse composed of a vast number of parallel universes."

"So, wait, maybe we're here and there?" I ask.

"At the same time." Sid says.

"How can I say that I know this for certain?" I ask.

"That's the next logical question," Sid says. "I'm glad to see you've moved on from thinking about Tic-Tac-Toe and Othlello. But let's not go there just yet."

"Why not?" I ask.

"This infinite-container-filled-with-finite-stuff theory isn't the only way that you can come to the conclusion that we may really be just one tiny part of an unfathomably huge multiverse."

"It's not?"

"That's one of the most intriguing parts about studying multiverse concepts in detail. There are numerous ways in which one can come to the conclusion that we're really part of an expansive multiverse. You can look at the data in different ways and, while my completed path may look different than yours or the other person's, we can all end up with the same conclusion: that this universe that we're in right now is not the only one."

"What other person?"

"It was just hypothetical, Grey. All I'm saying is that you can take different approaches and different routes and end up at similar destinations."

"Don't start talking riddles here, OK? I've already had enough of riddles in the last 24 hours."

"More calls from the underground?" Sid asks.

"No, I mean, yes, but let's not get into that right now."

"OK, well then I'm going to move on then."

"I'm ready as long as there are no riddles."

"Sure, of course, no riddles. OK, so another concept of the multiverse comes from what's called inflationary cosmology. Basically, inflationary cosmology, or cosmology theory, is kind of like the Big Bang theory on steroids. According to inflationary theory, space is in a constant state of expansion. Within this constant inflationary expansion, smaller bursts of spatial expansion occur seemingly at random. And these smaller bursts of expansion create separate bubbles or pockets within space."

"Bubbles?" I laugh.

"Yes, within this so-called inflationary expansion, which, of course, goes on forever, individual fields are scattered throughout. And each of these fields may or may not have the perfect conditions, so to speak, to experience a separate inflationary burst, which would ultimately create a separate bubble. But in each field that has the perfect conditions, a separate entity will be created, which is actually an individual universe. So, our universe that we currently know and love may be but one single component within the vast expanse of space. Not surprisingly, each separate universe created with the framework of inflationary cosmology is typically called a bubble universe or pocket universe."

"Hey, don't you think it would be awesome if I was able to shrink you to a tiny size and carry you around in my pocket?"

Sid pauses briefly and then answers.

"I get the shrinking part, I think. Maybe not, but, anyway, why would you want to carry me around in your pocket?"

"You'd have your own tiny tin can, so you wouldn't be just swimming around in there or anything."

"Well, that's good, I think. But, Grey, you can stick me in your pocket and even in a tiny tin can in your pocket, but I will still have access to infinite spacial extent no matter how small I am or how many pockets I'm in. And with access to infinite space, not even time can place limits on reality in its truest form."

"What're you saying exactly?" I ask. "I don't understand, does that mean it would be awesome or not? I actually found a tiny tin can that would be perfect."

"No, it would not be awesome to be in your pocket. For starters, I don't want to be even remotely associated with your wardrobe."

"Let me guess: you like pirate jokes, too?"

"How did we get talking about tiny tin cans and pirates? Let's get back on track here, OK?"

"Sure."

"Anyway, that's my current understanding of inflationary theory. Those are the basics as I see them. Oh, and there is one more interesting component to this inflationary theory that predicts the existence of a vast number of bubble universes. Basically, this theory does a bit of blurring of the difference between infinite and finite."

"Oh, no, not that again."

"Within each bubble universe, some physicists posit that the intelligent life within believe that their universe in infinite despite the fact that it's really just one finite part within an infinite collection of counterparts. Thus, inflationary theory may not be the answer but it could be part of the answer."

"I think I may now be infinitely confused but within a finite brain."

"I agree, this whole multiverse concept is huge. I think we've established that fact pretty well with just this short talk about space and time and bubbles and pockets."

"And tiny tin cans," I add.

"I mean, we're talking about infinity and concepts so large large that it's tough to fathom." Sid says. "And we're talking about a universe filled with hundreds of billions of galaxies each with hundreds of billions of stars, and then another universe on top of that and perhaps another on top of that and so on. Or, I should say, next to that and next to that.

"Despite the grandness of these theories and the sheer scale and scope of the predictions, the best way to actually arrive at a solid multiverse hypothesis may actually be - in my opinion, anyway - to stop looking big and, instead, look small. Perhaps we should look very small. I'm talking about looking at the smallest of the smallest particles that make up our existence."

"Wow, you mean like moisture ants? How do you stop those from coming in your windows, anyway?"

"No, I'm not talking about ants," Sid says. "I'm talking much, much smaller than ants. I'm talking about the most minuscule particles that make up everything around us, as studied through quantum mechanics."

"Awesome, does that deal with robots and whatnot?"

"No, quantum mechanics is not the study of robots, unfortunately."

<!--what happened to that robot tv show?-->

"Grey, please don't let your mind stray here and start thinking about that robot TV show again."

"I'm not thinking about any robot TV shows. So, you were saying something about small stuff, small wondrous particles?"

"No, I didn't say anything about small wonders, but I was getting into quantum mechanics. We're not talking robots here, we're talking quantum mechanics."

"Which is not the study of robots."

"Right."

"OK."

"Good, so quantum mechanics deals with subatomic particles and describes the behavior of matter and its interactions on very, very, very small scales. Quantum mechanics attempts to explain the world around us, and also the world way out there, with the use of a series of quantum rules. And quantum rules are really just probabilistic laws of particle behavior."

"Particles misbehaving?"

"Quantum mechanics makes use of the uncertainty principle in an attempt to explain our world. That is, quantum mechanics takes our world and describes it as a series of probabilities. Problem is, the uncertainty principle states that when dealing with subatomic particles it's impossible to precisely measure both the position and momentum of a particle at the same time."

"You're losing me here," I say.

"The uncertainty principle takes our world and explains it using a series of probabilities. So, for example, you don't just get from point A to point B and once the A-to-B journey is over that's it. No, you see, there was only a certain probability that you would get from point A to point B but there was a also a certain probability that you would go from point A to point C."

"OK, I am glad that you're dumbing it down to ABC's. That helps."

`<!--this much I know for certain?-->`

161

"So if A-to-B does indeed happen, the question is: what happens to the A-to-C outcome?" Sid asks.

"What do you mean 'what happens to it?' Nothing happens to it. It doesn't happen," I say proudly. "It's gone forever, or it never even happened. It was always gone. It was never there."

"I don't know about that," Sid says. "Maybe it does happen, you know? How do you know that it doesn't happen - for sure? Maybe it happens elsewhere, perhaps in another space. Perhaps it occurs in another universe."

"Are you saying that it happens both here and there?" I ask.

"At the same time," Sid says.

We sit silent for a moment. Sid seems pleased that I'm actually following along today.

"So, the next logical question is: How do you travel from a set of probabilities to a certain outcome? The easy answer is that there are multiple outcomes, as I mentioned just before. That is, each and every possible outcome of each and every set of probabilities actually happens in its own separate universe. And in that separate universe where either A-to-B or A-to-C occurs, it seems like the outcome that occurred is the only outcome. That is, in the A-to-B universe, you are unaware of A-to-C happening in the A-to-C universe and vice versa."

"And vice versa," I say.

<!--realized that repeating the last few words of last sentence while nodding implies that I am following closely-->

"So if you look at the A-to-B/A-to-C scenario, each possible outcome actually occurs in its own parallel universe."

"So what does that mean?" I ask.

<!--realized that asking ridiculously vague questions works, too-->

"Indeed, what does it mean?" Sid asks.

"I have no idea."

<!--this much I know for certain-->

"Let not get ahead of ourselves here," Sid continues. "There's yet another multiverse theory that involves what physicists call membranes. I won't go into too much agonizing detail here, but this theory basically predicts that we live on one membrane while other membranes float alongside us simultaneously in space."

"Membranes float," I say.

<!--danger alert: choosing words from the middle of the sentence-->

"My knowledge is a little on the weak side when it comes to membranes and the associated theories that go along with membranes," Sid says. "I only recently came across membranes, or brane worlds, as some term them, so I need to research this area a lot more. But I do have a good basic understanding."

"Brain worlds - that's funny," I say.

"Why?"

"I don't know."

"Yeah, well don't add that to your stand-up routine. It is spelled b-r-a-n-e, by the way."

"Yeah I knew that."

"Right. Well, think of these different brane worlds as floating in space, surrounded by dark matter."

"OK if I picture them floating in grey matter?"

"Sure, that's fine. Picture each membrane as maybe one card in a deck of cards. And there are maybe four of these individual cards floating close to each other, almost like vertical stacking with a little space in between."

"OK, I'll go with the Ace of clubs, the 6 of spades, the Ace of diamonds and the 8 of hearts."

"Great, this isn't a magic trick, but, sure, that's fine. And, just to paint a clear picture: if you were to exist on one membrane, you could look sideways and peer directly into another one of the branes. I mean, you can't do that, but just for visualization purposes, try to picture that."

`<!--I am sideways man-->`

"The best part of this membrane theory, or of *these* membrane theories, I should say, is that they may actually be testable. You see, when particles collide out there in space, some astrophysicists think that there is a minute but detectable amount of energy lost in the interaction."

"Lost in the interaction," I repeat.

"You know, you repeating the last few words of my last sentence doesn't automatically make me believe that you're actually following."

"Actually following," I say.

"Right, so where does this lost energy go? Where does it end up? It's very possible that this lost energy persists but only in another dimension, a dimension that we have yet to be able to detect. Take that a step further and think about not another dimension but another universe. So, if physicists are able to measure that a minute amount of energy is indeed lost during particle collisions, it could very well be evidence of the existence of multiple membranes, and, thus, multiple universes."

"The multiverse!" I exclaim.

"Correct. So, now let's consider some everyday implications of what we've been talking about."

"Sure, OK, yeah let's go ahead and do that."

"OK, well what if every decision, every choice exists much like when you focus too hard on one object and your eyes cross a little? When you do that, multiple variations of that object float next to each other in a momentary space. You can kind of see it but you're often not sure exactly what you're looking at and you definitely can't touch or feel all of the variations."

"Yeah that happens a lot."

"Every choice in our life doesn't have but one single, definite outcome. No, each choice has multiple outcomes and, beyond that, possibly multiple outcomes that exist out there in multiple universes. That is, each choice that we make, each thing that happens to us, is made and occurs both in our reality and out there in another world. 'Many worlds' is what some like to call it."

"Many worlds," I echo.

"So, the existence of the multiverse is really but a byproduct of life itself. How can life be summarized other than as a collection of unique experiences? And how can unique experiences, as a whole, be summarized other than as a collection of unique choices?"

"I honestly have no idea."

"Grey, the multiverse is real, very real, because we live and experience this very life in front of our eyes through a collection of unique choices. We choose to be *here*, yes?"

"Yes."

"But our unsuccessful but yet very possible other choice to be *there* doesn't cease to exist as a result of our victorious choice to be here. No, I think it is becoming increasingly obvious - crystal clear, even - that we are both *here* and *there*..."

"At the same time," we say in unison.

Cut the pie any way you like, "meanings" just ain't in the head.

Hilary Putnam

To: grey <maxwellgreyson@yahoo.com>;
From: sid <sidsays0@yahoo.com>;
Subject: re: zeroes

Message:

grey~

---zeroes 0.6---

Take two zeroes and place them next to one another. They're twins, no? Perhaps they're even identical by some definitions of the word? Keep in mind, though, that whether they're fraternal twins or identical twins is really of no matter here. So, I'll go ahead and say that the two zeroes are, in fact, twins. But, I ask, what about their shadows? Is the shadow of a zero identical to that of its twin zero? I suppose the answer to that question depends, again, on definitions available to you at any given time. Oh, here I go again! I must apologize. Please, carry on without notice, without a mention. You heard nothing, saw nothing, felt nothing, remember nothing. Nevertheless, the sun has set so this conversation will have to be had another day.

~sid

"I'm sorry I'm late," I say to the voice. "I got caught up at Sid's place and lost track of time."

"What was happening at Sid's?"

"He was telling me his latest theories about many universes and multiple worlds and brains and whatnot."

"That all sounds interesting."

"Not really, he ended up talking about bubbles and ants and

started making pirate jokes like everyone else. It was pretty confusing."

"That does sound confusing. So, how have you been otherwise?"

"A lot has been going on recently," I say. "I'm not even sure where to start."

"More trouble with the old man who got mugged at Green Lake?" the voice asks.

"No, not that. Other stuff."

"What happened with the alleged mugging of the old man?"

"Nothing, I don't think. I mean, I'm not sure."

"That's good. Hopefully that incident is behind you now. So, is it the phone calls, then? Are you still getting calls and voicemails?"

"No, not really. Well, I mean, I guess, sort of. The voicemails are still coming in, but other things are happening, too, like in the real world or whatever."

"You don't consider the phone calls and voicemails as occurring in the real world?"

"I don't know, I mean, the people are like dying and whatnot. I don't know. But other things have been happening for sure."

"What's been happening?"

"I went for a hike."

"A hike? That's great. Where did you go?"

"Well, I hiked up this one really, really steep trail and then there was this mailbox up at the summit and it had mail in it for me. It was a post card about compulsion or something, and I forgot to nanozero what that word meant."

"And then there were like two red gloves in the mailbox but only one of the gloves matched the red glove from the old woman who reads at night. The other glove I'm not sure about. I'm not sure what the deal is with that. And there were these rude hikers making jokes about me but I could care less what they think."

I do say that it is of absolutely no matter to me, and I feel that truth with every ounce of my being. But once I speak those few trivial words it all suddenly takes on the utmost of importance. Out of my way, scoundrel, I'm off to the underground!
-Frodrick Gray

"Oh, and Higgs brought me in to the police station yet again because he claims the old woman who reads at night is dead or whatnot but I know the truth. I was at her house and the yard was all overgrown with weeds and whatnot but she was there. I walked her up the hill and I saw her reading in her porch, too."

"Well, that's definitely a lot of stuff, like you said," the voice says. "That is *a lot* of stuff. Maybe you could start with the old woman: Can you tell me more about your encounter with her?"

"OK, yeah, well there was this old woman who walked by me at Cafe Entropy and mumbled something about a red glove. And then, strangely enough, I saw her again later in the day when I was out taking a long walk. I saw her twice after that, actually."

"So you saw her three times in one day?"

"Yeah, I saw her at the coffee shop and then reading on her porch and then she needed me to help her walk up this hill to her house."

"That does sound pretty coincidental, for sure."

"I guess, but the strangest part was that after I walked her home, Officer Higgs showed up at the curb and started harassing me."

"The same officer as before? The one from the lake?"

"Yeah, it's the same guy. He always seems to show up at the worst times and impede any progress that I might be making. His mere presence is the equivalent of walking around with a weighted vest on. In any case, he tells me that I'm trespassing and that Ms. Kaluza-Klein died like a decade ago or whatnot."

"He said that she was no longer alive?"

"Yeah, but I know that's not true. I don't know if she faked her death or what. But, anyway, in her mailbox there was a postcard that told me to go to Mailbox Peak and so I did and there was a mailbox at the peak and it had stuff in it and now I'm really confused."

"That is confusing. Do you have the postcards or the gloves with you right now?"

"No, sorry, I left them at home. I'll bring them next time. So, what do you think it all means?"

"I don't think either of us can answer that question very well right now. Let's talk some more and I'll see if I can help you sort things out. We'll see if we can get to the bottom of this all."

I spend the next 16 minutes or so telling the voice all of the specifics that I can remember from the last few days with as much detail as possible. But it's of no use; she's of no help. After going over all of the very fine details, she moves the conversation to a more general topic.

"Have you been writing every day like we spoke about?" she asks.

"I have. I guess I've enjoyed the writing part of this all. I've definitely enjoyed it more than I thought I would."

"You haven't shared any of your writings with me so far. Would you care to do so now? I'd love to see them."

"I don't think so. What's in the past is in the past, you know?

"Are you sure? I'm really an easy critic."

"I'll think about it. But, you know, I have been thinking of trying my hand at writing a screenplay. Maybe I'll work on that and then you could take a look at it?"

"I'd like that. What's the screenplay going to be about?"

"It's a little hard to explain."

"What's the general story?"

"It involves a garage sale."

"Do you collect antiques?"

"No, but I like garage sales."

"Well, I look forward to reading it soon."

"I'll try to finish it up for our next meeting."

"That sounds wonderful, Grey. I'm looking forward to it. I have to ask, though, why a screenplay? I've never heard you speak of it before. I'm always curious as to why writers choose to go with one style or one type of writing over others."

"I'm a writer now, huh?"

"Well, you are writing, so, yes, that makes you a writer."

"I don't know about that but it is time to shake things up," I say. "It's definitely time for some changes."

```
<!--this much I know for certain-->


\\+rx1618:

irth [sic]

Unearthed
Birthed
What comes first?
You brought
```

a sheet of paper
filled with idioms
I took it to heart
I met my doppelganger
that day
Filled with fear
of fearlessness
The paper got lost
I would prefer a sketch
any way

\\-grey

To: voice <cassini2358@yahoo.com>;
From: grey <maxwellgreyson@yahoo.com>;
Subject: !olleh

Message:

Have you happened across your doppelganger recently?

www.twinberth.com

Reception level: Average (2 out of 4) ||

```
function GoToScene(event:imeyeself):void
```

{

I am an old bowl shattered to pieces after one unfortunate
accident. My color is a shade of green that no bowl would
ever want to call its own and I'm scarred from gross
overuse. Dropped on slate tile, my pieces fragment such
that I'll never be completely whole again. My obvious and
permanent cracks are fused with a combination of polluted
air and toxic glue. Each time I'm filled with a liquid of
any kind, I share my toxicity with the molecular structure
that I temporarily house. I serve solely to contaminate
through contact, battling fiercely against leaks large and
small only so that I may continue distributing my
misfortune evenly through space and consistently through
time. Go ahead and place me in a microwave; the minute
fluctuations and unpredictable temperature changes will
coerce me to melt into futile oblivion.

}

8. Only on sail [sic]

I want sleep to come and go, smoothly.
Like passing out of the door of one car
into another. And then to wake up!
Find tomorrow in my bedroom.
I'm more tired now than I can say.
My bowl is empty. But it's my bowl, you see,
and I love it.

Raymond Carver

Something must change. Some thing or some things have to change. An element or two of everyday life needs to be altered, thrown out, burned, revised, flipped, remedied, reworked and/or recreated.

<!--see also: all of the above-->

I must figure out a way to shed this feeling of complete and utter uncertainty. I simply cannot go through the motions any longer.

I walk through a thick and sweet-smelling layer of low-lying fog, arms outstretched and eyes closed, hoping that a hidden message will condense on my finger tips or permeate my eyelids to help me draw a sketch of what's to come. I walk slowly and methodically as if on a direct and definite path but the hidden truth is that I really have nowhere to go.

I don't blame you if you don't want to hear any more about my ridiculousness. I can feel that you're very tired of this all, but, alas, I'm forced to care because it is I, myself that I'm dealing with here.

In any case, I'm aware that I'm on my own here and also that my whole bit is a bit tiresome but sometimes you just reach a new low point, you know?

<!--under the underground?-->

define: low point
A transparent floor that gives a clear view of what is below

And reaching that low point then necessitates change, you know?

When one reaches the lowest of lows, turns and then looks down again from another angle, one can often see even lower. If one looks hard enough, people can often be seen crawling on the ceiling.

Focus is a thing of the past, and is now replaced with a combination of blurred certainty and clear uncertainty. I feel as though my eyes are permanently crossed a slight percentage, which makes it nearly impossible to achieve true clarity of any kind.

Everything is hazy and untouchable. Surely it is all there in some type of muddled reality but I cannot grasp it and I'm not even entirely sure what it is.

\\+rx1618:

Soulfell [sic]

unknown mass to the masses; hidden behind stagnant tears; lips dried and cracked; speaking certainty; disintegration of needless air; thoughts of an unsteady sea; the brightness of night; beginning to see; only the soulful;

\\-grey

To: grey <maxwellgreyson@yahoo.com>;
From: sid <sidsays0@yahoo.com>;
Subject: re: zeroes

Message:

grey~

---zeroes 0.7---

Free is nothing more than zero cents, no? And how you say that zero is worth nothing! I won't go so far as to call you a fool, because I don't really believe that. You are no fool, at least not in the purest sense of the word. So, if twice-free equals zero, and free minus free also equals zero, then zero must have a value of which I personally cannot fully comprehend. But to which ultimate solution does the evidence point, I have to ask, when you consider that it's very possible that the value of zero can be comprehended by zero percent of people? I say nothing to that because perhaps that makes me the fool. I am no fool, though, although I hesitate to say there's a zero percent chance of that statement being false. Quit this foolish behavior, already! Go and find me a sale, put in on a scale and tell me what it reads. One guess: zero?

~sid

---

maxwellgreyson: BUZZ!!!
sidsays0: hello, old friend!
maxwellgreyson: hold up, which sid is this?
sidsays0: indeed
maxwellgreyson: how do I know whether this is the real sid or not?
sidsays0: indeed! but all variations r very real
maxwellgreyson: what would twin sid be named?
maxwellgreyson: tid? bid? skid?
sidsays0: why do twin names have 2 rhyme?
maxwellgreyson: lid? zid? kid?
sidsays0: again, why must they rhyme?
maxwellgreyson: dunno, but u need 2 prove this is the real sid
sidsays0: ive seen ur hammock
maxwellgreyson: but uv never rested in it
sidsays0: good pt
maxwellgreyson: my first ever!
sidsays0: :?
maxwellgreyson: my first ever good pt
sidsays0: u may b correct on that 1
maxwellgreyson: stars are aligned
sidsays0: y?
maxwellgreyson: correct & making good pts in same day
maxwellgreyson: stars must be aligned for that to happen

sidsays0: the stars are always aligned, old friend
maxwellgreyson: :1
sidsays0: :0
maxwellgreyson: been thinking about ur theories
sidsays0: multiverse?
maxwellgreyson: yeah - here & there – all that
sidsays0: good, glad 2 hear that i got ur brain up & running
maxwellgreyson: u mean my brane
sidsays0: no i dont
maxwellgreyson: think ive experienced it
sidsays0: what?
maxwellgreyson: being here & there at the same time
sidsays0: is that right?
maxwellgreyson: yeah i think ur on 2 something here
sidsays0: & there
maxwellgreyson: yeah here & there
sidsays0: at the same time
maxwellgreyson: & i might b able 2 help
sidsays0: how so?
maxwellgreyson: not sure. any ideas?
sidsays0: well 1st i need 2 know more about what ur talking about
maxwellgreyson: good pt
sidsays0: not my 1st
maxwellgreyson: no def not
sidsays0: lemme think about it
maxwellgreyson: sure, l8r
sidsays0: lets meet & discuss - have new multiverse thoughts for u 2
maxwellgreyson: ok. not 2day tho. got something else going on
sidsays0: boosters?
maxwellgreyson: no
sidsays0: how are the boosters doing these days?
maxwellgreyson: not sure
sidsays0: why not?
maxwellgreyson: got 2 much other stuff goin on
sidsays0: like what?
maxwellgreyson: dont have time 4 boosters
sidsays0: u better find time
maxwellgreyson: ?
sidsays0: boosters wont b there 4ever
maxwellgreyson: is that right?
sidsays0: esp @ this rate
maxwellgreyson: yeah yeah yeah

maxwellgreyson: anyway, I finished it up
sidsays0: what?
maxwellgreyson: the latest project
sidsays0: the windows?
maxwellgreyson: no, havent worked on the windows in a while
sidsays0: no idea what ur talking about
maxwellgreyson: windows r on the backburner
sidsays0: whats up w/ the windows?
maxwellgreyson: windows r on hold right now
sidsays0: what project r u talking about then?
maxwellgreyson: the screenplay
sidsays0: screenplay??? :0
maxwellgreyson: remember I was writing 1? :1
sidsays0: 0 memory on that
maxwellgreyson: ill send it over now
sidsays0: on edge of my seat
maxwellgreyson: just put finishing touches on it
sidsays0: screenplay?
maxwellgreyson: yep
sidsays0: about what?
maxwellgreyson: kind of tough to explain
sidsays0: doubtful
maxwellgreyson: a little tough
sidsays0: cant be that tough – u wrote it
maxwellgreyson: lol
sidsays0: when are u casting?
maxwellgreyson: LOL
sidsays0: ill call my people
maxwellgreyson: :|
sidsays0: no have ur people call my people
maxwellgreyson: will send it over now
sidsays0: plz do
maxwellgreyson: take a look
sidsays0: alright
maxwellgreyson: lemme know what u think
sidsays0: always do
maxwellgreyson: tru
sidsays0: u can always count on that
maxwellgreyson: thx
sidsays0: np
maxwellgreyson: l8r
sidsays0: l8r

If only I could sail away, O I would head out to the seas in an instant. In an instant, I say! But first I must find a sale, for I cannot fathom rocking to and fro for full price.
-Frodrick Gray

"GARAGE SALE DANCE PARTY"
Screenplay by Maxwell Greyson

EXT. URBAN, DOWNTOWN, LARGE APARTMENT BUILDING - DAWN (PRESENT)

Night is becoming morning. The sun finds a path through clouds and peeks through gaps between a couple tall buildings. A few people walk on the street. For the most part, the city still sleeps. Camera follows a cab for a couple of blocks, moves to close-ups of footsteps on the sidewalk and then proceeds to travel up a tall apartment building to one particular window as the sun works its way up the building.

INT. INSIDE APARTMENT, BEDROOM

The sun finds the window and peeks through the side of the shade, shining light on the face of OSKAR, who is peacefully lying on his back in his bed. OSKAR's eyes open and he sits up on the side of his bed, scanning his white room: White walls, white ceiling, white carpet, white bed sheets, white pillows, white lamp, white furniture and white curtains. He wears a white t-shirt and white boxer shorts.

EXT. DOWNTOWN

The muffled sound of city traffic gets louder and clearer, and pedestrian foot traffic gets heavier. Camera once again focuses on footsteps on the sidewalk and then travels back up the apartment building to OSKAR's window.

INT. INSIDE APARTMENT, BEDROOM

OSKAR gets out of bed turns and walks to the bathroom where he stands expressionless, brushing his teeth. Once finished, he walks to a window, opens the shade and looks out at a sign blinking "24 hours" down a few stories below. He then walks out of the bedroom, down the hallway and into the kitchen.

INT. INSIDE APARTMENT, KITCHEN

The kitchen is white: White cabinets, white laminate floor, white countertops, a small white round table and two small white chairs. A small white radio sits atop the countertop. OSKAR turns on the radio.

While the radio is on: OSKAR opens up a drawer and takes out a metal spoon. He opens a cabinet door and on the shelf with all white plates and white bowls is a lone green cereal bowl. He picks up the green bowl and carefully carries it to the table and places it on a white placemat.

He walks over to another cabinet, opens and removes a box of generic blueberry cereal and carries it to the table and sets it next to the bowl and spoon. He also gets milk from the refrigerator and places it on the table.

ON THE RADIO:
The disc jockey is in the process of making a prank telephone call. The DJ dials, you hear three rings and then the call is answered by a man.

DELI WORKER (DW):
Hello, 24-hour Deli. How can I help you?

DISC JOCKEY (DJ):
Uh, yeah, uh what time do you, uh, open? (barely holding back laughter)

DW:
We are open 24 hours, sir.

DJ:

OK, uh, good, good. What time do you close then? (still barely holding back laughter)

DW:
Excuse me, sir?

DJ:
What time do you CLOSE, then?

DW:
Uh, we are open 24 hours, sir.

DJ:
Right, 24 hours. Got it. BUT WHAT TIME DO YOU OPEN?

DW:
Uh...I don't understand.

DJ:
WHAT? TIME? DO? YOU? OPEN?

DW:
We're always open 24 hours, sir!

DJ:
Do you sell cold cuts?

DW:
Cold cuts? Yes, sir, we have cold cuts - 24 hours.

DJ:
But what time do you close?

DW:
Uh...sir?

Emotionless, Oskar walks over to the radio and unplugs it from the wall. He then sits down at the table with his back turned to the radio. The unplugged cord dangles. He fills the bowl with cereal and milk and takes a bite.

DW (ON THE RADIO):
24 hours, sir!

Startled, OSKAR spins to look at the radio, knocking his green bowl and spoon off of the table. The bowl shatters in SLOW MOTION.

The spoon spins in the air in SLOW MOTION and bounces until finally settling on the white floor with the shattered remains of the bowl.

OSKAR sits motionless and emotionless, staring at the dangling radio cord. He turns and looks at the table. He focuses on the box of cereal.

GHOST ON THE BOX OF CEREAL:
BOO!

EXT. URBAN STREET, MORNING

CLOSE UP of the cereal box of cereal dissolves, transforming into street art of a ghost on the side of a large, brick building in a downtown, urban setting. OSKAR is driving his pickup truck. The ghost street art disappears in the background as OSKAR drives away from the city.

OSKAR drives for a short time and then turns on the radio.

DW (ON THE RADIO):
24 hours, sir!

OSKAR turns the radio off immediately and drives in silence. The surroundings change from an urban setting to more of a suburban setting. Various shots of "24-hour" signs are mixed in to various street settings. Billboards, storefront signs, bumper stickers, a panhandler's sign made of a piece of cardboard and black marker all exclaim: 24 hours, sir!

OSKAR sees a sign for a garage sale, follows the directions, parks, and gets out.

EXT. GARAGE SALE IN DRIVEWAY OF SUBURBAN LOCATION

OSKAR browses the tables filled with shoeboxes of baseball cards, piles of old magazines, used jeans, a ten-speed bicycle for "best offer." He doesn't find what he's looking for. After looking over the available items for some time, he picks up an old, red toy phone with a plastic red coil cord and brings it to the lady sitting behind the table.

OSKAR:
How much?

LADY:
Honey, you can have that old thing for free. Take it or leave it!

OSKAR:
Take it?

OSKAR walks back to his truck, places the phone on the seat next to him and continues to drive. He drives for a while, passing by numerous "garage sale" signs but pays no attention until one reads "Garage Sale: Open 24 hours." He follows the directions, parks and gets out. As he starts looking at the items, an old woman approaches.

EXT. GARAGE SALE IN DRIVEWAY OF SUBURBAN LOCATION, II

ELEANOR:
Hello, I'm Eleanor. Are you looking for anything in particular?

OSKAR:
Not really.

ELEANOR:
Well, if you have any questions, I'm the one to ask.

OSKAR:
Wait, are you the same...

ELEANOR:
No.

ELEANOR turns and walks away. OSKAR searches until he finds a table of kitchenware. There it is: an exact copy of his shattered green bowl. He picks it up and looks at in awe. He stands there startled for a moment and then starts to carefully look over the bowl, examining every centimeter.

In the truck parked out on the street, the red phone starts to ring. With the green bowl in hand, he slowly walks back to the truck in a stumbling, confused haze. He gets to the car and puts the phone receiver to his ear.

DW (ON THE PHONE):
24 hours, sir!

Eleanor appears right behind OSKAR. She followed him to his truck.

ELEANOR:
You're gonna have to pay for that, you know.

OSKAR:
On, yes, I'm sorry, it's just that the phone started ringing.

ELEANOR:
Come with me, we'll take care of this lickity split.

Eleanor takes OSKAR by the arm and leads him back to the main table where the cash box sits.

ELEANOR:
That'll be zero dollars.

ELEANOR holds out her empty hand.

OSKAR:
Excuse me?

ELEANOR:
Nothing's free in this world, honey. Zero dollars - take it or leave it!

OSKAR looks around, confused, then opens his wallet, fakes taking money out of it and puts nothing into ELEANOR's outstretched hand. ELEANOR takes the invisible money and places it in the empty cash box.

ELEANOR:
Thank you Oskar, please proceed.

ELEANOR rotates her body counterclockwise 100 degrees and points the garage motioning with her right hand outstretched, palm facing up.

Over at the side door of the garage, a bouncer stands with arms crossed guarding the entrance. The main overhead garage door is closed. OSKAR cautiously walks up to BOUNCER. Loud dance music can be heard coming from inside the garage.

BOUNCER:
ID?

OSKAR alternates blank stares between BOUNCER and the door.

BOUNCER:
ID?!

OSKAR takes out his invisible wallet and removes an invisible ID, placing it in the bouncer's hand. BOUNCER looks at the invisible ID, tosses it on the ground to the left and then opens the door, revealing a loud, dark room with a large dance floor in the middle filled with dozens of people. They are all dancing.

NARRATOR (OSKAR):
Ah yes, the orange glow.

OSKAR, bowl in hand, walks slowly into the dance party. As he walks in he lifts the bowl over his head, holding it with both hands. The garage door closes to reveal a sign nailed to the door "24 hours, sir!"

FADE TO BLACK

THE END

And those who were seen dancing were thought to be insane by those who could not hear the music.

Friedrich Nietzsche

maxwellgreyson: BUZZ!!!
maxwellgreyson: watcha think?
sidsays0: terrible, awful, wretched
maxwellgreyson: gr8 thx
sidsays0: at least it wasnt a romance novel
maxwellgreyson: no it def isnt that
sidsays0: was worried that ruby would make an appearance
maxwellgreyson: hmm, interesting idea for screenplay #2
sidsays0: no no it isnt. no.
maxwellgreyson: seriously? it was that bad?
sidsays0: no, no, not bad
maxwellgreyson: bad or not bad? dont mess w/ me here
sidsays0: not
maxwellgreyson: not bad?
sidsays0: yeah, I actually thought it was NOT bad
sidsays0: tru story
sidsays0: has some potential
maxwellgreyson: really?
sidsays0: a little potential
maxwellgreyson: :!
sidsays0: yeah suppose so
maxwellgreyson: nicest thing u ever said 2 me!
sidsays0: settle down, old friend
maxwellgreyson: :!!!
sidsays0: never knew u were such a fan of garage sales
maxwellgreyson: indeed
sidsays0: or dancing
maxwellgreyson: indeed!
sidsays0: maybe u can become 1 of those overachievers u always complain about now
maxwellgreyson: overachiever? me? not possible
sidsays0: is that right?
maxwellgreyson: always under
sidsays0: always?
maxwellgreyson: always prefer the underground

Welcome to the latest edition of The Grey Matter Report, where Grey fills you in on what matters, what really matters and what's the matter.

This week's term: Underachiever

Being an underachiever is an admission that has seemingly gained popularity in recent years with all of the self-branding and entrepreneurship that infests present-day society. For these reasons, underachieving is a topic that calls out for careful examination and, thus, is the one and only topic of this edition of Grey Matters.

Let us begin our dive into the topic of underachieving by first looking at the underachiever's ugly cousin, the overachiever. The overachiever is one who attains stature above and beyond what was allotted to him or her in the blueprint of society. The overachiever is a peculiar and exotic creature to the rest of us. Dare we even say that the overachiever could be alien? Is alien? Indeed, the overachiever is not to be trusted and should be left out on the stones of the shore to shrivel in the searing heat that accompanies low tide.

The underachiever, on the other hand, is you, me, your neighbor, my neighbor, it is all of us. We are one and we are all. Whether you take the stairs, elevator or escalator is of no importance. The underground is the ultimate destination of choice.

To be an underachiever in the truest sense of the word, the following must be true:

1. One must possess intelligence, talent, skill and/or other ability above and beyond that which the average person owns.

2. One must, in turn, choose to not make use of this special ability - just because.

The underachiever is to be applauded, revered and loved. The underachiever can sit on the shore or ride the next wave tall and proud. Or the underachiever can opt out of participating in enjoying that next wave - just because. He or she is in ultimate control.

Note: Problems may arise when the simple hyphenated phrase "self-proclaimed" is placed in front of our glorious term of the week (e.g. self-proclaimed underachiever). Why? Number two on the aforementioned list can certainly be proved. That is, it can easily be proven that one chooses not to do something.

But what about number one on the aforementioned list? That is, how can it be proved that someone does indeed possess intelligence, talent, skill and/or other ability above and beyond that which the average person owns? If the underachiever has ALWAYS chosen NOT to make use of his or her special abilities, just because, how can we be certain these special abilities even exist?

I believe that we have found a flaw in our beloved theory outlined here today. I could explore this question, this flaw, even further as I have the ability to do so, but I choose not to.

Just because.

Move over, take three steps to your left to expose the trap door; I'm off to the underground!

Until next time, stay somewhere 'tween black & white.

Headline: Self-proclaimed underachiever refuses to admit that he's just average

sidsays0: seriously, when u casting?
maxwellgreyson: not sure yet
sidsays0: keep me posted
maxwellgreyson: hmm
sidsays0: im going 4 the role of oskar
maxwellgreyson: u know, thats not a bad idea
sidsays0: yeah i could easily pull off oskar
maxwellgreyson: no, ur not a good fit 4 oskar
sidsays0: def a good oskar right here
maxwellgreyson: no way
maxwellgreyson: good idea tho
sidsays0: what r u talking about then?
maxwellgreyson: casting
sidsays0: ?
maxwellgreyson: casting = good idea
sidsays0: was just kidding
maxwellgreyson: im sure u were!
sidsays0: grey u might want to think this 1 thru
maxwellgreyson: ok
sidsays0: good
maxwellgreyson: just did
maxwellgreyson: time to cast
sidsays0: that was quick
maxwellgreyson: casting starts today!
sidsays0: dont do it
maxwellgreyson: doin it!
sidsays0: this has trouble written all over it

maxwellgreyson: when it comes to me, it almost always does
sidsays0: does what?
maxwellgreyson: trouble written all over it
sidsays0: never have figured that mystery out
maxwellgreyson: i am mysterious?
sidsays0: not really
maxwellgreyson: itll be fine
sidsays0: no it wont
maxwellgreyson: smooth sailin ahead
sidsays0: hows that?
maxwellgreyson: got an idea
sidsays0: ?
sidsays0: oh no
maxwellgreyson: ?
sidsays0: stay away from cafe entropy!
maxwellgreyson: oh good idea!
sidsays0: grey!
maxwellgreyson: brb
sidsays0: gray!
maxwellgreyson: l8r [btw: with an e]
sidsays0: GRAY!
maxwellgreyson: E!
sidsays0: BUZZ!!!
sidsays0: BUZZ!!!

I don't like dancing. In fact, I've always hated dancing. But I do like garage sales.

And I'm ready to get going with this whole screenplay thing and this casting thing and this film thing, too. Sid himself said that my screenplay had potential and I, myself, said that I need to shake things up. I'm pretty sure that I complained and moaned about mixing it up and changing things for quite some time, in fact.

This is definitely my chance.

What better than to let some boosters fund this next project of screenplays and casting and short films and chairs for actors to sit on and tables of food for in between sets and whatnot? The screenplay is already done. Next up is casting and then on to the next and then the next. I'm not really sure exactly what "the next" would be but I've got plenty of time to figure that out. We're talking about the most minor of details there. The major details are already outlined, the blueprint is in place, and all we need now is someone to take the reigns.

That someone is me.

This is my chance to break free. I can feel it. Once the casting gets rolling I'll have everyone begging to be part of my inner circle. I won't even have to try and infiltrate other inner circles any more. Mine will serve just fine!

"Grey, how are you?" Ruby asks.

<!--welcome, friend, to the inner circle!-->

"Good, good. You?"

"I'm amazing, amazing. Thanks for asking. So, are you sticking with the red eye these days?"

"Yeah I'll go with a red eye, Ruby, thanks."

"What's new?" she asks.

<!--candidate for executive-level member of inner circle right here!-->

"Not much really going on. No, not much at all. Hardly anything, really. Haven't really got anything new to tell you about or anything. Nothing, really."

"That's pretty much status quo for you, isn't it?" Ruby asks.

"What's that?"

"The whole 'not much going on' thing?"

"Yeah, maybe it is. Maybe it is. You might be right there. But you know what?"

"What?"

"Uh, oh nothing much. There's just a, uh, nothing. It's just that ... hey, what's new with you?" I ask.

"Why?"

"Why what?" I ask.

"Why do you want to know what's new with me?"

"I don't know, just being conversational, I guess."

I've been working on being more of a conversationalist lately. I thought it might help.

"Hey did you fly in on your crow again?" she asks. "You have a pet crow, right? Isn't that what you told me?"

I stand and stare with no response. I've been trying to talk less these days. I thought it might help.

"Grey? Hello? Don't you have a pet crow or something like that?"

"No, I don't have a pet crow. I don't remember telling you that, but, then again, I may have told you that. In any case, I definitely don't own a crow."

"Sorry, my mistake."

<!--don't let the door hit you on the way out!-->

"Well, here's your red eye."

"Hey check this out: I just finished my first screenplay this morning," I say. "I guess it's not really my first screenplay, but it's the first screenplay that I've completed from start to finish, I guess. I've started others but never really finished them to my liking."

"Wow, a screenplay? I didn't know you were a writer."

"Yep, I'm a writer. I'm definitely a writer. And a project manager, too. Or maybe that makes me just a project manager because I manage my writing projects. I still haven't figured that one out, I guess."

"Don't tell me, the screenplay is a dark comedy about living on Patch Court?"

<!--can feel the gnats swarming again-->

"Or is it a mockumentary chronicling your stand-up performances at coffee shops throughout Seattle?"

<!--are there no screens in these windows?-->

My first instinct is to turn and flee much like the voice wanted to do the first time she met me. But, no, my feet are cemented firmly on the floor of Cafe Entropy for now. The voice stayed back then and I'll stay now. I won't allow myself to abort this mission. I must go through with this casting call, as it may be my one and only chance to create my own inner circle.

If I don't get from A to B here, what exactly is A to C?

"No, the screenplay is not about living on Patch Court and it's not about any stand-up routine, either."

"OK, then, what is it about? Do tell."

"Uh, well, it's pretty much about this guy who like breaks his green bowl and then sort of tries to find a new one at a bunch of garage sales. And then he finds it, he finds a new one."

"I don't get it."

"Well, the story behind it is a little complex. You see, he loves his green bowl and then he breaks it accidentally. He then goes looking for a bowl replacement at a couple of garage sales and finds a dance party."

"Sounds ... interesting."

"Maybe I'm not doing a great job of explaining it."

"Hopefully you're a better writer than talker."

"Yes, I think I am. I'm most definitely a better writer than talker.

I've been told that very thing. In any case, I'm starting casting for the film today."

"Wow, you just finished the screenplay this morning and now you're casting for the film this afternoon? That was quick."

"Yes, yes I am. And yes it is. Are you interested?"

"Interested in what?" she laughs. "Acting in the broken bowl movie? Are you serious?"

"Yeah, I'm serious. I'm starting casting right now. So if you or anyone else you know might be interested, be sure to let me know."

I give Ruby a handful of the business cards that I quickly created and printed out before heading over the Cafe Entropy. She walks to the back of the shop and has a quiet conversation with two of the laptop clones that have been sitting behind me listening in on our conversation.

I'm glad I stuck it out and stayed even though my first instinct was to turn and run. My plan is working! Everything is now in motion.

So this is what A to B feels like.

Ruby looks over at me and points her index finger up. I read her lips: "one minute," she says and then she disappears to the back room.

What a glorious day! First I complete the screenplay and now the formation of my very own inner circle is beginning right before my very eyes. I wonder who she might bring in from her inner circle for casting. Her network is so wonderfully deep that I can't even imagine who might surface. The merging of circles could produce an explosion unheard of in the history of this universe.

I pace back and forth parallel to the laptop-clone counter sipping my red eye. With my back turned to the door, I stop and contemplate what my next screenplay will be. There are so, so many possibilities and the door is but cracked open at this point.

With hand on chin, I feel heavy footsteps behind me. Whoever it is has a lot of keys and some heavy boots on.

Someone taps me on the shoulder. I turn and look: it's Officer Higgs. Of course it is.

So this is what A to C feels like.

"Maxwell, so we meet again."

"My name's Grey."

`<!--this much I know for certain-->`

"We just got a call about some creepy guy trying to recruit people for a porno film at a local coffee shop."

"A porno?!" I exclaim.

"And, of course, the description of the creepy guy that was called in fits you exactly, yet again."

"No one even calls it porno, Higgs. It's called porn, I believe."

"Ah, so you admit it!"

"No, I don't admit it. What is with you people and porns? My film is titled 'Garage Sale Dance Party.' It's not adult entertainment. It'll probably be rated PG."

"Is that right, Maxwell?" Higgs says, not even attempting to hide his sarcasm. "And what is this dancing movie about then?"

"It's about this guy who goes to a garage sale to find his bowl and there's a dance party there."

"Likely story. I'm bringing you in. Let's go."

"Seriously, what is with you people? You all think about porn and spam all day? First, everyone thinks I'm a spammer and now this!"

"Oh, so you're a spammer, too! That makes perfect sense. It's all coming together now, Maxwell."

"No, it doesn't make sense! Not at all. I am no spammer and I am no adult film creator! And my name's Grey!"

"I said I'm bringing you in. Let's go."

"Bringing me in? For what?"

"Indecent exposure."

"Indecent exposure?!" I ask, confused. "What did I expose?"

"Yourself," Higgs says

"How so?"

"You exposed yourself, meaning that you showed up. You were here."

"And what is indecent about that?"

"You."

"Me?"

"Yeah, you."

"That makes no sense."

"It makes sense to me."

"Why are you always impeding my progress, Higgs?"

"That's Officer Higgs to you, Maxwell."

"My name's Grey," I repeat. "You know, it's like I'm comfortably strolling through life and then you show up and it's like I'm trying to go for a run in an Olympic-sized pool."

"You mean go for a run and mug an old guy. I didn't forget about that, you know."

"I didn't mug any old guy, I'm not a spammer and I don't make adult films."

"Well, I have a different take on things. Let's go, I'm taking you in to the station."

"Look, here is one of my business cards," I say as I hand one to Higgs.

Maxwell Greyson
Project Manager

"Project manager? What the hell does that mean?"

"That I manage projects."

"Right, sure, like sending out spam emails and filming pornos. That sounds about right."

"Wrong, like writing screenplays about garage sales and selling boosters."

"Boosters? That's it! I'm taking you in to the station."

"I'm not going anywhere."

"We can do this the easy way or the hard way."

"Listen Higgs, I know you have it out for me and whatnot, but my movie is about a guy who breaks his favorite green bowl that he uses to eat cereal each morning. He then goes looking for a new bowl at different garage sales. And he finds a dance party. That's it. It is not creepy or whatever you said. And I'm not casting for a porn. Whoever said that is lying."

"Right, Maxwell. As much as I'd like to believe you, I need to go on the information I have at hand. And this information tells me that you need to come with me, right now."

These gnats are unbearable in here. He cuffs me and we leave.

I can hear laughter, I think. I don't even know for sure.

maxwellgreyson: BUZZ!!!
sidsays0: hello, old friend!
maxwellgreyson: thx for bailing me out
sidsays0: sure, np. how u doin?
maxwellgreyson: not bad, i guess
sidsays0: thats better than id b
maxwellgreyson: dont say it
sidsays0: 1 big 'told u so'
maxwellgreyson: not helpful
sidsays0: told u 2 stay away from entropy
maxwellgreyson: whole thing is ridiculous
sidsays0: thought u had good reception now?
maxwellgreyson: i need 2 bring my screenplay over 2 the station 2
sidsays0: y?
maxwellgreyson: prove that it exists
sidsays0: what r u waiting 4?
maxwellgreyson: afraid to go back there
sidsays0: wait til higgs is off
maxwellgreyson: good idea
sidsays0: how did they get the porn idea?
maxwellgreyson: no idea. some kind of sick joke or something
sidsays0: u need 2 stop spending so much $ on coffee anyway
maxwellgreyson: coffee habit only costs me about 2 boosters / week
sidsays0: again w/ the boosters
maxwellgreyson: yes, again w/ the boosters
sidsays0: what happens when the boosters run out?
maxwellgreyson: not gonna run out
sidsays0: everything runs out eventually
maxwellgreyson: not gonna happen
sidsays0: just sayin
maxwellgreyson: not gonna happen
sidsays0: if u say so
maxwellgreyson: i do say so
sidsays0: when was the last time u actually worked?
maxwellgreyson: dunno, maybe a few weeks?
sidsays0: dont u think maybe u should check up on things?
maxwellgreyson: yeah maybe, just dont have time, u know?
sidsays0: no I dont know
maxwellgreyson: just dont have time
sidsays0: u better find the time
maxwellgreyson: alright, alright
sidsays0: just sayin

```
maxwellgreyson: alright, alright
sidsays0: check in with me b4 you make any other decisions right now
sidsays0: ok?
maxwellgreyson: sure
sidsays0: l8r
maxwellgreyson: l8r
```

My head is throbbing. Why would Ruby sink to such terrible depths? I'm fully aware that I'm not a member of her inner circle but why must I be treated like a rodent?

Nevermore, I'm still at peace with it all. It's time to lie in my hammock and come up with a new plan, a better plan.

There are dozens of missed calls and voicemails on the snake. I haven't worked on my woodworking project in weeks. I have no idea how many cell phone antenna booster sales I've referred in the past month. I'm trying to make progress but it's like climbing a sand dune. With each step up I slide two steps down and my pace is not fast enough to turn that discrepancy positive.

The hammock isn't getting it done for me right now, nor is Patch Court. And Cafe Entropy is obviously not getting it done, either. I think it's time to take my ridiculousness to another place, a better place.

Second Beach is where I'll go. Yes, Second Beach is the destination! And here's the best part: I didn't get this tip from a mailbox or a voicemail or a postcard or a ghost or a ghoul.

I got it from myself. I, myself, came up with that very plan: I'm off to Second Beach and then on to the next, whatever or wherever that may be.

```
\\+rx1618:
```

```
steal [sic]
```

```
even stainless steel rusts
```

they call it oxidation
I call it oxidation
only because I know no better
|
oxidation:
age by oxygen
|
oxygen:
the breath of life
|
the breath of life
ages
and deteriorates
|
I stroll down my alley
palms up
consuming the breath of life
|
It's only four past midnight

\\-grey

To: voice <cassini2358@yahoo.com>;
From: grey <maxwellgreyson@yahoo.com>;
Subject: Sale – limited time only – open 24/7!

Message:

voice-

I did it! My very first screenplay is finished, done! But, of course,
things didn't quite work out exactly as planned. I'll have to explain
more when we meet next.

www.garagesaledanceparty.com

-grey

Reception level: Poor (1 out of 4) |

```
function GoToScene(event:imeyeself):void

{
```

I am an 18-year-old trash bin pressed firmly against a
grimy brick wall in an unlit alley behind an invisible
gourmet restaurant. Various rust spots scatter my
rectangular structure; A patchwork of different paints and
stickers have been placed at overlapping points in time to
cover up unintelligible graffiti, deteriorating metal and
a multitude of other unwanted blemishes of unknown origin.
Go ahead and flip open the warped black plastic lid.
Nothing is visible but a small puddle of errant rain water
in the bottom-right corner. I'm empty but the stench of
rotting food still fills the air. Gritty inner walls flash
memories of burned taste buds, midnight heartburn and
foiled criminal escape attempts. Close the lid and hide my
emptiness; the stench will linger for a while and then
dissipate in the wind as stale rain water slowly eats away
at my weakening base. My foundation is near collapse and I
have nothing left to plug the holes but abused and
apathetic air molecules.

```
}
```

9. My cents [sic] of taste

I suppose that I possess no senses: I believe that body, figure, extension, motion and place are merely fictions of my mind. What is there, then, that can be esteemed true? Perhaps this only, that there is absolutely nothing certain.

Rene Descartes

Second Beach will forever be my favorite place on this Earth.

This much I know for certain.

Second Beach: Where serene Pacific Northwest forest meets wild Pacific Ocean shoreline. There's a trail that travels down through about 0.62 miles of coastal forest to reach the ocean beach. I know the Second Beach trail so well that you could drop me on the far reaches of the planet and I would find my way home to that very trail, much like a well-trained homing pigeon.

If only I could pitch a tent here on a grassy perch above the shore and spend an eternity admiring the relentless tide and untamed elements of nature. I suppose I could do just that, and, to be completely honest, I've considered the pros and cons of such a life more than a few times. I'm still trying to come up with that first con.

Second Beach is northwest of Seattle, sitting on the western edge of the Olympic Peninsula. It's about a four-hour journey from door to door, or from patch to sand, I suppose. When the underground gets to be too much, this is where I go to figure things out.

The downward spiral I've been traveling down is relentless. To say that I embody ridiculousness is in danger of becoming an unforgivable understatement after this last series of events. There's no visible floor at the end of this strange tunnel to under the underground.

Now I want to see what the tides have to say about that.

```
\\+rx1618:

beech [sic]

if i could i would create a likeness of you out of bamboo
and straw and stick it in the sand gazing at the endless
tide. if i could i would remember the shadow of your
profile floating on uneven sand with the sunset looming.
ive always loved that thin layer of air that resides
directly above sand freshly washed by waves. it holds the
truth of nature and the nature of unknown in a temporary
space. if i could i would grab it and give it you to. ive
always wanted you to hold that in your palm to grasp. not
forever but for just one moment in time.

\\-grey
```

I wake up after a night on the beach with a clear head and all of my senses on high alert. The tides have spoken: it's time to bring Lavender Mongoose back.

Oh, yes it is!

Thank you Second Beach, you dear old friend! The wind and water and sand always combine to bring the answers I'm seeking. I immediately pack up and head back east to Seattle.

The four-hour journey from sand to patch is filled with thoughts of pastries and brisket, of roasting and grilling, of well-known spices and obscure cheeses, of sweet and savory, and more.

Yes - and more!

"Are you familiar with pop-up restaurants?" I ask the voice as I sit down in one of her comfortable chairs.

"Pop-up restaurants? Yes, I believe so. Are you referring to those types of secretive, exclusive gourmet restaurants?"

"Yes, they are both exclusive and elusive," I say. "It seems as though you're well-schooled on the subject of pop-up restaurants.

"They change location a lot, right?"

"Yes, pop-ups are kind of like underground supper clubs that bring the latest and greatest in the culinary world to a location near you. The one caveat - as you already mentioned - is that the location of the pop-up restaurant changes frequently."

"Yes, of course."

"And only the hippest of hip diners could ever even daydream of knowing the locations of top-tier pop-ups out there. You don't just have to be connected to know these locations, you must be the connection."

"I see."

"You can't be in the know, you must be the know, you know?"

"Yes, of course, those pop-up type of restaurants seem to be gaining popularity in recent years. I've never been to one, but I have heard of a few them. I've heard people discussing them quite a bit recently."

"Do you remember any of the names of the restaurants?"

"No, unfortunately none come to mind."

"Yeah, well, in any case, I wasn't all that familiar with pop-ups just a few years back, but I am now," I say.

"Oh, I see."

"It didn't really take all that long to become extremely familiar with them. In fact, I'm familiar with them in the purest form - I own one."

"You own a pop-up restaurant?"

"I do. It travels around with me like my own personal lap dog. It's called Lavender Mongoose. Have you heard of it?"

"Maybe. You know, the name does seem to be a little familiar. I'm not sure, though," she pauses and thinks. "Lavender Mongoose? The name does seem to ring a bell."

<!--of course it does!-->

"Would like to join us for dinner some time?"

<!--of course you would!-->

"Sure, yes, I could probably do that," the voice says. "How does it work? How do you plan everything and secure new locations?"

"I manage those projects to perfection."

"You've never mentioned the restaurant before," the voice says. "And I wasn't aware of your culinary expertise, either."

"My culinary experience pretty much begins with putting a metal spoon in the microwave and pretty much ends with buying a new microwave."

"Oh, so you're just the brains of the operation?"

"Well..."

"Or the project manager?"

"That I am. I do indeed manage this project. But I also have an invaluable partner through it all - Sid."

"OK, so Sid is in charge of the kitchen, then? He's never mentioned the restaurant to me, either."

"No, we both do it all."

"I see."

"Or we both do none of it all, actually."

"I'm sorry, I'm not following."

"Lavender Mongoose is but a figment of your imagination, my imagination, and all other imaginations. The restaurant is a fake, a ghost, a ghoul. It doesn't really exist but as a wild, untamed phantom. However, the best part is that many, many people do think that it exists."

"They do?"

"Actually, they don't think it, they know that it exists. Do you know why?"

"Why?"

"Because no one will ever admit that they couldn't find it or that they got duped, so the myth lives on! It's incredible, really."

"Let me see if I'm following you here: You operate a fake pop-up restaurant that you call the Lavender Mongoose."

"Yes, otherwise known as the 'goose."

"And this fake restaurant lives on because those who were supposed to eat there - and obviously never did eat there - have never admitted that it's a fake because they're too embarrassed to admit being fooled?"

"Yes! I know, it's crazy!"

"That sounds a little farfetched, even for you and Sid."

"I know. It does. I agree. I completely agree. It was supposed to be just a one-time gig that Sid and I came up with. It was supposed to be just a bad joke, really, but then it took on a life of its own. It took on a generation of lives."

"How did it come to be?"

"The first time, we tried to create a kind of buzz about the place, but we weren't sure if it would take hold. We then leaked the location, which, of course, was not real. And we made sure that the secret location was in a crowded part of the city so that we could watch the would-be diners wander around and flutter about while trying to find it. It was great!"

"I don't know if I'd call that great. Maybe strange, but not great."

"Strangely beautiful!"

"But how has no one figured out that it's a fake?"

"That's the true beauty of it all! It's crazy, really it is. I still have trouble processing it all."

"Well, it's certainly different."

"One of the keys, I've learned, is to have the Lavender Mongoose take long, unannounced breaks and disappear for months at a time with no explanation. It only adds to the intrigue of the 'goose."

"How do you make something that doesn't really exist disappear? Isn't The Goose already not there to begin with?"

"It's the 'goose, and, by the way, the 'goose doesn't play by the rules."

"Right: The Goose."

"Wrong. It's the 'goose, all lowercase with an apostrophe, not The Goose with capital letters and no apostrophe," I say.

"How can you ..." the voice starts to ask.

"I know, I know, it's crazy But, believe me, I'm telling you the absolute truth here. In any case, I'm bringing the 'goose back this week."

"Is that right?"

"Yep, the plan is already in motion, but with date, time, menu and location to be determined, of course."

"Grey, do you really think it's a good idea to be misleading people like this, to be fooling strangers and wasting their time simply for your own amusement?"

"Sure, why not?"

"Well, you're consistently worried about your relations with others, am I right?"

"How so?"

"What I mean is, you're convinced that people have a tendency to not like you very much. You have a little of the 'me against the world' mentality. Would you agree with that?"

"Yeah I guess. People hate me - is that what you're talking about?"

"Well, don't you think that maybe doing things like this could potentially diminish your likeability?"

"I don't know about that, but I do love the 'goose!'"

"Grey, I think I need to advise you against continuing on with the Lavender Mongoose."

"But we have a great menu in store for this week."

"Grey..."

"Listen, I appreciate the advice, but I need to run. Sorry to cut out early today. But I thought you might like to hear about the 'goose.'"

"Grey, I strongly advise against this type of behavior."

"I guess I was wrong."

"Grey, this can lead to nowhere good."

"Nowhere good? I like that. I think I've heard that somewhere before. Thanks for the advice!"

"I liked your screenplay, by the way," the voice says as I get up to leave. "Garage Sale Dance Party: I liked it. Thanks for sharing."

"Oh, thanks. But it didn't really work out that well in the end."

"What didn't work out in the end?"

"Well, I kind of got taken in to the police station again when trying to cast for the short film."

"The police? Again!? What happened?"

"It's kind of a long story."

"It wasn't the same officer, was it?"

"Officer Higgs? Of course it was," I say. "The whole incident was confusing and made no sense. I'll have to fill you in later."

All credibility, all good conscience, all evidence of truth come only from the senses.

Friedrich Nietzsche

It's time to get back on track. Tomorrow I'll check in on the boosters and I'll also start planning the exact details of the much-anticipated return of Lavender Mongoose. Tonight, though, I'll head over to my woodworking class in Ballard. I don't care if the haters in the class will ridicule me even more now that I've missed so many classes or not. I'm really at peace with it all.

They have no idea of the sheer comfortableness of my hammock.

Right now is all about me getting back on track; it's about straightening out this crooked, misdirected, jagged path. It's not about debating which circles of friends I'm part of and which I'm not.

And it's definitely not about debating the differences of tap water.

In any case, joining an inner circle of woodworking friends is not high on my priority list right now, nor is tasting tap water.

Walking toward the Ballard Bridge at a brisk pace, I notice that the bridge is stuck in the open position. No people or cars can pass. This happens from time to time and I've never really tried to figure out exactly why it happens. Sometimes the bridge gets stuck open after allowing a tall boat or two to pass but then it eventually just gets unstuck and that's that. It can take a few minutes or an hour, so I'm hoping for the minute-long variety here.

I walk up to the pedestrian barrier and lean against the steel rail, admiring the Cascades to the east as the sun is lying down to rest with the Olympics behind my back. A few small boats float below but there's really nothing special to speak of. Hopefully the bridge gets unstuck soon. I don't want to be late for class.

"You're late! You're late!"

I hear an angry voice yelling but it doesn't completely register as I take in the scenery.

"You're late! YOU ARE LATE!"

"Yes, I am going to be late if this bridge doesn't get unstuck soon," I think to myself as I stare off to the east.

I turn and look. A man is standing on the other side of the bridge pointing in my direction. At first glance he looks to be a homeless man, perhaps a free passenger coming from the freight trains not far from where we are now. He looks dirty; his clothes are old and worn; his shoes are really nothing more than pieces of fabric flapping around with each step. He stands there yelling and pointing at me across the four lanes of the bridge.

His half of the road is empty, as the south-going traffic is currently stuck on the northwest side of the bridge. The two lanes on my side are packed with cars waiting for the bridge to close and traffic to resume as normal.

"YOU ARE LATE!! You're late!" he screams and he climbs over the barrier and starts hobbling in my direction.

He has a pronounced limp; it appears as though one leg is much shorter than the other. He doesn't walk so much as he stumbles and then swings the other leg around and snaps it in place. With each step it looks as if he'll trip and fall face-first into the concrete. As he gets closer I can see him more clearly. His hair is long and unruly. He looks extremely agitated and despondent. His eyes are bloodshot and he's missing a few teeth.

"You're late! You! Are! Late!" he shakes his head from side to side and wags his finger at me as he slowly makes his way across the four lanes.

I'm paralyzed and have nowhere to go. I could turn and head back to Patch Court but I really want to make it to woodworking class tonight. The bridge starts to go down. Soon, I'll be able to cross to safety.

"You're late!"

He comes right up to me, with his finger wagging and drool dripping from his lower lip. He struggles his way over the barrier and we stand toe-to-toe.

I stand my ground.

"YOU ARE LATE!!"

His finger touches my nose and bits of saliva spatter my face. I don't budge.

"You're late!"

I have never seen a human look less human.

"You! Are! Late!"

The bridge is down. The lanes and sidewalks are now open for foot and car traffic. I turn and run as fast as I can to the other side of the bridge.

I sense that my senses are in need of a tune-up, perhaps even an overhaul, for they have been mutating. Does this mean that I own a sixth sense? A seventh, even? Old friend, exactly what unseen creature has formed here in the underground? I speak not and hope that my newfound senses mix with the absence of words to bring me good fortune.
-Frodrick Gray

At the bottom of the other side of the bridge, I stand hunched over with hands on knees trying to catch my breath. There's no way that the crazy guy obsessed with punctuality could catch up with me, at least not for a while. He can't move fast enough with the limp. I'm safe, I think.

After a quick rest, I start walking again while trying to catch my breath at the same time. Up about a block a strange presence flows along with the slight breeze. The presence has a slight glow, it appears, too. Yes, this presence is, so to speak, kind of flowing and glowing down the street. As I get closer I can see that it's a person.

I want our paths to cross.

No, I need our paths to cross.

"Ruby?" I say, stunned.

"Grey?! What are you doing here, I mean, where are you..."

"I live right over the bridge, remember? Patch Court?"

"Oh, right, Patch Court," She says. "Wait, really? You live there? I thought you were joking."

She seems nervous. She's not standing behind the safety of the counter at Cafe Entropy. She's out of her comfort zone.

"No, I wasn't joking, as I told you many times before. And don't worry, I'm not following you or whatever new bizarre fable you're going to come up with next. I'm just going to my class over there." I point.

"So, you really live on Patch Court, huh? And I didn't say you were following me, by the way."

"Well, I wouldn't put it past you. I'll say that much. Goodbye." I turn and start walking away, hoping that something doesn't appear out of thin air to impede my progress yet again.

I have a bad feeling that this is some sort of sting operation led by Officer Higgs.

"Grey, listen, I'm sorry!" Ruby yells. "I'm truly sorry. It wasn't me. It wasn't me who called the police, and it wasn't my idea, either. I had nothing to do with it."

"Sure," I say, still struggling to catch my breath.

"Are you OK?" she asks.

Yeah ... I just ... there was this ... I was late ... and he was ... yeah, I'm fine."

"You know, it wasn't me who called the cops. I had no idea. I'm sorry about that. Really, I am. That was horrible, terrible. You didn't deserve that. No one deserves that."

"Yeah, well you have no idea," I say. "That officer - Higgs or whatnot - has it out for me or something. You really have no idea. You really screwed me over. I mean, you really screwed me over - big time."

"I really am sorry, Grey," she says. "Maybe we can put this past us and you can stop by for a coffee on the house. Tomorrow?"

"Uh, yeah I don't think so," I say. "Listen, I'm not that dense and I also don't even care about your inner circle or whatnot anymore."

"Inner circle?"

"Nevermind. It doesn't matter. I'm not going back to your lame establishment of caffeinated beverages, ever."

"Well, think about it. I understand that you're still upset and I just want to tell you that you're always welcome."

"Where? Here?"

"No there."

"There?"

"Yes there, you know, Cafe Entropy?"

"Yeah, right. I'll be sure to stop by right away. I'll just be certain to bring enough money with me to cover bail from now on. Or maybe I'll just call the cops myself before I head over so that they can meet me there before I even set foot in the place."

"And don't forget to bring your crow, too."

"That's not funny," I say. "And I'm supposed to be the funny guy, anyway."

"Right, the stand-up routine," she says. "Don't quit your day job."

`<!--LOL-->`

I check the snake: I still have a few minutes to make it to class on time. The snake also tells me that I have 18 new missed calls and 16 new voicemails. I've lost control of virtually every aspect of life. I can't even keep up with all of the phone calls anymore. My project managing skills have deteriorated to the lowest of lows.

To: grey <maxwellgreyson@yahoo.com>;
From: sid <sidsays0@yahoo.com>;
Subject: re: zeroes

Message:

grey~

---zeroes 0.8---

Food can have zero taste, no? Indeed, food can have zero taste. I think it's safe to say that we've all experienced that unfortunate scenario. But what about the experience of nothing tangible that leaves a really bad taste in your mouth? See, this is where it gets all complicated. The answer is an easy one, though: Zero is being ill-treated; Zero is being neglected. The wrongful campaign against zero is moving ahead at full speed, looking to obliterate the poor, unsuspecting chap. I'm here for you old friend! You'll always have a safe haven here on my shelf. Stay a while, if you will. Or stay a while longer even. It'll bring one single tear of joy to my eye.

~sid

---

sidsays0: hello, old friend!
maxwellgreyson: u coming 2nite? should i count u in?
sidsays0: uh, sure
sidsays0: where?
maxwellgreyson: lavender mongoose
sidsays0: excellent! ur bringing the 'goose back?
maxwellgreyson: yep, remember where it is?
sidsays0: uh yeah - zero st right?
maxwellgreyson: something like that
sidsays0: oh ill b there!
maxwellgreyson: good menu 2night
sidsays0: will def b there
maxwellgreyson: top menu, best ever maybe
sidsays0: got some saffron-spiked aioli?
maxwellgreyson: yeah
sidsays0: fennel-infused tapenade too?
maxwellgreyson: yep
sidsays0: herb-crusted?
maxwellgreyson: done
sidsays0: frizzled?
maxwellgreyson: sure

sidsays0: what else u got for me?
maxwellgreyson: menu crushes it
sidsays0: like crushed heirloom yellow pepper flakes?
maxwellgreyson: yes! menu blows others out of the water
sidsays0: like freshly prepared organic mango lassie presented in blown glass vases?
maxwellgreyson: nice one, may use that
maxwellgreyson: or 11-cheese fondu with free-range lentil cakes?
sidsays0: lentils cant be free range
maxwellgreyson: at the 'goose they can be
sidsays0: tru
maxwellgreyson: mango lassie wins
sidsays0: agreed
maxwellgreyson: i.e. food for the foodie
sidsays0: like that
maxwellgreyson: thought u might
sidsays0: what time do u want 2 meet?
maxwellgreyson: not sure yet, will let u know
sidsays0: please do
maxwellgreyson: foodies will be pleased

Welcome to the latest edition of The Grey Matter Report, where Grey fills you in on what matters, what really matters and what's the matter.

This week's term: Foodie

The foodie (i.e. one who has a concerted interest in both the knowledge and consumption of all types of food) used to be more of a rarity - a novelty, even - but has, in recent times, been multiplying in volume like mosquitoes in swampland in May.

Despite the higher likelihood of encountering wannabe foodies in this day and age, it's important to note that encountering a true, certified foodie is still not a particularly common occurrence. When coming across a possible foodie candidate, consult the following list to ultimately determine that individual's status.

To truly own the title of foodie, not just in name but also in practice, one must:

- Possess an above-average yearning to obtain wisdom of food and food-related topics.

- Have an unadulterated enthusiasm for preparing, eating, and talking about food.

- Be willing to ridicule others for their juvenile and simplistic views on consuming food.

- Have no problem berating aspiring chefs for creating subpar quiches and soufflés.

- Enjoy eating asparagus with every course of every meal for one month straight.

- Mention ceviche a minimum of twice per hour during important meals.

- Be able to interject the term "mise en place" into any conversation regardless of context.

Before debating the need for foodies or cursing their existence, stop and think: What would all this be without foodies? Sure, we would still chew and swallow, but at what cost? Much lower cost, you say? You might be on to something there.

Until next time, stay somewhere 'tween black & white.

---

maxwellgreyson: hey check this out
sidsays0: ?
maxwellgreyson: i ran across ruby last night
sidsays0: what?! ur crazy!
maxwellgreyson: whoa, calm down. why?
sidsays0: u went to entropy!
maxwellgreyson: no, it was on the street
sidsays0: oh, ok. thought u really lost ur mind there 4 a sec
sidsays0: still, not good

maxwellgreyson: literally ran into her
maxwellgreyson: was running away from something
sidsays0: from what?
maxwellgreyson: not sure exactly
sidsays0: alright, well, what did she want?
maxwellgreyson: she apologized & asked me 2 come back
sidsays0: come back?
maxwellgreyson: yeah 2 entropy
sidsays0: wha?!
maxwellgreyson: can u believe it?
sidsays0: no. stay away man
maxwellgreyson: i know, dont have 2 tell me
sidsays0: good
maxwellgreyson: she kept saying how sorry she was & that i should come back
sidsays0: no way man. stay away <--> far away
maxwellgreyson: agreed
sidsays0: dont trust her
maxwellgreyson: agreed
sidsays0: as far away as possible
maxwellgreyson: yes
sidsays0: what time later for the 'goose?
maxwellgreyson: will let u know in a bit
sidsays0: hold up
maxwellgreyson: :?
sidsays0: just had a good idea
maxwellgreyson: :??
sidsays0: very very good idea
maxwellgreyson: :???
sidsays0: u & i are gonna meet @ entropy this afternoon
maxwellgreyson: lol
sidsays0: no seriously
maxwellgreyson: LOL
sidsays0: ruby will 'find out' about the 'goose
maxwellgreyson: oic plz tell more
sidsays0: yes, ruby will find out & tell her people about it
maxwellgreyson: yes! payback!
sidsays0: well, a little payback
maxwellgreyson: i like it
sidsays0: me 2
maxwellgreyson: a lot
sidsays0: :0

maxwellgreyson :1
maxwellgreyson: what time?
sidsays0: ill head over at @ 1
maxwellgreyson: ok
sidsays0: u dont show til 2 tho
maxwellgreyson: why?
sidsays0: gotta give me a cushion
maxwellgreyson: 4 what?
sidsays0: dont want u 2 get there b4 me
maxwellgreyson: good pt
sidsays0: indeed
maxwellgreyson: sounds good
sidsays0: cya
maxwellgreyson: l8r

It has been said that the only thing that is certain is uncertainty. That is, that all we know is that we know nothing at all. Fair enough O'doers of deep thought. I shall devise a language of complex gibberish and travel the world with a team of gnats. The gnats will swarm the heads of unsuspecting thinkers and transform the gibberish into coherent concepts for all to consume like decade-old cheese.
-Frodrick Gray

As I approach Cafe Entropy, I'm consumed by one thought: This would not be a good time for one of Sid's patented pranks. Walking up to the door of Entropy I feel a tap on my shoulder. My heart sinks.

I turn slowly with eyes closed and open my eyelids one by one: Sid.

Sid!

My heart is pumping like crazy. He still managed to throw a prank in even though he stayed good to his word. Only Sid can be the most horrible enemy one instant and then a most trusted confidant the very next. We walk into Entropy together and head immediately to the counter.

"Grey!" Ruby tries to sound excited.

"Hey," I mutter. "This is my friend Sid."

"Sid? I know Sid! I didn't know you two knew each other."

<!--[:?]-->

"That we do," Sid says. "I've actually known Grey for a long, long time."

"I had no idea," Ruby says. "I haven't seen you in forever, Sid, what have you been up to?"

"Oh, you know, just this and that," Sid says.

"Zero," I say with zero acknowledgement from zero people.

"I'm glad you came back, Grey," she says with pathetic acting skills. "Like I said, I'm really sorry about what happened before."

"Yeah, OK, I'll have a red eye."

"This one's on the house," Ruby says.

She turns to Sid: "What kind of 'this and that' have you been up to?"

"Just working on new theories and whatnot," Sid says.

<!--whatnot is my word-->

"Hey, have you ever heard of the Purple Goose or something like that?" Sid asks. "It's a restaurant."

<!--purple? come on, come up with something better than that-->

"You mean Lavender Mongoose," Ruby corrects him. "I've heard it's amazing but I've never been. Have you?"

<!--whatever works-->

"I haven't personally been to the 'goose, but have I got a tip for you!" Sid says.

He asks her for a piece of paper and writes down an address.

"Hey, what are you guys talking about? The zoo?" I ask.

"Oh, nothing, Grey, it's nothing," Ruby says.

"I'm just telling her about ..." Sid attempts to include me in the conversation.

"He's telling me about nothing important," Ruby interjects. "Seriously, it's nothing. Nothing at all. Don't worry about it."

"Not worried," I say as I walk away.

"Thanks, Sid, how did you get the address?" she asks Sid.

Sid starts to fill her in on all of the fabricated details of the invisible restaurant in all of its glorious fakeness. I take my red eye and head out the door, saying goodbye to no one in particular. That was easy. It was almost too easy, in fact

Thanks to Sid, the plan is taking shape.

```
maxwellgreyson: BUZZ!!!
sidsays0: hello, old friend!
maxwellgreyson: nice work earlier 2day
sidsays0: yeah that was nice work if i do say so myself
maxwellgreyson: well done
sidsays0: piece of cake
maxwellgreyson: seemed that way
sidsays0: 2 easy really
maxwellgreyson: agreed
sidsays0: she bought it tho
maxwellgreyson: think she will show?
sidsays0: def
maxwellgreyson: mos def?
sidsays0: yeah mos def
maxwellgreyson: still on 2 meet @ 9 near pike & broadway?
sidsays0: im out
maxwellgreyson: lol
sidsays0: no im out
```

maxwellgreyson: LOL
sidsays0: no 4 real, ur on ur own 2nite
maxwellgreyson: :???
sidsays0: gonna rain so im out
maxwellgreyson: gonna rain? says who?

"FOUR CAST"
Screenplay by Maxwell Greyson

ACT 1, SCENE 1

EXT. TV NEWS STATION SET – NIGHT (PRESENT)

JOE THE WEATHERMAN looks very tired and bored on set and is
slouched over his desk as ANCHOR1 and ANCHOR2 discuss the
happenings of the day.

ANCHOR1
(Laughing) So true, so true. Stranger than fiction (laughing). Well,
I hate to spoil the mood but I think I saw some clouds rolling in
earlier tonight.

ANCHOR2
(Laughing) Yes, I saw those, too. I think it's time to take a look at
the weather with meteorologist Joe Kepler. Now to you Joe.

JOE THE WEATHERMAN (annoyed)
You think you saw clouds rolling in earlier? Are you serious?!
You've got to be kidding me! This is Seattle, so, yes, I think those
were clouds! (shaking head)

Joe the Weatherman places his head down sideways on his desk
while tapping a black permanent marker on the desk with arms
outstretched.

The camera pans to ANCHOR1.

ANCHOR1 (confused)
Uh, yes, Joe. They are definitely clouds. Uh, I know that much. So,
what does the weather have in store for the next few days?

Joe the Weatherman lifts his head slowly from his desk, then bangs it on the desk three times and looks up. His forehead is red from the banging.

JOE THE WEATHERMAN (even more annoyed)
What? Does? The? Weather? Have? In? Store? For? Us? Well, let's see here!

Joe the Weatherman tosses the blank sheets of paper in front of him into the air and stumbles away from his desk. He has the permanent black marker in his hand. He walks right up to the camera and looks right into camera.

ANCHOR1 and ANCHOR2 mumble and whisper to each other. Muffled commotion is heard in the background.

Joe the Weatherman writes a backwards 5 on one of his cheeks with the black marker and writes a 0 (zero) on the other cheek.

JOE THE WEATHERMAN (staring into the camera)
See that! 5-0! 50! 50 degrees! That's what the weather has in store for us, people. It's 50 freaking degrees every day here! What are you watching the weather for? Sure it's like 75 for like a month and it's like 35 for a month, but the rest of the year it's 50 degrees! Every day it's 50 degrees. Got it?

A hand is seen grabbing Joe the Weatherman's shoulder. Someone is behind him trying to pull him back from the camera.

JOE THE WEATHERMAN (still staring into the camera but being pulled away)
Oh, and it will rain a little and then stop. And some clouds will roll in and then they will go away. Clouds roll in, mist, clouds roll out, repeat. Got it? Got it?!

Joe the Weatherman grabs the camera with two hands and starts shaking it.

JOE THE WEATHERMAN (shaking the camera)
50 degrees! 50 degrees! 50 degrees! 50 degrees! 50 degrees! 50 degrees!

Joe the Weatherman shakes the camera so fiercely that the camera falls on top of him. Shrieks of pain mix with shouting from a number of off-camera voices.

JOE THE WEATHERMAN
My legs! My legs!

CUT TO COMMERCIAL

FLASH FORWARD: EXT. TV NEWS STATION SET – NIGHT
(FUTURE)

Joe the Weatherman is in a specially designed wheelchair to accommodate his two broken arms and two broken legs. Each arm and leg is in its own cast. On the screen behind Joe the weatherman is the three-day forecast.

JOE THE WEATHERMAN
So it looks like a high of 50 degrees on Tuesday, then up to 51 on Wednesday and then a bit of a cold front shows up Thursday to push the high back down to 50. Back to you.

CUT TO BLACK

THE END

---

sidsays0: sorry man, im out
maxwellgreyson: thats ridiculous
sidsays0: no thats u
maxwellgreyson: fine, thats re:ridiculous
sidsays0: no thats u 2
maxwellgreyson: yeah i guess it is
maxwellgreyson: fwd:ridiculous ?
sidsays0: maybe
sidsays0: well let me know how it goes
maxwellgreyson: u know what sid spelled backwards is
sidsays0: dis
maxwellgreyson: !
sidsays0: nice 1 grey, ur brain really is working these days
maxwellgreyson: multiverse talk woke me up
sidsays0: from a deep slumber?
maxwellgreyson: something like that
sidsays0: good, ive got more multiverse theories
maxwellgreyson: still dont understand about 2nite tho ... ???
sidsays0: nothing 2 understand but rain

maxwellgreyson: what are you made of suede?
sidsays0: good 1
maxwellgreyson: you live in seattle & dont go out when it rains?
sidsays0: tru story
maxwellgreyson: makes no sense
sidsays0: it doesnt even really rain here 1/2 as much as every1 thinks
maxwellgreyson: shhhh, dont tell anyone
maxwellgreyson: they will all move here
sidsays0: oh right, I mean, it rains here all the time! downpours!
maxwellgreyson: better
sidsays0: like every hour of every day!
maxwellgreyson: much better
sidsays0: lemme know how it goes
maxwellgreyson: fine
sidsays0: thx
maxwellgreyson: lol
sidsays0: doesnt apply here
maxwellgreyson: LOL
sidsays0: l8r
maxwellgreyson: LOL LOL LOL

Tonight's menu is set:

Say "I do" to the 'goose
a carrot becomes so much more than just a carrot when it's
frizzled

Why go to all of the trouble of having your own wedding when
you can simply join us for a wedding-like feast? It'll be much
cheaper, much less time consuming and you won't have debate
whether or not to invite that one cousin who you know will show
up anyway.

Assorted Hearth Baked Breads
with sweet cream butter

Cornish Game Hens
marinated in marjoram, garlic and citrus zest and served with a
lemon and thyme jus

Roasted Garlic and Rosemary Filet of Beef
served with caramelized shallots and red wine demi-glace

Red Jacket Mashers

Savory Rice Pilaf

Potato and Herb Crusted Halibut
served with frizzled carrots and a roasted garlic and thyme aioli

Wild Mushroom Ravioli

Grilled Vegetable Medley
includes saffron-seasoned asparagus

Baby Field Greens
with white balsamic and honey vinaigrette

Seasonal Fruit Selection

Imported and Domestic Cheeses

I station myself about a block away from the fake location that Sid leaked to Ruby at Cafe Entropy earlier today. Usually, 62 percent of the fun is picking out which people on the street may or may not be searching for the 'goose, but tonight is different.

Tonight, I'm looking for one person and one person only. I want to see Ruby struggle and be humiliated in front of top-ranking members of her prized inner circle.

This much I know for certain.

Yes, her cronies will abandon her like a broken old trash can in a hidden alley. Yes they will! Scanning the street, I'm looking for her flow and glow. Or maybe that flow-glow was but a one-time event? I have no idea, really. It's pretty crowded out here on the sidewalks and it's hard to tell if any of these wanderers are searching for the 'goose or not.

And it's not raining at all.

<!--:|-->

I stopped and bought a pair of black plastic glasses with attached eyebrows, nose and mustache to help disguise my presence. But the mustache already fell off and the nose looked really obvious so I removed it. I added some orange tape in between where the two lenses would be on black plastic frames, but then removed the fake eyebrows because they looked ridiculous.

So my disguise now consists of a pair of black plastic thick-rims with no lenses and piece on orange tape on the bridge.

Scanning the Pike Street, I finally pick out Ruby. She has no flow. She has no glow. I'm not sure what that was about last night, because she looks very pedestrian tonight. She's flanked by a handful of the laptop clones from Cafe Entropy as she strolls casually to the invisible underground restaurant.

It's pretty late already and I've already seen a couple of extremely confused and unhappy people searching for a nonexistent door. According to the intelligence that Sid spread, the location of the 'goose was behind a newly-painted orange door near this intersection.

I wasn't sure that Ruby would show. But there she is and it's all worth it now! I can't help but laugh out loud.

<!—LOL?-->

Being especially careful to keep my distance, I notice a sort of angry, agitated mob of people forming near where the Lavender Mongoose is supposed to be. Ruby is literally standing in the middle of her inner circle. She's talking loudly and animatedly about something or someone or both.

How strange it is to see a physical manifestation of her inner circle. The angry mob is small in size but I can feel the tension in the air. I think it's time to head home.

I turn to take the roundabout way back to Patch Court and a cyclist crashes directly into me. Bags and body parts and miscellaneous other items go flying everywhere.

I get up as quickly as possible and dust myself off. Making my way over to the cyclist on the ground I look up to see Ruby.

"Grey? What are you doing here? Are you OK?" she asks.

The cyclist mumbles some obscenities under his breath, gathers his items, gets back on his bike and leaves.

"Why are you wearing those glasses?"

"Not sure," I say.

My brain is frozen in glacial ice.

"Hey, were you spying? Were you listening in on my conversation with Sid earlier? Is that why you're here? I knew it!"

"No, I don't know what you're talking about. I'm not even interested in the Lavender Mongoose or whatnot."

"Ah ha!" she says. "So you were listening!"

"No, everyone knows, I mean, Sid told me anyway."

"I doubt that," she says.

"He did, anyway, what's the big deal? I don't even want to eat their frizzled fare over there anyway."

"Over where?" she asks.

"There."

"You mean here."

"Sure."

"Well, I think Sid's information was wrong or something, because it isn't here," she says.

"What isn't here?"

"The Lavender Mongoose, it isn't here."

"It isn't? Sid's always right, are you sure?"

"Yes, I'm sure," she says. "We've searched every inch and the 'goose is nowhere to be found."

"That's strange."

"Either it's not happening here at this place tonight or it's just not happening at all."

"What do you mean it's not happening at all? Of course it is."

"Some of these people are even wondering if there's even a Lavender Mongoose at all anymore."

"Really, I had no idea that the 'goose was fake. That's strange. Who would have ever guessed that the whole Lavender Mongoose thing was a fake? Not me."

"What do you mean it's fake?" she asks suspiciously.

"I don't know," I say. "That's what you said."

"No, that's what YOU said!" she yells.

"What?"

"That!"

"It?"

"It was you, wasn't it? This was some sort of twisted payback!"

Ruby turns and looks at the angry mob. She turns back, finger outstretched and a veins popping from her forehead.

"It's him! It's him!" she yells, pointing at me. "This is the guy who made us all out to be fools! There is no Lavender Mongoose! He's playing some kind of lame prank!"

The angry mob surrounds me instantaneously. Within another instant, I'm picked up off the ground and carried to the nearest alley amidst the chaos. The mob collectively tosses me in a trash bin and shuts the black plastic lid emphatically.

I feel as though I'm the main character in low-budget, late-night cable movie. And it feels like a poorly-made film with bad acting, at that. Perhaps sexy aliens will rescue me at any moment and cook me up a pot of lentil soup.

What's that smell? My left foot is immersed in a bulk container of rancid mayonnaise. At least I hope that's what it is.

\\+rx1618:

Pyour [sic]

I look like anyone
you choose to see
Oh, keep searching
for purity of being
Do not deceive yourself
I may walk forever

\\-grey

To: voice <cassini2358@yahoo.com>;
From: grey <maxwellgreyson@yahoo.com>;
Subject: Feeding frenzy!

Message:

Have you eaten at the lavender mongoose recently, by chance?

www.lavendermongoose.com

-grey

Reception level: Poor (1 out of 4) |

```
function GoToScene(event:imeyeself):void
```

```
{
```

I am a pre-owned display case. Don't dare call me used. My glass face is peppered with partial fingerprints that are only visible when the light is just so. The shadows of past inhabitants layer each of my scuffed shelves so that current items float a minute fraction above what was before. My aluminum corner protectors are loose, jagged and ready to pierce the nearest skin at first opportunity. Never content, I'm always searching for new contents to fill my surprisingly deep void. I'll take what you have to offer - and without judgment, at that. But don't turn around and judge me like that, all the same. Open the shades and let in a bit of that summer sun. This is I and I am not afraid to exclaim it to the world: Displaying is the great explainer.

```
}
```

10. I've been heir [sic] before

My body is a torn mattress
Disheveled throbbing place
For the comings and goings
Of loveless transients.
The whole of me
Is an unfurnished room
Filled with dank breath
Escaping in gasps to nowhere.
Before completely objective mirrors
I have shot myself with my eyes,
But death refused my advances.
I have walked on my walls each night
Through strange landscapes in my head.
I have brushed my teeth with orange peel
Iced with cold blood from my dripping faucets.
My face is covered with maps of dead nations;
My hair is littered with drying ragweed.
Bitter raisins drip haphazardly from my nostrils
While schools of glowing minnows swim from my mouth.
The nipples of my breasts are sun-browned cockleburrs;
Long-forgotten Indian tribes fight battles on my chest
Unaware of the sunken ships rotting in my stomach.
My legs are charred remains of burned cypress trees;
My feet are covered with moss from bayous, flowing
across my floor.
I can't go out anymore.
I shall sit on my ceiling.
Would you wear my eyes?

Bob Kaufman

The windows project is finally complete! I stayed up all night woodworking after returning from my first ever dumpster-diving experience. I just put the finishing touches on the windows as the clock reads 4:18 p.m.

Working on my beloved windows project was the only way that I could even temporarily forget about the stench of rotting trash that has been stationed stubbornly in my nostrils since the disappointing and abrupt end to the 'goose last night.

All told, the finished project consists of eight rudimentary wooden window frames. But even creating rudimentary window frames has been a monumental task. I drew up the plans for this very set of eight windows one night after waking from a dream or perhaps a daydream of sorts. The exact origin is unknown. But whether the instruction came from a dream, a daydream or somewhere between is really of no importance now.

When the end appears as white into black, the grey beginning disappears.

Instructions and specification for grey windows:
- Eight wooden window frames must be built.
- Each window must measure precisely 1.618 feet by 1.618 feet.
- Each window must be created from identical materials.
- The frames must be hung at shoulder height from a metal wire.
- Each frame must hang exactly 1.618 feet from the next.
- The hanging of the windows must take place on August 12.
- The windows can be used shortly after midnight on August 13.
- At 2 minutes and 2 seconds past midnight I must begin.
- I must place my hands through the first frame.
- I must start with the window on my left.
- In my right hand will be a blank notepad.
- In my left hand will be a pen.
- I am to keep my hands in each until it is time to move to the next.
- Repeat.

Each of the eight windows is precisely the right size. I'm certain of that. I took painstaking efforts to make certain of that. In the end, this project took many hours to complete and cost many boosters.

But that's all in the past.

Here - in the present - the project is nearing completion. I'm not sure what the end result will ultimately be but I've taken care of my part, at least. Everything is identical: I used the same type of wood and screws for each. I installed a sturdy steel cord across my entire basement, supported at even intervals, and hung each window frame exactly 1.618 feet from the next. The blank notepad and pen are sitting on the ground underneath the first window. Everything is ready to go.

This much I know for certain.

Exactly what this all is ready for I'm really not too certain of. For now, the hammock is calling, as I need to rest my eyes and clear my head as much as possible before midnight strikes. I'll set the alarm on the snake to ensure that I don't oversleep.

To: grey <maxwellgreyson@yahoo.com>;
From: sid <sidsays0@yahoo.com>;
Subject: re: zeroes
Message:

grey~

---zeroes 0.9---

I have inherited a zero. There, I said it. I feel much better now! But what is one to do with a zero that pretty much shows up on one's doorstep unannounced? Or dare I say both unannounced and unwanted? I suppose I'll do nothing for now, but that strategy surely cannot last forever. I fear that if I leave my newfound zero sitting there untouched for too long, anything can happen. Well, not anything, but something. Something will surely happen. Nothing will happen, you say? Have you not been listening? This is not an old friend we are talking about here! All zeroes are old friends, you say? Fool! I will bury this zero in the backyard next to old bush back there. Yes, that's what I'll do.

~sid

At midnight, the snake buzzes and rattles. I roll out of the hammock and head down to the basement. I left all of the windows and shades in the basement wide open. I don't even have to turn on the lights; I can see perfectly fine.

I look up to the full moon in the sky and see patterns and details

I've never noticed before.

The night sky has never been this clear.

O nighttime you are my sunny, blue-skied, white-sand beach. I shall build a sandcastle of moonlight and dark matter and watch the waves of stars slowly consume it as we spin to the the next.
-Frodrick Gray

It isn't so much that my eyes are adjusted to the dark as it is that the night and I are one and the same.

`<!--I am a clear night sky-->`

Two minutes and two seconds pass by one deep breath at a time.

I pick up the pen and paper and slowly put my hands through the first window.

(left hand through, right hand through);
```
I stand there looking into the night sky. I have no
intention of looking down.
```

(left hand through, right hand through);
```
I pause and reach far inside to the depths of my limited
knowledge.
```

(left hand through, right hand through);
```
We talk about universes and such. We discuss aliens and
parallel worlds.
```

(left hand through, right hand through);
```
I don't really want to believe it.
```

(left hand through, right hand through);
```
But I don't not want to believe it, either.
```

(left hand through, right hand through);
```
If yes, then no. Or is it the other way around?
```

(left hand through, right hand through);
```
I'll believe it if that is what it takes in this life.
```

(left hand through, right hand through);
```
Otherwise, I'll just sit here a while and consider what
ought to be.
```

The pen falls from my grasp and hits the floor; the pad of paper drops directly atop of the fallen pen. I can't feel my hands and have no control of their movement. The rest of my body is functional. It's just my hands - they're limp and lifeless. I sit down on the ground a few feet away from the eighth and final window with my arms bent carefully around my knees. With my palms facing me, I stare at my wilted hands for a moment and then bury my head in my bent arms and close my eyes tightly.

Light flashes speckle my eyelids and form a sketch of something more infinite than me.

I often dream elaborate memories about not being able to see, and it frightens me so. O let me see it all just one more time. Just once more! When I awake, I'll close my eyes for a good long while, waiting for the perfect time to take it all in for the first time again.
-Frodrick Gray

I hear something. No, I feel something.

Slowly, I lift my head and shift slowly but surely so that I am sitting with my arms hugging my knees even more tightly. My hands are still limp and lifeless.

He comes right up to me, crouches down and looks me in the eyes: "I, I want to know, uh, where I'm going to?"

She is behind me on the other end of the basement but I can hear her clearly: "I'd love to hear from you. Be sure to give me a call now. Have a good day now, goodbye."

She is floating above me: "I like it here, I want to stay."

He paces back and forth repeating: "Do me one favor: Tell him that I knew it was his worst day."

She is standing at one of the windows, peering at the moon: "I don't know where I am right now, can you come and pick me up, please?"

He is on his knees facing away from me: "From where am I supposed to gather what is to be gathered? It's empty."

In the darkest corner of the basement, a voice is slowly repeating the same thing over and over: "Reformat. Carry on."

I can't speak. I'm stuck somewhere between here and there and I don't know how to get unstuck. I can see, hear, feel and move in a limited way but I can't fully make sense of it all and I certainly don't have full control of what I'm doing or what's happening around me.

I can't see what or who is over in the corner. The voice does eerily sound a lot like mine but I can't tell for sure. My mind may very well be playing tricks on me at this point.

"Reformat. Carry on."

<!--I am sideways man-->

I should have done more. I ignored their calls. I couldn't even find time to check my voicemail. I didn't respond at all - not at all. I didn't even try. I should have helped them. I don't know how or why but I should've done more. I did nothing. I sat in my hammock and did nothing. Nothing!

<!--this much I know for certain-->

It's decided: I will sit here on the cold floor and listen and hear and see and watch and feel for as long as it takes. I owe them that much. I'm at peace with it all; what will happen, will happen.

I sit there and listen until the moon finally vanishes and the first glimmers of the sun rise over the Cascades. The feeling is gradually returning to my hands.

Hold tight, hands. I need you now more than ever, if only until I can just figure this all out.
-Frodrick Gray

sidsays0: BUZZ!!!
sidsays0: hello, old friend!
sidsays0: friend?
maxwellgreyson: ?
sidsays0: how goes it?
sidsays0: how did it work out with the 'goose last nite?
sidsays0: ???
sidsays0: ………
sidsays0: u there?
sidsays0: did ruby show?
sidsays0: hello?
sidsays0: come on man, ur killing me here!
maxwellgreyson: hard 2 type
sidsays0: whats going on man?
sidsays0: u there?
sidsays0: grey?
maxwellgreyson: goin away
sidsays0: where u going?
sidsays0: :?
maxwellgreyson: pck smthn up
sidsays0: need a companion? ive got nothing going on
maxwellgreyson: no
sidsays0: where r u going to exactly?
maxwellgreyson: N
sidsays0: :?
maxwellgreyson: north
sidsays0: canada?
sidsays0: … :??
maxwellgreyson: no
sidsays0: where then?
sidsays0: :??
sidsays0: zzzzzzzz
maxwellgreyson: up hwy 99
sidsays0: whats up aurora ave?
sidsays0: ive been up hwy 99 a lot & never really found much
sidsays0: at least not much worth mentioning
sidsays0: hello? grey?
sidsays0: …….
sidsays0: zzzzzzzzzzzzzzz
sidsays0: grey – u there?
sidsays0: BUZZ!!!
maxwellgreyson: p

maxwellgreyson: a

maxwellgreyson: w

maxwellgreyson: n

sidsays0: pawn?

maxwellgreyson: s

maxwellgreyson: h

maxwellgreyson: o

maxwellgreyson: p

maxwellgreyson: .

sidsays0: pawn shop?

sidsays0: what?

sidsays0: pawn shop?

sidsays0: BUZZ!!!

maxwellgreyson: 1 sec

sidsays0: if memory serves there r a lot of pawn shops up on 99

maxwellgreyson: tru

sidsays0: which 1 u goin 2?

maxwellgreyson: dunno

sidsays0: why are u goin 2 a pawn shop?

maxwellgreyson: :1

sidsays0: confused

sidsays0: :??

maxwellgreyson: long

maxwellgreyson: story

sidsays0: sure u dont want company?

maxwellgreyson: y

sidsays0: need me to lend a helping hand?

maxwellgreyson: n

sidsays0: ok man, u know where to find me

sidsays0: if u need me

maxwellgreyson: ty

sidsays0: np

maxwellgreyson: brb

sidsays0: thats doubtful

sidsays0: you wont brb

sidsays0: not if you head up hwy 99 as slow as u type right now

sidsays0: ...

maxwellgreyson: brb

sidsays0: ok l8r

sidsays0: if i don't hear back from u in 24 hrs ill send search dogs

maxwellgreyson: l8r

sidsays0: L8R

One cannot lose something of which has infinite value. For to lose infinity you must first comprehend infinity. And to comprehend infinity you must step away from reality into an illusion far beyond the scope of value.

Immanuel Kant

"PAWNSUMER"
Screenplay by Maxwell Greyson

EXT. NEAR HIGHWAY 99, a.k.a. AURORA AVE – SEATTLE, WA - DAWN (PRESENT)

NARRATOR (GREY):
It dawns on me as I tight-rope it down the railroad tracks that I can't go on like this. I have to go back. I have to go back as soon as possible. I have to go back right now. I don't even have a choice. Really, I don't. There's only one way: One foot in front of the other. Left in front of right, right in front of left. Repeat. I just keep doing what I do because that's what I do. And that's what I'll be doing: Left in front of right, right in front of left. Repeat. That's the only way. At least, that's the only way that I know. I just keep doing what I do because that's what I do.

GREY falls backward slowly onto the tracks into a sitting position and rests on the ground motionlessly and emotionlessly with his arms tucked into the pockets of his coat. It is an overcast day with a slight mist falling. Traffic from Highway 99 can be heard not far away. GREY is close to the highway but not yet walking alongside it, as he soon will be.

NARRATOR (GREY):
Unfortunately no trains are coming right now. I can't even remember the last time I did see a train going down these tracks. I need to keep heading north. I know that it's time to go back. And I knew this day would come eventually. Why not, right? I'll just do what I do best: Left in front of right, right in front of left. I just keep doing what I do because that's what I do.

GREY stands up, dusts himself off, leaves the railroad tracks and walks to a sign that confirms that he's on the correct path:

"Highway 99." He takes a good, long look at the sign and then starts walking alongside the road. Across the street a neon sign flickers "Open 24 Hours" in no particular pattern.

NARRATOR (GREY):
Time to go back. Time to get them back. It's definitely time. I know this.

GREY walks slowly alongside HWY 99, taking in all of his surroundings with heightened sensitivity. He looks in every window he passes by but there's really not much to see. He receives a few blank glances and stares from people inside of various buildings but sees nothing else of note. GREY stops, looks up to the overcast sky and takes a deep breath.

NARRATOR (GREY):
Ah yes, the comings and goings. It's been a while since I've been down this road, but not much has changed. Yep, this is how I remember it. Is there any other way to remember Highway 99?

GREY continues to walk down HWY 99 deliberately with his arms tucked into the pockets of his coat. He stops, turns counterclockwise 90 degrees and watches the traffic on HWY 99 go by in SLOW MOTION for an instant.

NARRATOR (GREY):
I don't know if I can find my way back. They all look the same, you know?

A car passes by in SLOW MOTION, a child in the back seat has his right hand pressed up against the window with fingers spread out.

A finger taps GREY on the shoulder, startling him out of his temporary SLOW MOTION existence. GREY first focuses on the finger and then turns to see a frail, dirty, disheveled-looking homeless man standing behind him.

HOMELESS MAN:
Excuse me kind sir, have you happened to have seen my bag?

GREY looks at HOMELESS MAN silently and thoroughly for a moment, and then answers with slow and careful words.

GREY:
No, I have not seen your bag, but I will keep an eye out for it. What

does it look like?

HOMELESS MAN:
It looks like my bag.

GREY:
I'm going to need a better description than that.

HOMELESS MAN:
Give it back!

GREY:
I'm sorry but I haven't seen your bag and I certainly don't have your bag.

GREY turns to walk away but HOMELESS MAN grabs his shoulder and forcefully turns him back around. HOMELESS MAN then sticks out his filthy index finger out and points it centimeters from GREY's face.

HOMELESS MAN:
Give me my bag!

GREY:
Listen, I don't have your bag.

HOMELESS MAN:
Give it to me now! Or else!

HOMELESS MAN puts up his fists and takes a fighting stance. He's frail and sickly and looks as if a strong wind would easily knock him over. GREY stands in place, staring motionlessly and emotionlessly with his arms still tucked deep into his coat pockets. He has yet to remove his arms from his pockets.

HOMELESS MAN:
Put up your dukes, let's get this over with! Now!

GREY:
I don't think so.

HOMELESS MAN:
Put 'em up!

GREY:

I don't think you really...

HOMELESS MAN:
Now!

GREY takes his arms out of his pockets. He has no hands.
HOMELESS MAN, startled, falls backward to the ground and
starts to crawl away in horror. GREY looks down at his wrists and
shakes his head. HOMELESS MAN is frightened and muttering
incoherently as he tries to get away.

GREY:
Yeah, I know.

NARRATOR (GREY):
I need to get my hands back.

HOMELESS MAN gets to his feet, looks GREY over once more and
then turns and runs.

HOMELESS MAN:
I'm outta here!

GREY stares at his handless arms for a moment and then
continues his deliberate journey up HWY 99. He passes by a
number of motels, convenience stores and pawn shops. GREY
stops at one particular pawn shop, turns and take a long look. He
walks to the entrance.

NARRATOR (GREY):
Noiseless. The door doesn't creak as I open it. It's completely
noiseless. It's crazy to think that he applied enough WD-40 to
bring permanent silence to this door. What would bring him to do
such a thing?

GREY walks in and PAWN SHOP OWNER immediately recognizes
him.

PAWN SHOP OWNER:
Well, well, well, Mr. Grey? So good to see you, my man. My man!

PAWN SHOP OWNER clasps his hands together joyfully and then
- with wide eyes and eyebrows raised and head nodding - points to
a "24 Hours, Sir!" sign hanging on the wall behind GREY.

PAWN SHOP OWNER:
I'm always open 24-7 for you, Mr. Grey. My man!

GREY:
How have you been?

PAWN SHOP OWNER:
I just keep doing what I do because that's what I do.

GREY:
That's my line.

PAWN SHOP OWNER:
Haha Mr. Grey - I guess it is, I guess it is. You are right about that, my man. It is your line. So, my man Mr. Grey! (laughing and clasping his hands together) How have you been and whatnot?

GREY:
That's my word.

PAWN SHOP OWNER:
Yes Mr. Grey, it is, it is. That is your word. You are correct about that. So how have you been?

GREY:
I can't go on like this anymore. Enough is enough.

PAWN SHOP OWNER:
Well, you certainly came to the right place, then, Mr. Grey. If you need a change of pace, you've entered the right place to find it. I can tell you that for sure. Oh yes, let me tell you that. Let me assure you of that, Mr. Grey.

GREY:
Thanks, I appreciate that.

PAWN SHOP OWNER:
What is it that you need exactly, Mr. Grey? What can I help you with? Like I said, you've come to the right place. Let me assure you of that. But what exactly are you in need of today?

GREY walks up to the counter and removes his boots one by one. Toes to heel. Toes to heel. He places the boots on the counter one by one, balancing them carefully between his wrists. He then stares at his right wrist.

GREY:
I'll take the right.

PAWN SHOP OWNER:
I've gotta tell you, man, I didn't think you'd be back. My man! Mr. Grey!

NARRATOR (GREY):
He smells like a flooded cigar store.

GREY:
Well, I'm back, so I guess you thought wrong.

GREY holds up his right wrist for PAWN SHOP OWNER to see up close.

GREY:
I'll take the right.

NARRATOR (GREY):
Just give me my hands back.

PAWN SHOP OWNER:
Sorry man, your hands are long gone, my man. I mean, I'm sure I can help you find an alternative that will suit your needs. But your hands are long gone. Long gone.

GREY:
Long gone? You're kidding, right?

PAWN SHOP OWNER:
I would not kid you about such things, Mr. Grey. I've been called a few bad names in my years but I would not sink to that low of a level to kid you about such things that are of such importance.

GREY:
What do you mean they're long gone?

PAWN SHOP OWNER:
I mean that they're gone, Mr. Grey.

GREY:
How do hands just disappear? Where have they gone to?

PAWN SHOP OWNER:

I'll tell you what, Mr. Grey, now that's a good question. Now that's a *very* good question. And let me tell you the answer to that very good question: Some guy who looked an awful lot like you came in about a fortnight ago and bought them both, old friend.

GREY:
A guy who looked like me? Bought them?

PAWN SHOP OWNER:
I kid you not, Mr. Grey. As I said, I don't kid about such things.

GREY:
A fortnight ago? Who says fortnight?

PAWN SHOP OWNER:
You're looking at him, my man. You are looking right at him. And, like I said, this guy looked an awful lot like you. You hear what I'm saying, Mr. Grey? Maybe you can help to explain that one to me, Mr. Grey? Because, like I said, I'm here to assist you but I have to tell you that in order to assist you to the fullest I'll need your full cooperation. Let me repeat, Mr. Grey: I need you full cooperation.

GREY:
Well, I don't think I can explain that to you. I don't know anything about a fortnight or about a supposed identical twin.

PAWN SHOP OWNER:
Is that right, Mr. Grey? It's been more than 90 days, anyway, so your hands were fair game to any fine customer with the cash, regardless of their appearance, you know?

GREY:
Right. Got it. Well then, what else have you got for me?

PAWN SHOP OWNER opens the case with the key rubber-banded around his wrist, takes out a left hand and puts it on top of the glass case.

PAWN SHOP OWNER:
For those piece-of-crap boots you're only getting a left.

NARRATOR (GREY):
That's the one I wanted anyway. I'm left-handed.

GREY takes the left hand, tries it on and nods softly.

GREY:
I think this will do.

NARRATOR (GREY):
It's a little stiff, but not too bad. It's been too long.

GREY removes a small prescription bottle from his left pocket and places it on the counter. PAWN SHOP OWNER opens the bottle and the sound of birds chirping emerges. He places the cap back on and the sound is muted. PAWN SHOP OWNER opens and closes the bottle a few more times - first slowly, then quickly - as a grin emerges.

GREY:
OK, I said I'll take the right.

PAWN SHOP OWNER pauses momentarily and then removes the corresponding right hand from the glass case. He pauses again before placing it on top of the glass case. GREY tries on the right hand.

PAWN SHOP OWNER:
As I've told you, Mr. Grey, I can't give you *the* right, but here is *a* right for you to try on. It's the best right hand I got.

GREY:
This will do.

NARRATOR (GREY):
It feels good. These will definitely do.

PAWN SHOP OWNER :
So now you have your hands back. La-dee-freakin-dah. Now what are you gonna do? (laughs) My man! Mr. Grey! (laughs)

GREY, looking down at his hands, slowly turns his right hand clockwise and his left hand counterclockwise so that his palms are facing up. GREY turns and leaves without comment.

NARRATOR (GREY):
The door still didn't make a sound.

Inside the pawn shop, the "24 Hours, Sir!" sign on the wall falls to the floor. Outside, GREY walks away from the shop.

NARRATOR (GREY):
I'll just keep doing what I do because that's what I do.

GREY walks south on HWY 99 until he blends into the overcast mist.

FADE TO BLACK

THE END

---

maxwellgreyson: BUZZ!!!
sidsays0: hello, old friend!
maxwellgreyson: im back
sidsays0: whered u go?
maxwellgreyson: to get them back
sidsays0: :?
maxwellgreyson: my hands - i got them back
sidsays0: ok, ill just pretend i know what ur talking about & move on
maxwellgreyson: they feel pretty good
maxwellgreyson: not bad at all
sidsays0: good, im glad
maxwellgreyson: feel a bit strange but they r a good fit
sidsays0: wonderful
sidsays0: so ... ?
maxwellgreyson: so ... what?
sidsays0: so did I miss some good action with the 'goose last nite?
maxwellgreyson: no u did not
maxwellgreyson: u def did not miss some good action
sidsays0: :?
maxwellgreyson: they figured it out
sidsays0: what?! when? who? figured out what??
maxwellgreyson: yep & they threw me in a trash bin
sidsays0: who is 'they' exactly?
maxwellgreyson: an angry mob led by ruby
sidsays0: whoa, not good
maxwellgreyson: no, def not good
sidsays0: how did they know it was u?
maxwellgreyson: no idea
sidsays0: u used ur pathetic black-plastic-glasses-with-orange-tape disguise didnt u?
maxwellgreyson: no

251

maxwellgreyson: maybe
sidsays0: & u prob stood right there, like 3 ft away?
maxwellgreyson: no
maxwellgreyson: maybe
sidsays0: & then u prob said something u shouldnt have didnt u?
maxwellgreyson: whatever u shouldve been there
sidsays0: forecast said rain
maxwellgreyson: it didnt even rain
sidsays0: tru
maxwellgreyson: u shouldve been there & u know it
sidsays0: yeah it prob woudnt have happened if i was there
maxwellgreyson: mos def
sidsays0: sorry man, they threw u in a trash can? seriously?
maxwellgreyson: a trash bin to be exact
sidsays0: ugh
maxwellgreyson: i.e. bigger & nastier than a can
sidsays0: sorry man
sidsays0: truly sorry
maxwellgreyson: cant get the stench out of my nose hairs
sidsays0: gross
maxwellgreyson: sad thing is thats the least of my worries right now
sidsays0: hows that even possible?
maxwellgreyson: believe me its possible
sidsays0: higgs showed up 2?
maxwellgreyson: NO - thankfully
sidsays0: what then? whats worse than being tossed in a dumpster?
maxwellgreyson: finally checked up on the boosters & its not good
maxwellgreyson: not good at all
sidsays0: whats goin on w/ the boosters?
maxwellgreyson: no 1 is buying boosters anymore
sidsays0: why not?
maxwellgreyson: nanozero booted me
maxwellgreyson: & created their own page to sell boosters from
sidsays0: I dont understand
maxwellgreyson: they kicked me off nanozero completely & took over
sidsays0: booted u from where & took over what exactly?
maxwellgreyson: now when some1 nanozeros 'antenna boosters' my
site doesnt show up
maxwellgreyson: now the nanozeroer is sent to a nanozero-owned
boosters page
sidsays0: I still dont understand
maxwellgreyson: not much 2 understand really

sidsays0: can they even do that?
maxwellgreyson: guess so
sidsays0: how can they do that?
maxwellgreyson: no idea
sidsays0: so they pretty much stole from u in broad daylight?
sidsays0: & then kick u out 4 no good reason?
maxwellgreyson: indeed thats precisely what they did
sidsays0: i wont say it
maxwellgreyson: go ahead
sidsays0: no, u already know it
maxwellgreyson: go ahead
sidsays0: told ya so
maxwellgreyson: great thx! LOL
sidsays0: whatre u gonna do now? can u fix it?
maxwellgreyson: dunno, nanozero wont respond 2 my emails or calls
maxwellgreyson: looks like this was their master plan all along
maxwellgreyson: learn how sites make $, then blatantly copy them & kick them out of the index
sidsays0: not good
maxwellgreyson: pretty sure they are doing this 2 other sites 2
sidsays0: so lemme get this straight
sidsays0: within the last 24 hours:
sidsays0: u got screwed over by nanozero
sidsays0: u pretty much lost ur boosters business
sidsays0: u got tossed in a trash can
maxwellgreyson: bin
sidsays0: trash BIN
sidsays0: u cant stop smelling trash
maxwellgreyson: rancid trash
sidsays0: right
sidsays0: lavender mongoose vanished 4ever
maxwellgreyson: pretty much
sidsays0: something unknown happened to ur hands
maxwellgreyson: something is an understatement
maxwellgreyson: but yes that all sounds about right
sidsays0: thats what u call a bad day man
maxwellgreyson: agreed
sidsays0: u need to stop this downward spiral
maxwellgreyson: been trying 2 trust me
sidsays0: stop by l8r
maxwellgreyson: why?
sidsays0: got more multiverse stuff 4 u

maxwellgreyson: anythings better than more trash
sidsays0: cya
maxwellgreyson: l8r

\\+rx1618:

Myne [sic]

```
I go to sleep
thinking of the sound
of waves crashing.
Asleep?
I wake up
dreaming of the smell
of sun on sand.
Awake?
Looking down,
I feel sand between my toes.
Looking up,
I see it.
I smile at a ray of
summer's sun.
Tomorrow,
but not now.
Why ask for myne?
```

\\-grey

Not being able to visit Cafe Entropy for my daily coffee fix has been problematic for a couple of reasons. For starters, I have nowhere to go to pass the time. Passing the time is such an important part of my daily routine.

And my problems with headaches have now worsened, I think, because of caffeine withdrawal.

Patch Court and my hammock are still not getting it done, either. It's not enough. All of it. Or none of it. Or something like that.

I suppose this means that I have no choice but to take Sid up on his offer to stop by and talk about this and that. I don't really want to stop by his place given his ridiculous behavior yesterday, but, really, what other choice do I have?

<!--I don't know where I'm going to-->

After demanding a pot of freshly-brewed coffee, I sit comfortably on Sid's couch so that I can peer out of the window and watch the boats travel back and forth.

"Did you figure out what to do about Antenna Boosters 'R' Us?" Sid asks.

"No, I'm pretty much screwed. Actually, I not 'pretty much' screwed at all. I'm completely and utterly screwed. I'm a screw that's been turned and turned and turned so that there's no realistic chance of getting it out. There's nothing I can do."

"I'll help you brainstorm about that later. There's got to be a way to keep the boosters going," Sid says.

"It's a lost cause."

"Do you smell something?"

"Yeah, me."

"Oh, right, the trash bin. Sorry about that. I should've been there."

"Yes you should have."

"Well, for now, let's get back to the multiverse. Let me start by asking a question: You mentioned that you thought you had experienced being here and there at the same time, right? What did you mean exactly?"

"Yes I have been here and there at the same time. You have no idea," I say. "I have most definitely been here and there at the same time."

<!--this much I know for certain-->

"How so? I mean, how're you so sure?"

"Well, I finished the windows yesterday and ..."

"You finished the windows!? You didn't tell me."

"I didn't know you were so interested."

"What're you talking about? I've always been interested."

"That's like the most interest you've ever shown about anything associated with me - ever."

"Hey man, you've been working on that project for a long time. I'm just happy for you is all."

"Sure, right, you're happy for me. That sounds about right. In any case, I finished the windows and set them up exactly as instructed and ..."

"As instructed by whom? I thought it was your own personal project, no?"

"You know, I'm not sure where the instructions came from exactly. I guess it was a dream or something. In any case, I set up the windows and went through the steps one by one ..."

"The steps?"

"Let me finish. Stop interrupting me."

"OK, sorry. Go ahead."

"So, anyway, I went through the steps one by one. I stuck my hands through the windows one by one and wrote out eight lines on this notepad here," I take the notepad out of my backpack and toss it to Sid. "And then I was most definitely here and there..."

"at the same time," Sid finishes my sentence.

"They were all there. They were all there in my basement."

"Who?"

"The people from the voicemails, you know, the ghosts or ghouls or whatever."

"Hold up here one sec, Grey," Sid says as he reads the words on the notepad. "You're telling me that you built the windows, set them up, and then went through some series of instructions that produced these words and then ..."

"Yes, and then all of the voicemail people were kind of like in my basement with me. Yes."

"And you're not kidding me at all? This isn't some kind of prank that you're trying to pull, is it?"

"No, that's what you do," I say.

"You do it, too, just not as often," Sid says.

"The strangest part of the whole experience, which, believe me, was all very strange, was that I kept hearing a voice coming from the darkest corner of the basement. I couldn't see who or what was in that corner but I could hear what he/it was saying. But it sounded eerily like my own voice."

"What was the voice saying?"

"Reformat. Carry on."

"Carry on?"

"Reformat and carry on. That's what it was saying. It kept repeating it over and over. What do you think that means?"

"I'm not sure, Grey. The whole thing sounds insane. The whole thing is completely mind-blowing. What do you make of it all?"

"What do I make of it?" I ask.

"Yeah, what do you make of it?"

"That it's time to reformat and carry on?"

"What does that mean?"

"Well, for starters, I need to drop the voice and move on with my life. My meetings with the voice are doing me more harm than good. I know that much."

"What does Cassini have to do with anything?"

"I don't know, but I'm going to head over there and tell her that I'm not coming by anymore. I'm done with it. I'm done with it all!"

"Grey, don't back out now, she's helping you."

"No way, my downward spiral has only sped up since I started talking to her!"

<!--out of my way, I'm off to the underground-->

I'm out the door and on my way out of West Seattle before Sid has a chance to try to talk me out of it. I'm on a straight path to the voice's office.

It feels as though the answer is so very near but yet I'm not even sure what the question is.

\\+rx1618:

laff [sic]

walking down the street tripping over every crack [] i switch to the sidewalk [] same thing [] tripping over every crack that i see [] i need to stop looking for cracks [] the air is unusually cool [] the sun is out of order [] date of repair unknown [] wind comes and goes with an unnatural consistency [] leaves cease rustling [] tree branches moan [] flower petals laugh [] a distant dog bark starts to skip [] exposing the myth [] where am i? [] or, better yet, where am i supposed to be?

\\-grey

To: voice <cassini2358@yahoo.com>;
From: grey <maxwellgreyson@yahoo.com>;
Subject: used goods!

Message:

I got them back!

www.pawnsumer.com

-grey

Reception level: Excellent (4 out of 4) ||||

```
function GoToScene(event:imeyeself):void

{
/*
---:1---
*/

}
```

11. 0 prophet [sic]

When we try to pick out anything by itself, we find it hitched to everything else in the universe.

John Muir

There's an unfortunate consequence that comes along with living at 1618 Patch Court: trash. Garbage, refuse, junk, waste, rubbish: trash.

I have yet to figure out exactly what it is about driving around slowly in a circular motion on concrete dotted with yellow lines that makes people want to discard half-full mango/pomegranate smoothie cups and wrinkled fast-food wrappers with remnants of Canadian bacon stuck to hardened mild cheddar cheese onto my fine patch of land. Perhaps there really is no logical conclusion.

Do all of these passersby always happen to finish their meals on wheels at the very moment they reach 1618 Patch Court or do they hoard trash and kick it around while they drive throughout the week in order to scatter it on my prized property when the time's right?

Nevermore, I'm at peace with it all. Really, I am. I'm a part-time volunteer garbage collector and that's that

---

To: grey <maxwellgreyson@yahoo.com>;
From: sid <sidsays0@yahoo.com>;
Subject: re: zeroes

Message:

grey~

---zeroes 0.1.0---

Question: When you add an additional decimal point to a sequence, does it change the meaning of the sequence? After all, it's merely a point, no? Does the simple presence of a point make that great of a difference? Take "point" and "pt." – the two have the same meaning, no? Does the presence of a point - or a pt. – really change anything? Let us ponder: what if the sequence is composed of only zeroes? Or, even further, what if the sequence contains only ones and zeroes? Am I mad, you ask? You call me mad through an unspoken question that may or may not be rhetorical and I'm the fool? Or was your use of the word mad referring to anger there? In that case, again, perhaps I'm the fool. You must forgive me, as my head is cluttered with varying levels and variations of zero. As I near the point of nothingness the answer is, unfortunately, nowhere clearer or closer. At least I don't see it. This empty room that I speak to while standing at this here virtual podium seems oh so quiet. Hello? Is anyone there?

~sid

---

maxwellgreyson: BUZZ!!!
sidsays0: hello, old friend!
maxwellgreyson: ive got all the answers
maxwellgreyson: all of them
maxwellgreyson: i think
sidsays0: is that right?
maxwellgreyson: yeah it took a few years but ive got em all
sidsays0: how many years?
maxwellgreyson: all of em?
sidsays0: how old r u anyway?
maxwellgreyson: u know, im not sure
sidsays0: thats a little odd, even for u
maxwellgreyson: thx!
sidsays0: np
sidsays0: so what have u got for me?
maxwellgreyson: the answers, somewhere between some & all
sidsays0: ... = ?
maxwellgreyson: it starts & ends w/ zero
sidsays0: tell me something i dont already know
maxwellgreyson: will do
sidsays0: go ahead
maxwellgreyson: not just yet
sidsays0: when u gonna start?
maxwellgreyson: start what?
sidsays0: telling me?

```
sidsays0: explaining it all?
maxwellgreyson: now
sidsays0: im all ears
maxwellgreyson: I found zero
sidsays0: did u now
maxwellgreyson: this is <---> true
sidsays0: good, so ... ?
maxwellgreyson: will fill u in after i go break up with the voice
sidsays0: thought u already did that
maxwellgreyson: not yet, heading over this afternoon
sidsays0: what time?
maxwellgreyson: not sure
maxwellgreyson: gotta run
sidsays0: grey, when u heading over there?
maxwellgreyson: maybe in an hour or 2
sidsays0: ttyl
maxwellgreyson: l8r
```

I pass by the Fremont Troll on my way to the voice's office half expecting the large mass of cement to go directly into a deep belly laugh once I appear and half expecting the strangely complacent creature to be wearing the missing red glove.

Neither of my expectations is met.

It's of no matter, anyway, as I have more important things at hand. This voice experiment is over. I'm looking forward to saying goodbye and going back to the way it was before. Yes I am! I can't help but crack a smile as I walk toward the voice's office door for the very last time.

I turn the knob and swing the door open. There they are.

"You've become too advanced for your own good," Sid says immediately as I enter the voice's office.

Sid's sitting there in the office, right next to the voice.

Of course he is.

And he's sitting in my favorite comfortable chair, too.

Of course he is.

I should've seen this whole thing coming from miles away, many miles away.

Speechless for a moment, I point to my chest and glance over my shoulder to make sure no one is standing behind me.

"Advanced?" I ask.

"Yes," the voice says.

"Me?"

"Yes, Grey, you've become too advanced," Sid says.

"Haha, yeah, good one. I get it," I say.

They both sit there and stare without a smile, without a word, without motion.

"Wait, you know what? I don't get it. I don't get it at all. Not at all."

I turn to leave.

"And I don't care."

"Grey..." the voice starts to speak.

"Seriously, I don't have time for this today. In fact, I don't have time for this ever!"

"Grey, everything you know and see and hear and feel and experience is not exactly what you think," Sid says.

"Yeah, hasn't that been established, what, 1.618 million times before already?" I ask.

"Hasn't what been established?" the voice asks.

"That what I know is not what I think? Is that not but a simple fact of life at this point?"

"Grey, we're being serious here," the voice says. "Please have a seat so we can talk, so that we can have a productive conversation about all of this."

"We're here to come clean," Sid says.

"Come clean? What is this, one of your patented pranks, Sid? Listen, I've had it with all of these games and riddles and whatnot!"

"This is no game," Sid says.

"Wait, let me guess: you set me up with the whole Lavender Mongoose and dumpster incident. Yeah, sure, big surprise there. Tell me something I don't already know, please."

"No, I had nothing to do with that," Sid says. "Seriously, I had nothing to do with it. Well, at least not purposely."

"That makes no sense!"

"What makes no sense?"

"You don't! I told you I don't have time for this!"

"You need to find time for it, trust me."

"I have no time for games today!"

```
<!--well, maybe for Reversi-->
```

"Again, this is no game, Grey."

"Grey, please have a seat so that we can talk," the voice says.

"Talk about what?!"

"Please, Grey, just take a seat," the voice says.

"Why? Just spit it out!"

"Grey, this is serious," Sid says.

"Got it, it's serious. But do you mind, you know, maybe filling me in about what exactly is so very serious? Maybe you could, you know, explain to me what you're talking about?"

"All of it," the voice says.

"All of this," Sid says.

"All of what?"

```
<!--:??-->
```

"This. Life. All of this," Sid says.

```
<!--
define: lyfe[sic]
this; discomfort that will turn into pain later
-->
```

"I think it's time for me to leave and go somewhere far away," I say.

"No, Grey, please don't leave," the voice says.

"No, I'm out of here. Goodbye."

I turn and open up the door to leave.

"You are a robot," Sid says.

I slowly shut the door, turn around and look very carefully at Sid and the voice.

"Say again?"

"You are," Sid says.

"A robot," the voice says.

"You are a robot," Sid repeats.

"I am a robot?"

"Yes," they both say. "A robot."

"Grey, you're a robot."

"I don't understand."

"Yes, I know," the voice says. "Give us a chance to explain."

"Perhaps I could start not with an answer but with a question instead," Sid says. "I think that this will be the best way to proceed, the best way to explain, the best way to ease your mind."

<!--here we go-->

"Grey, who is Rx1618?" Sid asks.

I look at Sid, then at the voice, then back at Sid, then back at the voice.

"What do you mean, who is rx1618? She is who she is. What're you trying to do, torture me here or what? You're going too far this time, even for you."

"She is who she is? Is that right?" Sid asks.

I look at Sid, then at the voice, then back at Sid, then back at the voice.

"Do me a favor and go ahead and describe to me exactly what Rx1618 looks like," Sid says.

"I know ... I just know what I know."

<!--this much I know for certain-->

"Could you please just describe Rx1618 to me, Grey?"

"I'm not going to sit here and describe every detail of rx1618. I can't anyway, did you forget about my prosopagnosia?"

"Right, right, your prosopagnosia," Sid says.

"You don't believe me?"

"No, I believe you," Sid says. "But your prosopagnosia is just an example of ... difficulties, Grey."

"Yeah, OK Sid," I laugh.

They are not laughing.

"Right, you're a robotics engineer and I'm a robot."

"That's not what I said," Sid says.

"Grey, please calm down and listen to what we have to say," the voice says.

"OK, let's forget about the whole robotics thing for just one minute," Sid says. "I don't mean to be patronizing here, but could you please describe Rx1618 to us? I assure you this is a serious question and not a prank in any way, shape or form."

"Fine. Sure. Whatever."

They both sit and stare.

"I don't know - she is everything and anything at the same time. Nothing else matters. Once we reunite, all will be right, everything will be correct once again."

"Grey, Rx1618 is not a 'she' but rather an 'it.' The true question is not 'who is Rx168?' but rather 'what is Rx1618?'- do you understand?"

"Who, what, when, where, how, how much," I say. "Who cares? I know what I'm talking about. I'm not crazy."

"We didn't say you're crazy," the voice says.

<!--I just do what I do because that is what I do-->

"This is insane," I say.

"You exist here, or you're here for, one ultimate goal," Sid says. "Grey, you're supposed to use what you're given and what you learn about the world and then what else you're given after you learn about the world to find it."

"It?"

"Yes, it," the voice says.

"Why are you talking about learning and finding and whatnot? That makes no sense at all."

"You don't even know the correct name - it's Rx1618 with a capital R," Sid says. "You always chose to use a lowercase r, which is incorrect, but I left it alone because you liked it that way."

"L-O-L. What, is this like the clowns on the chalkboard in elementary school? Trying to make me look the fool yet again?"

"Elementary school," Sid laughs.

"Let me guess, elementary school is yet another figment of my memory or you forgot to fuse my circuit board on one week and my hard drive failed?"

<!--getting the hang of this now-->

We sit there silently for a moment and I wait stubbornly for someone to say something.

I have nothing more to say.

"Grey, do you recall that you had a mysterious bout of selective mutism when you were, uh, younger?" Sid asks.

The voice sits up straight in her chair.

"Yeah, I was selectively mute. Of course I remember that. I didn't talk for like a year or two or something like that."

"591. To be exact, you couldn't talk for 591 ..."

"But who's keeping track?" I interrupt.

"It's not that you didn't want to, it was that you couldn't. You

271

didn't have any control over it, really. Something went wrong. That's when Cassini came into the picture."

"The voice?"

"One and the same," Sid says.

The voice smiles.

"Hold up, what are you saying exactly?"

"Why do you think you call her 'the voice' anyway?"

"Because she talks and talks and talks and talks and talks and talks but doesn't listen?"

"No, you call her 'the voice,' Grey, because she gave you yours back."

"It's true, I helped you find your voice," the voice says.

"We're coming clean," Sid says. "This is the absolute truth."

"You deserve it. You deserve the truth," the voice says.

"OK, so did I succeed in finding it, then?"

"Yes, you did to a certain degree," Sid says. "You made great progress. But..."

"Are you familiar with Frodrick Gray?" the voice asks.

"Yeah, he's like a writer or an old philosopher or something. Everyone knows him."

"Not everyone - just you," Sid says.

"What, he's like my imaginary friend or something? Does he live in my closet?"

"No, he is you," the voice says. "In a parallel universe."

"There's no way that Frodrick is me," I say.

"Yes, there's a way," Sid says. "It's not a direct way, but there's a way."

"There's just no way."

"Why not?" the voice asks.

"That dude is like smart and whatnot, that's why,"

"Not that smart," Sid says. "And a little strange."

This much I know for certain.
-Frodrick Gray

"It was predicted that you could potentially become advanced enough to connect with a Twin Earth version of yourself given enough time and resources," Sid says.

And also, I am sideways man, too.
-Frodrick Gray

"Robots, Twin Earth, resources, got it," I laugh. "What exactly are these mysterious resources that I'm utilizing here, Professor Sid?"

"Well, the resources..." Sid starts to answer.

"Wait, the boosters?"

Sid and the voice look at each other and shrug their shoulders with a smile.

"It wasn't known exactly how you would do it but it was predicted that you would find the resources that you needed some way, some how," Sid says.

"And you did," the voice says. "But you really did get too advanced for your own good."

"You're getting too sophisticated too quickly," Sid says. "You've already begun to do things that hadn't been expected. You're reaching new levels, new territory."

"The voices? The voicemails?" I ask.

"Yes, that's one good example," the voice says.

"What is that all about, anyway?"

"Well ..."

"Hold up, Ruby's got to be real. No way she's from some other world. She's very real in the flesh," I say.

"Well ... the thing is," the voice says.

"OK, seriously. It's time for me to leave. I used to be certain that I was ridiculous, but this ..."

"We do have a theory," Sid says.

"You discovered Cafe Entropy, and we think it's a major piece of the puzzle," the voice says. "You see, entropy is generally thought of as disorder. Or, rather, the degree of disorder that something owns - its level of unpredictability."

"Right," I say.

<!--:??-->

"But that's not necessarily true," the voice says.

"What's not true?"

"Well, all I can tell you is that what entropy really is: information that has yet to be discovered," Sid says. "Or, information that has been discovered but is hidden for one reason or another."

"OK, so what hidden information does Cafe Entropy have other than the fact that their coffee beans aren't really organic?"

"When you talk about entropy you almost have to talk about black holes, too," Sid says.

"You do?"

*The stars brought me light but silence filled the empty space.
Dimness is a way of life 'round here, you see. Ask me three times
what I want and you'll get two answers.
-Frodrick Gray*

"Yes, we believe that you discovered a gateway between brane worlds, Grey," Sid says.

"B-r-a-n-e," I spell it out.

"Very good, old friend."

"Cafe Entropy is a gateway? To what?" I ask.

"Yes, it's likely that Cafe Entropy is connected to a black hole that gives access to a parallel universe."

"Don't black holes just destroy everything or something like that?" I ask. "Don't they consume all and let nothing out?"

"That's traditional thinking," Sid says. "That every black hole has an event horizon that is pretty much a point of no return. What goes in stays in, so to speak."

The voice finishes Sid's thought, "but what we're saying is that maybe black holes aren't so much holes as they are funnels. Perhaps black holes take information and matter and funnel it into another dimension, another universe."

"Grey, you may very well have found the gateway to a Twin Earth, or to a very important part of a very important parallel universe. We think that you found a black hole funnel at Cafe Entropy that leads to access to a parallel brane universe."

"I can't even beat Sid at Reversi, how could I do that?"

"Problem is, you're moving much too fast," the voice says.

"We need you to slow down," the voice says.

"How can I slow down when I already feel like I'm crawling in slow motion?"

"That's why we're talking to you right here, right now."

"OK, so stop confusing me, then, and actually explain some things."

"It's all about numbers, Grey," Sid says.

"The zeroes again?"

"Think about it: If numbers underlie every single component of our life as we know it, if numbers are at the base of everything we look at, hear and touch, then what's the logical conclusion, Grey?"

"That we're way more boring than we'll ever admit?"

No, the logical conclusion is still being formulated."

"This just isn't possible," I interrupt.

"It is," Sid says.

"It really is," the voice says.

"No way, it just isn't. Take everyday life, for example. It is so mundane that is has to be real. Take Higgs, for example."

"Higgs?" Sid asks with surprise. "I'm glad you brought him up."

"Yeah, I suppose that if anyone is a robot, it's got to be Higgs," I say.

They both laugh.

"Higgs is here solely to slow you down," Sid says.

"Of course he's here to slow me down. Are you implying that you put him here to slow me down?"

"I'm not implying that I put him here, but I'm telling you, without an iota of doubt, that he's here to slow you down."

"Don't you mean here and there?"

"At the same time," Sid says.

"I am a robot?" I ask, laughing uncontrollably.

I turn and leave. I never hear the door close.

Look to the stars, my friend: old connects with older and the young are but complex collections of recycled connections. I can only hope to be but a mere string holding a subsection of your bent time.
-Frodrick Gray

```
<!--will you remember my orange glow?-->
```

```
\\+rx1618:
```

```
Profet [sic]
```

```
If today I went to see a prophet,
She would tell me,
"Your soul is broken."
Gently caressing her grey crystal ball,
Her 110-proof breath cutting into my eyes.
But is it beyond repair?
I would ask.
"Your soul is hurting. It hovers above you,
displaced from burned taste buds."
Feeling my tongue, it is unusually smooth.
But is it beyond repair?
"You need not tools
and it cannot be replaced.
Pain has no safe hiding place.
The oasis for hurt is overbooked."
Today, if I went to see a prophet
She would understand.
```

```
\\-grey
```

To: voice <cassini2358@yahoo.com>;
From: grey <maxwellgreyson@yahoo.com>;
Subject: thx for nothing

Message:

Now that I know what I know and also what you know, I know that you've been here before, you know?

www.sidsays.com

-grey

Reception level: Excellent (4 out of 4) ||||

12. imeyeself [sic]

Even now, to focus on absolute true nothingness makes my heart sink. Total nothingness, from our familiar vantage point of somethingness, entails the most profound loss.

Brian Greene

To: sid <sidsays@yahoo.com>;
From: grey <maxwellgreyson@yahoo.com>;
Subject: re: zeroes

Message:

---zeroes 1.618---

sid <

I think I have, to use your own words, zeroed in on the answer here. Take two equal parts: One is positive, one is negative. What do you have? I will agree with you, Sid, that this is indeed an interesting question. But others may think differently. Perhaps others think that the question of the true nature of zero is, in fact, quite an uninteresting question.

You know what? I don't blame the others for thinking that. You know why? All of this zero-this and zero-that talk can really be quite tiring and unexciting. But it does help that no one is really listening to our discussion, you know? How do I know this? Stop and listen: do you hear that? Neither do I.

In any case, why question the question, right? In my estimation, asking that question is simply too easy. Questioning the question is, in fact, often the path of least resistance. Nevermore, others will say what they will say; or they will ask what they will ask. I'll take zero for what it is. It is here now, and, in any case, there is no denying its existence.

We could, of course, bury zero in the snow but it's only a matter of time before it gets pushed down by melting snow and ice and new layers of snow only to surface on the ceiling somewhere down below. It could be a long, long time - I understand this - but it will resurface. This I know with a high degree of certainty.

Maybe that's it - maybe it's all just a matter of degrees. Shift a few degrees here or there, right? First, you must determine the proper degree, then you must adapt to that. Yes, and there are some who are more adept at adapting. "Welcome home, friend!" is really only slightly off from "Go away, scoundrel!"

"But how many people really use the word scoundrel?" You'll ask, of course.

You see, people like to use "zero" and "nothing" synonymously but that couldn't be further from the truth. Nothingness only exists in the absence of numbers.

You taught me that, Sid. Reality is bigger than what you or I or us as a collective whole see and comprehend and, thus, nothingness is smaller than what we can comprehend?

Zero is a mountain peak to nothing's cavern.

I say now that it's time to put this all to rest. The information is all there and I have zeroed in on the answer. I can see it right there! You can't see it? Right there! Zero is not nothing but something. I do believe!

> grey

I long for the city:
Sidewalks uneven like my visions
Streets noisier than my thoughts
Brick walls scarred like my half-memories
Urban purification:
I lie down in the nearest alley
Which one need not matter
Fading sirens blend with distant trains
Heretical chorus:
A murmured drumroll

culminating in a memoir
that is mine and wholly mine
-Frodrick Gray

"KNOW MAD"
Screenplay by Maxwell Greyson

EXT. DOWNTOWN – SEATTLE, WA – LATE NIGHT (PRESENT)

GREY walks slowly down an unknown block late at night in downtown Seattle with his hands tucked carefully in his coat pockets. Kicking one slow step at a time, he stops, looks up at the sky, and then back down at the street. A few strangers pass by without even a simple glance in GREY's direction.

NARRATOR (GREY):
As I walk the streets I think of the cliché: these streets are crowded but lonesome. A nomad, I wander the city blocks in search of my next home. The next home will be the one. Whether or not I find a home is not in question. Why I search for my next home is not in question, either. It's simply a matter of when and where. I'll find my next home. It's time.

GREY stops to watch trash swirl in an unknown storefront door in SLOW MOTION. The miscellaneous remnants of everyday life seemingly start and stop spinning in no particular pattern.

NARRATOR (GREY):
Is there a pattern? If so, I certainly can't recognize it.

GREY starts walking down the street once again.

NARRATOR (GREY):
I wander the streets in a state of desensitized stupidity. A few people pass by and then more pass by. And then even more people pass by. Was that the same person as before or not? They all look different and similar at the same time.

GREY stops at a storefront door. He carefully removes his hands from his pockets and closely examines each hand.

NARRATOR (GREY):
Good, I've still got them.

GREY picks up two pieces of trash from ground: an empty coffee
cup in his left hand and a clear plastic wrapper in his right. He
restarts his casual stroll with the trash in each hand.

NARRATOR (GREY):
We are not humans in the flesh. We are not here right now. Were
we ever? We are but energies floating through time and space
doing our best to avoid collisions. How do I know something is
here? Or there? Or both? My eyes are surely opened but I'm not
really looking for anything real.

Strangers continue to pass by with no interaction.

NARRATOR (GREY):
How is it that I always shift away at just the right angle and
moment in time to avoid that opposing energy floating
unpredictably toward me?

A stranger bumps into GREY, knocking him back a step. GREY
catches himself, drops both pieces of trash simultaneously, looks
up and sees an "Open 24/7" sign blinking down a dark alley. GREY
walks directly to the sign, which hangs directly above an
unmarked grey door in the alley next to a trash bin. He tries the
handle; the door is unlocked. He opens it and walks in.

And OLD MAN sits at a small table smoking a cigarette in the
corner of a dark room with a single incandescent light bulb
hanging from the ceiling above the table. OLD MAN motions to
the empty chair across the table with his free hand.

NARRATOR (GREY):
It looks like an interrogation room gone wrong in a low-budget,
late-night, made-for-TV movie.

GREY:
Seriously? You're going with the single, dangling light bulb?

OLD MAN:
Who are you?

OLD MAN says something else but the words are unknown.

NARRATOR (GREY):
The words are mumbled. The words have become something
other.

GREY looks at OLD MAN carefully as he carefully takes a seat in
the open chair.

OLD MAN:
I am not a fly, but when it turns cold out I do die.

GREY:
Uh, thanks. That's good to know.

OLD MAN:
Rub that fake snow all over, do not miss a spot. You are coming
with me.

GREY:
Where are we going?

NARRATOR (GREY):
I'm not ready yet.

OLD MAN:
Who are you?

The old man is now trembling.

GREY:
I am the prophet seeker.

OLD MAN:
Are you trying to reach the capitol?

GREY:
Yes, I am.

OLD MAN:
Have you been there?

GREY:
Not yet.

OLD MAN:
You're not still searching for it, are you?

GREY:
No, definitely not.

NARRATOR (GREY):
I'm not entirely sure of that.

OLD MAN:
Well, then, have you found it yet?

GREY:
What am I trying to find?

OLD MAN:
The divine prescription.

GREY:
I don't know if I've found that.

OLD MAN:
You do. Or you will, at least.

GREY:
How will I know?

OLD MAN:
You'll know because the search will cease.

GREY:
I have stopped searching.

OLD MAN:
Then you've found it.

GREY:
The divine prescription, you say?

OLD MAN:
Yes.

GREY:
I think I've got something for you.

GREY removes a small prescription bottle from his left pocket and places it on the counter. OLD MAN opens the bottle and the sound of birds chirping emerges. He places the cap back on and the sound is muted. OLD MAN opens and closes the bottle a few more times - first slowly, then quickly - as a grin emerges.

GREY:
Take it, it's yours.

OLD MAN:
Yes, I know.

NARRATOR (GREY):
I am ready.

Camera pans up and zooms slowly on the single light bulb.

CUT TO BLACK

THE END

\\+rx1618:

Hello, world!

//-grey

To: voice <cassini2358@yahoo.com>;
From: grey <maxwellgreyson@yahoo.com>;
Subject: [0]

Message:

www.imeyeself.com

-grey

Reception level: Excellent (4 out of 4) ||||

```
function GoToScene(event:imeyeself):void
```

{

I am a rusty door hinge. I've been opening and closing
with prideful mediocrity since 1942. Oddly, I'm completely
satisfied with the noise that I make when performing my
duty. I have just two directions: this way and that way. I
sport the remnants of numerous second-rate paint jobs and
am the proud owner of a handful of nicks and scratches
that scatter my tiny surface. Spray oil to silence me and
I'll leave a trail of dark brown grime on the nearest
surface behind the direction that you spray. I serve the
purpose of letting people come and go as they wish with
little trouble, although the noise and filth that I
produce easily offset any good qualities that I may claim
to possess. I think I shall stay here a while longer,
perhaps until time injures me further. Yes, I will hang
around, going this way and back that way, all the while
yelling obscenities at passersby. It pleases me so.

}

13. Hear [sic] and their [sic]

He in his madness prays for storms,
And dreams that storms will bring him peace.

Mikhail Lermontov

I'm done. It's over.

I'm done with Ruby. I'm done with my hammock. I'm done with the voicemails. I'm done with Higgs. I'm done with Sid. I'm done with the voice. I'm done with them all.

I'm done with Cafe Entropy. I'm done with Patch Court. I'm done with it all.

I don't believe it. I don't believe them.

```
<!--rx1618: light the way with my torch of tears-->
```

```
\\+rx1618:
```

```
man maid [sic]
```

```
I am tamer now. Some might bestow a tag of domesticated,
as it were. Out and in, I see you now.
```

```
<!--Fibonacci: 1,2,3,5,8,13,21,34,55-->
```

```
\\-grey
```

I've got an unbearable stinging sensation in both of my eyes again. It's nearly impossible to see anything that I need to see.

I head back to Patch Court lie down in the hammock one last time to rest my eyes a bit before the journey.

The Mountain is out. And that's good, because I plan to be on The Mountain shortly. There's no place but up at the present time. I have no choice, but, honestly, even if I did have a choice I would still make this very same choice.

If given a say in the matter, I'll always choose a path that takes me closer to the sun and the moon and the stars.

A man may be born, but in order to be born he must first die, and in order to die he must first awake.

Carl Sandburg

I take the bus from Seattle to Puyallup and then a bus from Puyallup to Eatonville. Now I must find a way to get from Eatonville to Ashford. The town of Ashford sits at the base of Mount Rainier.

In my time, I haven't had much luck with hitchhiking but I'll have to give it another shot here. I'm aware that any attempt could very well end with a trip to the local law enforcement station, but this is out of Higgs' jurisdiction so I should be safe.

Higgs could have a cousin or some other family or friend connection out this way, but I'll take my chances. I have no choice but to take my chances. I don't have it in me to make it all the way to the base of The Mountain and then all the way up, too.

From Ashford, it will be all foot in front of foot. The walk from the entrance of Mt. Rainier National Park to the Paradise visitor center alone will include maybe 4,000 feet of vertical gain. From Paradise, I will then be ascending about 9,000 vertical feet to the summit.

The top of Puget Sound, and nearly the top of the lower 48 states, awaits. I'm ready.

<!--this much I know for certain-->

```
\\+rx1618:
```

sence [sic]

When soul eclipses thought
You have two overlapping beings
Both greater than you
Their sum equaling exactly
your essence

```
\\-grey
```

The driver says his name is Karl. He pulled over right away - a younger guy driving a nondescript, decade-old car - and didn't seem too concerned with who I am or where I'm going. He says he's a mountain guide and has been guiding on Rainier for years. Thing is, he doesn't look much like a mountaineer. But I must admit that I don't really have a great idea of what a mountaineer does look like.

"So this is your first time, huh?" he asks.

"No, no, I've hitchhiked a ton of times," I lie.

"No, I mean The Mountain. It's your first time trying out The Mountain, huh?"

"Oh, right. It's that obvious?" I ask.

"I don't know about it being obvious," he laughs. "But I've been doing this a long time and my first instinct is usually right."

"It's the backpack, isn't it?

hiker1: he's still using that same ridiculous pack!
hiker0: OMG! LOL! LOOSER!
hiker2: Poor guy, maybe I should offer him my old pack?
hiker0: LOL! Offer him a new life! ROTFL!!!!!

"Uh, maybe your backpack could be upgraded, but no worries."

He starts to ask more details about my hike, my journey, my ascent, my climb, so I try to reroute the conversation. I tell him about Mailbox Peak and the actual real-life mailbox up there. He seems somewhat intrigued but I don't think he completely believes me, either. It's doubtful he'll ever find out for himself. He's seems too busy with the real peaks like Rainier.

Headline: Two non-believers sit two feet apart not believing a word, waiting for a sign to believe

We reach Ashford in about a half hour. We'll both be going up The Mountain in the morning, but that's where the similarities end. He just returned from a trip to Mount Everest.

Me? I was just told that I'm actually a robot.

"Good luck, man," he says.

I can only muster a nod of the head.

The next morning, after a cold night of sleeping outdoors in a tent rented from an outdoors outfit in Ashford, I'm able to catch a shuttle bus from the base of Mt. Rainer to Paradise with a group of climbers that are heading up Rainier with a couple of guides. I guess I must look the part as a beginner, given the backpack and all, so no one seems to notice my presence.

The first part of the climb is a 4,600-foot vertical trek up to Camp Muir from Paradise, where the bus drops us off. A large part of this initial section of the ascent is made up of the Muir Snow Field.

The hike up the Muir Snow Field is a formidable task for my novice legs. My thighs, eyes and lungs burn as I approach the stone huts and scattered tents that make up Camp Muir. The winds are fierce and bring flashing visions of natural disasters and other destruction.

After a few hours of rest but no sleep in my borrowed tent, I arise and start getting ready to head to the summit. The snake tells me that it is just a bit past midnight. A nanozero search told me that it's necessary to start the ascent while the ice and snow is still firm in the middle of the night.

I need every advantage I can get.

One of the guided groups has about a 10-minute head start on me. I plan to follow from a safe distance to avoid detection

It's a clear night and the stars are bright, so I should be able to see the group up ahead with little trouble. I have no idea where the route begins or ends, so I can't lose sight of this group that I'm secretly hitching a ride with.

About 16 minutes into the ascent, I'm already falling far behind. I stop, remove my pack and sit on it to carefully scan the area above for my free guides. I can hear the faint sound of footsteps but I can't hear any voices and I can't see a single headlamp, let alone an actual human.

Finally, I see the group again. Without hesitation, I pick my pack up off the ground and swing it back over my shoulder as I stride ahead. I stumble and fall face-first on the snow and ice at my feet. As I fall, I close my eyes, drop my pack and put both palms out to catch myself. The red glove on my left hand hits ground first and my bare right hand follows.

I lie there motionlessly for a few seconds in a push-up position with my face hovering over a small crevasse. The gap in the ice is only about 10 inches wide - not wide enough to fall into but wide enough to lose something in. I can't see the bottom.

As a stream falls from a single crack in a glacier
and its taste has two faces, one forward
one backward, and one is sweet and one hard,

so I die for the last time through each moment of these days,
and one way the old sighing frees me no longer,
and the other way the goal can no longer be seen.

Osip Mandelstam

295

After almost losing my surrogate guide group a few more times, I make it safely to what looks like a popular resting area of some sort. I sit down far away from the groups to avoid being noticed but can see a few people looking over in my direction.

They're on to me.

A few minutes after sitting down to catch my breath in the thinning air, I see two of the guides from the group ahead talking and looking in my direction. One of them starts to walk in my direction. I pack up and get heading out before he arrives. We cross paths.

"Hey, I know you," Karl says with a grin.

"Hey, you're the taxi driver from Eatonville, right?" I say.

"Are you up here by yourself?" he asks. "I thought this was your first time, no? Soloing? That's pretty bold."

I just keep walking.

"Be careful, there's a storm rolling in," he yells to the back of my head.

All I see is the faint glow of snow and ice everywhere I look.

Nevermore, there's no turning back now.

`<!--left in front of right; right in front of left-->`

In about an hour, my visibility has been reduced to maybe 10 feet. The clear skies and calm air of the past few hours are but a faded memory. I'm now encompassed by clouds and quarter-sized snowflakes are swirling in every possible direction and pattern. The wind picks up without warning and I'm now getting blasted with 30- to 40-MPH gusts.

I dig my crampons into glacial ice with an incline of about 38 degrees, ready to stand my ground and wait it out. Honestly, I don't know what else to do.

After 18 minutes or so, it's painfully obvious that the wait-it-out approach is no longer an option. My feet are cold and falling asleep. I have to go up. With each step I seem to lose two. Hunched forward to combat the wind, my crampons suddenly seem dull and inadequate.

<!--left in front of right; slide; right in front of left; slide-->

I'm absolutely depleted.

In the midst of the storm I take off my pack and set it down firmly on the glacier. I sit down atop the pack and hold my coat tightly against my body. Every part of my body is covered with snow and ice except my eyes, which I can now barely keep open. The wind is howling and snow is blasting me from all angles.

I am becoming glacier.

I should be frightened but cannot muster the energy for such a complex emotion.

In the wind, I hear the faint sound of voices. It's of no matter, I've been hearing and seeing illusions for some time now.

But the voices seem to be getting louder. No, it's my mind playing tricks on me. No, the voices are getting louder and clearer.

I open my eyes as wide as I can, wiping away the snow and ice as best as possible, and see two bodies standing a short distance from me. Focusing harder, I can see them huddling over a small device.

I stand up quickly but am so stiff that I immediately fall to the ground. My tumble catches the attention of one of the people above. He comes over to me. It's Karl, again.

Of course it is.

"Hey, come with us. I don't care if you were with us or not originally, you are now," he yells into the storm. "We need to get out of this whiteout. Our GPS tells us that we're only a few hundred meters from the crater rim."

I look up to see a white wall of nothing.

"Just a walk in the park!" He yells into the wind.

I nod my head slowly, pick up my pack, and walk over so they can rope me into the back of the group. Step by step, we make slow, steady vertical progress into the heart of the storm. My body hits levels of zero I never even fathomed.

The reserves of my reserves are long gone.

The rope connecting me to the group continues to tighten as I fall behind the pace. Periodic jerks from the rope help propel me up the steep incline.

With the wind still howling and the flakes still plastering every centimeter of empty space, I detach from the group and head directly to my left. I can barely make out a rock or a cover of some sort in that direction.

Or is my mind playing tricks on me once again?

I step and trip and lunge and crawl my way over and dive in.

It's a cave of some sort.

I crawl in a few feet and collapse to the ground, using my pack as a pillow. The ice cave is cold and uninviting but at least it's out of the blizzard.

To: voice <cassini2358@yahoo.com>;
From: grey <maxwellgreyson@yahoo.com>;
Subject: []

Message:

voice–

Thank you for your kind words and welcoming chairs. You have some of the best tap water in Seattle.

It's true: you gave me a voice when I had none. Or perhaps I had one all along but no one had the ability to hear me.

I want you to know that I found true comfort in absolute nothingness.

Oh, and I found the answer by erasing the question.

www.hearandtheir.com

-grey

After a long rest on my pack, I stand up and shake the snow and ice from my outer layer. I can still hear the wind howling outside of the walls of frozen water.

Thankful that my headlamp still works, I start exploring the ice cave one small step at a time. Not long into my journey through the ice tunnels, I notice something protruding from the ceiling of ice above.

It's red. It's a glove.

It's the other red glove.

I can't reach it – it's maybe 16 or 18 feet above my outstretched hand in the ceiling of the ice cave. I try to devise a plan to get to the glove but it's of no use. Its five dangling fingers taunt me with every cycle of the wind.

I pull the snake out of my pocket and immediately fumble it to the ice below. I pick it up, wipe the screen, and power it up.

No reception.

sidsays0: BUZZ!!!
sidsays0: hello, old friend!
sidsays0: friend?
sidsays0: gray?
sidsays0: GRAY?

```
sidsays0: grey?
sidsays0: GREY!
sidsays0: BUZZ!!!
sidsays0: :0
sidsays0: \:1
sidsays0: goodbye, old friend
```

Here, with eyes closed, I'm able to connect the dots into an outline of there. I lie back down on the floor of the ice cave and feel the ice near my temple melt a bit but freeze again in an instant.

My breath feels thicker than the surrounding air and I can feel that it's only feet away, maybe even centimeters away. In the pause between if and then I find a slow-motion reality so unbreakable that it spins forever in the interim of here and there.

Finding myself in a synthetic alter-interlude, I live 34 lifetimes in one-and-a-half breaths. I close my eyes and attempt to sort tiny specks of light as if trying to focus on microscopic dust particles swirling around in organized chaos at twilight.

Holding my red glove tightly in my left hand, I say goodbye for the first and last time.

Suddenly remembering the first time that I was here and there at the same time, I breathe ever-so-slowly to prolong the moment and impress the vision on my memory forever: A rough sketch of the ageless illumination of a ridiculous mind.

The past is but the smoke from an old, winter chimney.

The present is but the orange glow from a dull alley streetlamp.

The future is but a tree tossing and turning in the heart of an unrelenting storm.

My loneliness is broken, shattered, gone; it's now part of the wind, snow and rain.

I think I'll stay here a while.

\\+rx1618:

eternall [sic]

all the same
i know
it was always you
i always knew
i hold out my hand
it is filled
with nothingness
here
take my eternity
it is yours

//-grey

Reception level: unknown ([zero] out of 4)

14. [sic]

maxwellgreyson: i am a robot?
sidsays0: yes u r
cassini2358: 1 w/ feelings 2
maxwellgreyson: not many tho [?]
sidsays0: no, but not 0 either
cassini2358: u r a robot
maxwellgreyson: what, like a walking, talking computer?
sidsays0: not exactly
maxwellgreyson: i am a robot?
frodrickgray: 'tis a fact my trusted confidant
maxwellgreyson: where r u?
frodrickgray: somewhere 'tween here & there
sidsays0: at the same time
frodrickgray: O my time is always bent
maxwellgreyson: i am a robot?
rubyentropy: 1 w/ used coffee grinds 4 brains
maxwellgreyson: what r u doing here?
rubyentropy: was about 2 ask u the same thing
maxwellgreyson: so, like a metal head w/ flashing lights & batteries?
sidsays0: no, u r a collection of information
maxwellgreyson: inform me then
cassini2358: i gave u a voice
maxwellgreyson: when i had none
sidsays0: & i help u see clearly
maxwellgreyson: when i have trouble w/ transparency
sidsays0: & i help you hear
maxwellgreyson: when my memory runs dry
cassini2358: & i help you feel
maxwellgreyson: when clouds roll in
cassini2358: & ur soul drowns in endless mist
rx1618: & i help you dream
maxwellgreyson: when i need it most
rx1618: no i make you dream
maxwellgreyson: of what?
rx1618: of being here
maxwellgreyson: & there?
rx1618: at the same time
maxwellgreyson: for what?
rx1618: not what but where

maxwellgreyson: for where?
rx1618: u know where
maxwellgreyson: i am a robot?
rx1618: r u?
maxwellgreyson: 2 many ?s
rx1618: not a ? but a choice
maxwellgreyson: what choice, then?
rx1618: ur almost there
maxwellgreyson: but im still here
rx1618: not 4ever
frodrickgray: dimness is a way or life 'round here, old friend
rx1618: look to the stars
maxwellgreyson: i always do
rx1618: keep doin what u do
maxwellgreyson: because thats what i do?
rx1618: just take the next step
maxwellgreyson: how?
rx1618: who r u?
maxwellgreyson: im a thinker
rx1618: and a dreamer
maxwellgreyson: im a dreamer
rx1618: a believer?
maxwellgreyson: a dreamer i said
rx1618: no1 can take that from u
maxwellgreyson: imeyeself
rx1618: [sic]

ABOUT THE AUTHOR

Matt Mills currently resides in Chicago, IL with his wife, children and dog after spending many years in the Pacific Northwest. When not writing, he can often be found gazing at the stars and trying to picture what Chicago would look like with a mountain backdrop.

goodreceptionbook.com

http://facebook.com/goodreception
http://twitter.com/good_reception
contact@goodreceptionbook.com

www.ingramcontent.com/pod-product-compliance
Lightning Source LLC
Chambersburg PA
CBHW051239260626
47162CB00002B/514